THE
HYPNOTIST

THE HYPNOTIST

LAURENCE ANHOLT

CORGI

CORGI BOOKS

UK | USA | Canada | Ireland | Australia
India | New Zealand | South Africa

Corgi Books is part of the Penguin Random House group of companies whose
addresses can be found at global.penguinrandomhouse.com.

www.penguin.co.uk
www.puffin.co.uk
www.ladybird.co.uk

Penguin
Random House
UK

First published 2016

001

Text copyright © Laurence Anholt, 2016

Set in 10/14.5 pt Caslon 3 and 11.5/14.5 pt Adobe Garamond
by Falcon Oast Graphic Art Ltd.
Printed in Great Britain by Clays Ltd, St Ives plc

A CIP catalogue record for this book is available from the British Library.

ISBN: 978–0–552–57345–0

For Cathy

This Is How the Story Ends...

'I'm counting back now, Hannah ... eight, seven, six ... Your breathing slows ... Your eyes fall deep into their sockets ... five, four, three, two ... You are deeply, deeply relaxed ...'

'It's so hot tonight.'

'Where are you, Hannah? Tell me what you see.'

'I'm in my bed above the tool store. There's a strange light keeps flashing ... No, no, it's the storm brewin' outside and lightning crackling in the sky.'

'Go deeper now ... You can remember everything. Tell me, how old are you, Hannah?'

'I'm thirteen or fourteen years old – and I'm so afraid!'

'You know how to wake if you need to ...'

'I'm kneeling on my bed. Here's my dreamcatcher blowin' at the window an' I stare through its web at the yard below. There's a whole lot of noise out there, and suddenly I see a Jeep drivin' fast through the gates. I hear doors slammin'. The dog is barking in the doghouse . . . and now it's yelping – maybe he's kicked it.'

'Who is it? Who has returned so late?'

'Erwin. It's Erwin. Oh God! He's comin' into the tool store below. I hear him crashin' about downstairs. He's drunk – I can tell because he's stumblin' and cussin'. Now . . . Oh my Lord! He's treading up my stairs . . .'

'You remember everything, but you are quite, quite safe . . .'

'I always knew he would come – that's why I never go to my bed without heavin' the chest of drawers against the door.'

'Take it steady, Hannah . . .'

'I'm out of my bed, shivering in my nightgown, and outside the thunder is crashin'. Now I'm piling chairs and the laundry basket against the door – I need to stop him getting in. I'm trying to drag the bed, but he's so strong, the door is already opening . . . Oh Lord! I see one huge hand reachin' at me, and he's saying, "*Ah'm cummin' for ya, gal. Ah always tol' ya ah would.*"

'I'm whimperin' like the dog in the yard an' I'm callin', "*Pip, Pip, I need you now!*"

'Then I'm climbin' back into bed 'cos there's nowhere else to go. I'm pullin' the blankets way up to my eyes. Suddenly there's an almighty *CRASH!* – and Erwin is here! Right here in my room! Nearly seven feet tall. No matter how many times I see that man, I am shocked and terrified. I'm tryin' to disappear into the bed and he's lookin' down at me, bent beneath the ceiling, like . . . like a shrunken head on a stick.'

'Keep breathing, Hannah. Remember you can wake if you want to . . .'

'And now he's bendin' down, and my heart is beatin' so fast it may bust my rib cage. The smell of whiskey makes me wanna puke. His long fingers are tuggin' at my blankets, he's pushin' that tombstone face right up to mine, and he whispers, *"Ah 'magine yer 'bout the purtiest li'l woman ah ever seen."*

'Now he's untyin' his laces and pullin' down his dungaree straps – then he trips and hits the bed so hard it knocks the breath out of me. My mouth is dry – I can't find a sound, but my eyes – my eyes are . . . *screaming*!'

'But you remembered the words, Hannah? The words I taught you?'

'I'm trying to find the words, because I know they can save me. But I been silent for so long . . . I been mute for years now, and my jaw is frozen and my tongue don't work.

'Erwin's naked and slimy with sweat. There's a big ugly tattoo on his back: a blood-drop on a white cross.

'He's kneelin' on my bed, which almost gives way, and he's pressin' his mouth against mine and pushin' his tongue inside – I can taste the chicken and onions he had for his supper.

'I feel his stubble scrapin' my skin. I'm tryin' to twist my head away. Then he says, *"Ah ain't gonna hurcha, gal. Wal, not too much anyways."*

'And I know I'm gonna die . . . Right here. Right now . . .'

'That's grand, Hannah. You've done well. I'm going to wake you now. I'm going to bring you slowly back . . . and when you awake, you will remember everything, but you will feel calm and strong. I'm counting from one to ten.

'One, two, three . . . slowly awakening . . .

'Four, five, six . . . opening your eyes . . .

'Seven, eight, nine . . . Wake up now, Hannah, and join me back in the room.'

1

St Joseph Poor Boys' Orphanage, Spring 1963

Pip had been awake for hours when the flashlight snaked across the dormitory floor and picked out his bed and his face on the pillow.

'Pip, git yer clothes on. I wanna innerduce you to someone.'

While the other boys slept, Pip pulled on his clothes and walked across the linoleum into the corridor. He carried his book in one hand and his boots by their laces in the other. There was a cluttered office outside the dormitory with windows on three sides, where a TV crackled and the two men were drinking whiskey.

'Pip, this here is Mr Zachery. He's looking to foster a boy—'

'But it cain't be jes' any boy. Ah need a *strong* boy. Also, ah need a boy who cin read. Ah see ye got a book, son. Ye able t' read?'

'He's the only boy on the premises who truly can.'

Pip stood blinking in the flickering light as Mr Zachery turned him about by the shoulder like a cut of beef. The old man's beard was yellow with nicotine and the teeth were black within. It reminded Pip of something foul – a piss-hole in the snow.

'Pip, Mr Zach askin' if you can read. Why don't you tell him 'bout your book?'

'My mama give it me. It was her book. She tol' me I was named after the boy in the story.'

'What's the book, son?'

'*Great Ex'tations*, sir. Charl' Dickens.'

'Wal, ah don' know 'bout that, but if ye cin read, ah gotta place for yer. Lemme feel yer muscles, son.'

Pip rolled up his sleeve and flexed his bicep. Both men laughed – '*Snee, hee, hee!*' and '*Hur, hur, hur!*'

'He's small for his age, but he'll grow. He's a good kid. Edercated too. You wanna take him, Zach?'

'He'll do.'

'But listen, Zach, you gotta look after this one or the poh-leece will be knockin' on mah door. That's three o' my boys you misplaced now. I ain't forgettin' them twins a few years back.'

'Twins . . . ? Ah must have disremembered. Wal, ah cain't help it if the little critters run away. Anyways, ah 'preciate the drink. Me 'n Pip gotta long drave ahid of us.'

Chairs scraped the floor.

'Now then, Zach, here's a pey-un. I need a signature, right here . . . and another one here.'

When he had signed, the man named Zachery pulled out a wad of dirty dollars. Licking his fingers theatrically, he began to count – 'Twenny, twenny-farve, thurty, thurty-farve, fawty, fawty-farve . . .' – until there was a jumbled hillock on the table. Then there was more counting and recounting until the men shook hands and the money was shovelled into a drawer.

Finally Pip was pushed gently but firmly from one man to the other, as casually as you might pass on a pair of discarded corduroys.

'So long, Pip. You jes' do what Mr Zach says and be a credit to St Joseph. I hope you'll allus 'member the good times we had.'

Pip squatted on the office floor, his thin legs trembling as he worked on his bootlaces. Then he rose to his feet and followed Mr Zachery like a gangly calf at an abattoir along the silent corridors which he had mopped so often; down the granite steps, thirty-eight in all, each spangled like a starry universe, and into the courtyard of the St Joseph Poor Boys' Orphanage, where they were consumed by the drizzle of the night.

Pip carried no bag but he shoved his precious book deep inside his jacket. He watched Zachery climb into the cab of a battered brown truck. The engine chuntered, then the old man leaned across to push open the passenger door. But Pip did not move.

'What's troublin' you? Oh, the dawg. He won't hurt you none. Name's Amigo – bought him off a Mexie fer farve dollars. Jes' push him aside and climb on up. Best git acquainted, we three.'

The inside of the cab reeked of tobacco and dog and old man.

Zachery peered through the murky windshield and the truck jolted forward, through the great iron gates, past blind tenement buildings and black warehouses, trundling through slumbering clapboard suburbs and into the lonely countryside.

Pip tried to settle but the seat was cold and rough, with ripped leather and horsehair stuffing, and all the while the hound, Amigo, inspected each part of his body in turn, finishing by thrusting a wet nose deep within his ear.

As they drove, Pip's fingers stroked the cover of his mother's book, soft and worn by years of his unconscious caress. The only sound was the groaning and thumping of the wipers and a sniffing and coughing from Zachery.

After an hour the small truck entered a huge forest, where the weary headlights created dancing shapes amongst the foggy trees. In Pip's imagination the shadows took on the forms of dead men concealed behind every trunk, who lurched violently towards the windshield waving their elastic arms before disappearing again and again into the blackness. Why could Zachery not see them? Pip stared at the old man's cadaverous face, illuminated by the glow of a cigarette, and imagined that he was one of them – driving deeper and deeper to his dead man's lair.

'Wal?'

'Wal what, sir?'

'Wal, the dawg tawk more 'n you . . . Ye know how t' roll a cig'rette?'

'No, sir.'

Zachery hauled on the brake and, with blackened thumbnails, prised open a battered tin containing a wad of tobacco and a scrap of apple to keep it moist. Then he patiently showed Pip how to roll a cigarette. 'Pinch o' baccy, lay it 'long the paper, roll it real neat. You watchin' me, boy? Lick it here . . . Not too wet, dog darn it . . .'

Pip was a fast learner and glad of a diversion. With some pride he handed his effort over for inspection. Zachery turned the cigarette in his hands, sniffed at it, struck a match, exhaled a vast cloud of blue smoke, and they lurched on into the sodden night.

'Wish ah could fill the truck with some o' this rain. Don't git too much where we're headed. Now, ye gonna tell me how ye ended up in the Poor Boys' home – or 'm ah gonna guess yer daddy ran off with someone ails, an' yer mammy don't wan' ye no more?'

'That's a lie!'

'Sho it's a lie. That's why ah'm standin' in need of an explanation.'

Pip had never spoken of that fateful Sunday. Not to a soul at the orphanage, or to the childcare officers who had taken him there. But something about this strange night opened him up and he began to relate the tale of the drive to church, which started so happily, with hymns in the car and excited talk of his baby brother or sister curled snugly within Mama's belly.

Pip heard his own voice far away, describing the details of how he had crawled into the very back of the station wagon to retrieve his book, so that when the signals failed and Papa drove straight into the path of a speeding train, Pip

9

had miraculously survived, while his mama and papa had died in an instant, taking with them the sibling he would never know.

Having no other relatives, Pip had been passed by the preacher to St Joseph's where, although he had not been mistreated, he had waited and waited for something to happen, never knowing exactly what it would be.

If he had been older than ten years when he arrived at the Poor Boys' Orphanage, he might have been aware of some injustice at being labelled poor. Pip's parents had not been poor – his father ran a busy general store and they had lived in comfortable rooms at the back of the schoolhouse where his beloved mother was head teacher.

Pip's father had never trusted banks, and after his death, although the people searched and searched, no savings could be found. The store and eventually the schoolhouse were sold, but a number of parties came out of the woodwork claiming 'evidence of unpaid bills' or debts, which had 'accumulated interest'. By the time they had taken their share and the pastor had paid the triple funeral bill, there was nothing left, and young Pip had been sent away with only the clothes he stood up in and *Great Expectations* in his hands.

And now he was almost fourteen years old, and when he looked back in later life, Pip would realize that he had entered a kind of limbo in the orphanage years, like a chrysalis wintering in an attic.

'Dang burn it,' Zachery whistled. 'Sometimes life jus' iden right.'

In the brief moment before he fell asleep, Pip imagined

how he would tell the story to his father, getting every detail just right, and how sorry they would be for that poor family.

Pip dreamed of rumbling and jolting and an ever-increasing weight on his legs. He awoke to a ghostly dawn and the horrible realization that the story was true and he was that orphan, and that the weight on his legs was the sleeping dog, Amigo, who had drooled a copious quantity of saliva across his knees. His body ached, his throat was dry, his belly groaned for food. Then it came to him that the bearded man at the wheel, with drooping eyelids and cigarette hanging from lip, was named Zachery, and that for 'severnty-farve dollars' he had bought his life.

They lumbered to a stop at a gas station next to an all-night diner, seemingly nailed together with advertising signs. The rain had evaporated and a fierce heat was building like a threat.

'Ah need some aigs and grits,' muttered Zachery. 'You sit right here with the dawg and don't think about going noplace. Ye need t' piss, ye step over to them bushes, y' hear?' He climbed down, slammed the door, stretched himself and spat on the ground. Then, seeming to soften a little, he wandered round to Pip's side of the truck and thrust his bristly head through the windowframe. 'Listen, boy, y' know ah would take yer in if ah could. But see the sign? Clear as day, ain't it?'

It was indeed as clear as day:

NO COLORED ALLOWED BY ORDER OF MANAGEMENT

11

Pip waited with the panting dog. He figured he could jump down and head cross-country and he might not be caught. But the fact was, old Mr Zachery was pretty much the only person he knew in the world. He watched the old man take a seat in the bright diner, smoking more cigarettes over steaming mugs of coffee as the waitress brought him huge trays of food. As new customers arrived or left, Pip caught faint snatches of Country music from the jukebox inside.

A memory came to him of his father in a checked shirt on a holiday morning, singing loudly and breaking into little dance moves as he fried pancakes for the three of them. Pip's father was always cheerful, but that was a special day when father and son were heading off with a packed lunch to fish in their secret place near an old stone bridge. 'Pop and Pip time', his mama called it. It seemed then that the future would keep running on for ever like the endless water beneath his toes.

In the hot truck, with Amigo smouldering against his body, it suddenly struck Pip that if he looked at the big map of America pinned to his mother's classroom wall, he would not have the slightest idea where he might be. And even less idea of where he was headed.

'All righty, boy. What's that? Y' been cryin'? Jes' when ah got yer a bacon roll with ketchup 'n everthang. Yer wan' Co-Cola or Sebmup?'

He handed Pip a cold soda and a bag of steaming food, and tossed a scrap to the dog. Then Pip became aware of his hunger, which was the ravenous hunger that only a teenager knows.

Zachery refuelled and the old truck clattered on mile after mile, swallowing the endless ribbon of the road. Now they were in sparsely populated cotton country, where skinny dogs barked from dusty yards and skinnier kids swung from tyres in trees, and endless fields were spotted with the upturned buttocks of migrant workers.

'Ah bin thinkin',' said Zachery. 'Seems ah owe yer some expl'nation 'bout what ah got in store for ye. Me 'n mah family live 'bout four more hours from here. Ain't nuttin' special 'bout Dead River Farm – fawty-farve acres of thirst an' dust. My wife, Lilybelle, ain't in good health. Ah mean she cain't raise from her bed. That's why ah need a good strong boy like you, see? We give yer a place to lay yer head 'n all the food ye want. In return, you look after Lilybelle like she's yer own momma, Gawd rest her soul.'

He hawked and spat out of the window. 'Mah poor Lilybelle cain't do nothin' fer herself no more, so you gotta clean her, an' lift her, an' help her do all the things any human needs t' do. Way it works at Dead River – if Momma ain't happy, ain't nobody happy. Most 'f all you gotta read t' her, y' hear? Tha's why ah picked you outta all the kids ah coulda chose. If there's one thing Lilybelle love, it's a story. She laikes romance 'n all that, or ye cin start right away with that book yourn.'

'Dickens.'

'Yeah, Dickends . . . Things work out, y' cin help out on the yard, then ah might even roll a few nickels yer way. How's that sound, boy? Partners?'

He spat on his palm and reached out a mustard-coloured hand. Pip said nothing.

'Cain't hear ya, boy.'

Pip thought he detected a faint twinkle around the old man's eyes. What choice did he have? Surely life with Zachery and Lilybelle and Amigo would be better than the hard regime of the orphanage. However, that damaged boy was a long way off trusting another adult. He kept on staring at the outstretched hand, gnarled and leathery as a coalman's glove. But he would not shake it.

Zachery chuckled. 'Snee, hee, hee! Ah laikes a fella who knows his maind. You shake when yer ready t' shake an' not a day before.'

He brought his hand sharply back to the wheel, swerving violently to avoid a blaring eighteen-wheeler. The stream of curses from the old man's mouth would have cleared a church in an instant. When he had recovered, he lit the freshly rolled cigarette that Pip handed him.

'One last thang ah gotta tell ye,' said the voice within the smoke. 'Kinda warning, ah guess. You best stay clear of mah son. He's nainteen years now and . . . wal, ah don't rightly know what goes on in that gallumpin' head o' his. He don't do nuthin' for his momma. He's got hisself in with a crowd ah don't care for – too much liquor, too many guns. Heed mah warnin', boy . . . You jes' stay outta his way and Erwin won't do ye no harm.'

2

The Hypnotist's Tale

From the deck of my bungalow I watched the truck
shudder to a halt at Dead River Farm. I raised my hand,
but Zachery ignored me.

I had lived at the end of that track for several months
and I was beginning to get a picture of my neighbour: old
Zachery could be spectacularly rude, but beneath that
bristly surface I reckoned he was as decent as the next
fellow. It was clear that he had been driving all night
because he almost fell from the cab and limped across the
yard towards the farmhouse, coughing like he was
expelling his lungs. Then he kicked open the screen door
and disappeared inside.

Zachery was followed as usual by his dog – a lovely
flea-bitten old thing. The mutt knew better than to enter
the house; he paused to quench his thirst from a bucket
and crawled into the shade of his kennel by the porch.

Nothing unusual about any of this, you might say. But a moment later the passenger door opened a crack and I realized there was someone else inside the truck. Out he stepped – a lost-looking Black boy in huge boots, with bright eyes in his round face and sticky-up hair like a scrawny little angel. Even stranger, the lad was holding nothing but a large leather book.

He stood right in the centre of the cobbled yard, shielding his eyes from the raging sun. Then he began to turn slowly round and round, staring in bewilderment, but never once looking to where I sat, not two hundred yards across the way. The lad seemed to be taking in the small sounds – the shuffling chickens and the post-mortem contractions of the truck.

I'm not sure why, but I felt awful sorry for the tiny man, whoever he might be. I'd seen several farm workers come and go at Dead River, but there was something different about this fellow – an intelligence perhaps . . . I can't quite describe it. I was about to call out and see if I could help when he set off in Zachery's footsteps across the chaotic yard. He paused for a moment on the porch, with the book clutched tightly to his chest, and then he let himself nervously into the house.

But wait a minute! My ma would kill me . . . I should have started with the introductions! My name is Jack – Dr Jack Morrow, to use my full moniker, originally a native of Dublin. The reason I found myself so far from the Fair City is easy enough to explain – I had taken a job at the new university on the outskirts of town.

When I arrived fresh off the plane, a pretty young

leasing agent brought me to see that bungalow, the last in a line of identical properties – all newly built in white-washed clapboard, with a deck and a yard at the front. My rent would be slightly lower than my neighbours', she told me. No, she was not doing me a favour on account of my winning Irish charm; the fact was that my neighbours enjoyed sweeping views across the fields to the distant mauve mountains, whereas my bungalow looked straight into the rustic shambles of Dead River Farm. Every evening, when I had finished at the university, I sat with a cold beer and my feet up on the rails and gazed into that remnant of American history: the rickety farm buildings, the rusting motorcars, the spindly windmill on stilts, the skeleton of a tractor and the posse of poultry pecking amongst the weeds.

To tell you the truth, the view didn't bother me at all. I've always been more interested in people than fields. Besides, it gave me plenty of stories for the folks back home. Once a week I called my family, expensive as it was, and the many Morrows gathered around the phone to hear the latest instalment from Dead River Farm. They thought I was making it all up until I sent them a set of Polaroids – I even managed to get a sneaky shot of Zachery plucking a chicken wearing long johns . . . that's Zachery in the long johns, not the chicken!

Zachery made no secret of what he thought of the scholars and academics who were settling into his neighbourhood. I will never forget our very first encounter: the old man shuffled across the track, vigorously scratching his groin. Ignoring my outstretched hand, he

17

spat in the general direction of my car, stared long and hard into my eyes and said – if I can recall the expression – *'You look like y' wuz born at the top o' the ugly tree an' hit each branch face first on th' way down!'*

So much for Southern hospitality! But as far as I was concerned, the old man and his funny farm were nothing to do with me – I was an outsider; an accidental observer, if you like. Mine was a different world altogether; my world was the bright, new, pioneering America of the 1960s. Yes indeed, the times were definitely a-changin'.

I'll tell you what . . . to get the full picture, why don't you join me on a little drive to my place of work? It won't take long. Hop in and I'll give you a tour.

You've not said anything about my car. What you're looking at is a limited edition silver Alfa Romeo 2600 'Spider' with a reclining sunroof and all the trimmings. I'm not one to brag, but this beauty cost me half my first year's salary – not bad for a fellow from a Dublin terrace! I'll admit that one or two Polaroids of the Spider might have found their way across the Atlantic, and my youngest sister, Caitlin, described it as 'totally groovy'. All I can tell you is you'll get a smoother ride than you would in Zachery's old tin bucket.

I expect you'd like some music while we drive. The soundtrack of those years was the Beach Boys, Joan Baez and – especially exciting for me – a young British band called The Beatles . . . perhaps you've heard of them.

Now we're off . . . along the rutted dirt track, with the chaos of Dead River receding in the mirror and the warm wind blowing in your hair. To your right are the Toytown bungalows, each with a neat little lawn and a station wagon in the driveway. My neighbours are friendly enough, but you'd think their goal in life was to live in identical houses, watch the same TV channels and save their salary for a food mixer! As we pass, we are greeted with nice waves and friendly smiles . . . Did you ever see such white teeth?

To your left are the endless parched fields I mentioned, broken only by a colossal army of electricity towers marching towards the horizon. After a few minutes we reach the copse of poplar trees at the end of the dirt track, with the sweet smell of magnolia in the air. When there's a pause in the traffic, we turn right and soon we are cruising along Main Street. It's a brave new world all right! Here's a Drive-Thru McDonald's; and should you need it, there's a KFC next door. If you're still peckish, we've not one, but three supermarkets! And if you're looking for a place to take your lover on a Saturday night, why, there's the drive-in movie house, showing Hitchcock's *The Birds*. I went a fortnight ago and saw the new James Bond movie, *Dr No*, which was marvellous.

Would you look around at the bright and confident people? Of course, there are old timers in wrinkled suits, but what I notice is the young women with big hair, pillbox hats and oversized sunglasses. I see handsome men sporting paisley shirts with butterfly collars, flared trousers and white Stetson hats. Some of them have huge sideburns like the earwarmers Ma made us wear back home in winter.

You won't find many here in the South, but we're

hearing about a new species called the hippies, or flower children, who go about with bare feet and ragged clothes – I've heard they remove their clothing altogether at the pop festivals!

But that's not the whole picture: while half of America's men are growing their hair, their stubble-headed brothers are preparing for the bloody, wasteful war in Vietnam. Over the next decade many would return draped in the Stars and Stripes.

After a couple of miles we leave the town, and now you get your first view of the university . . . do you see it up there on the grassy hill? It's what the poet might call a citadel of concrete and glass, sparkling and gleaming like a ship from another galaxy. *This* is where I belong! For I am Dr Jack Morrow, Head of Neurological Research. Just thirty-two years old and I have my own designated parking space!

Without doubt this first year here in America has been the most exciting of my life. Why wouldn't it be, when I have free run of these state-of-the-art laboratories with the softly whirring machines and all the wires and monitors? I'm like a child in a sweetie shop and I get paid for the privilege! I think you could safely say that we've created the finest Neurology Department on the planet.

Right along here you'll find my office, with my name – DR JACK MORROW – on the door. My specialism is the astonishing field of Neuro-Linguistic Programming and Hypnotherapy, pioneered by a fellow named Milton Erickson, who is a bit of an idol of mine. The work that goes on here is – if you'll excuse the pun – mind-bending!

When I first arrived at the university I dare say I was a source of great amusement. I certainly heard a few nicknames – 'HypnoPaddy' was a good one, or simply 'The Leprechaun'; but they soon changed their tune when they saw me at work. One year on, it's standing room only in Dr Morrow's lectures!

To give a couple of examples, my team and I are currently investigating hypnosis as a means of pain control . . . Like the fellow under full hypnosis who had his appendix removed in front of two hundred people in the lecture theatre. Not so much as a squeak of anaesthetic and he was grinning like a babby throughout! And I've been known to do the same trick with dentistry, childbirth and even surgical amputations.

Another subject I'm interested in is the use of hypnosis with psychological problems. My team have done great work with deeply traumatized soldiers. We use a technique called regression, which takes them right back to the battlefield, so that we can release the anger or the fear. Ah, the look of gratitude on their faces when we liberate them from that absolute hell . . .

So you can see why I'm getting something of a reputation on the campus. When students see my demonstrations for the first time, it seems like sorcery . . . Morrow the Magician, they call me!

But of course the thing that has always set me apart – and led to so much teasing back at school – is my eyes. I suppose that's what old man Zachery was referring to when he said I was born at *the top of the ugly tree*. At home in Ireland, a straight-talking girlfriend once broke off our relationship by saying, 'Jack, you're a lovely gentle guy with the sweetest smile and you're not at all bad looking with that mop of curly hair, but all my friends tease me about . . . you know, your eyes! They give me the heebie-jeebies, Jack Morrow, so they do. Could you not see yourself wearing some sunglasses or something?'

Ah, my eyes! I suppose they are rather curious. Useful for my work, of course, but . . . take a look . . .

. . . and just relax for a moment while I slip on the old white coat. Now, if you know nothing about hypnosis, you are missing out on one of the true wonders of the human mind. Would you care to sit while I'm talking? The big chair reclines back like this . . . and feel free to pull off your shoes and give your toes a little wiggle. That's right . . . we keep things very informal in Neurological Research.

Just let my words float about in your mind, and although you may not understand every detail, the curious thing is that you'll retain everything that's important. Are you feeling a little drowsy . . . ? I can open a window if you want me to . . .

Where were we now? Ah yes . . . hypnosis. Hypnosis ranges from 'light trance' to 'deep induction'. Now, light trance is a part of your everyday life, although by its very nature you are not very aware of it. All that's happening is your brain is resting from all that activity. For example, we've just seen old Zachery and the boy returning from a long journey, remember? Along the way, the little fellow would certainly have glazed over as he stared out of the cab, just like the dog beside him. Zachery at the wheel would have fallen into trance too – just enough alertness to keep the wheels on the freeway (I'd like to think), but his brain patterns would have been very suppressed.

Light trance feels warm and pleasant, doesn't it now? Like drifting about on a fuzzy cloud of love! So don't hesitate to relax and enjoy the sensation as Dr Morrow dims the lights . . . It'll do you no harm and you look like you could do with a nice little relax, if you don't mind me saying.

It's as if you keep drifting away, but the point I'm trying to make is that the incredible state that we call 'deep hypnotic induction' is a heightened version of the light trance you may be experiencing now. As the hypnotist talks, the subject (that's you, for the sake of argument) becomes deeply relaxed . . . Perhaps you notice your limbs relaxing and the warm sensation of drifting down . . . down . . . down like riding in a velvety elevator . . . Now why would you want to fight that?

Deep induction is a *unique mental state* – I mean, it's not sleep (although some of my students might disagree) but it's very different from normal waking consciousness. I have found clear similarities between subjects in deep hypnotic trance and yogis in meditation. We had one in the laboratory a while ago – extraordinary fellow, he was!

Just for fun, imagine I am hypnotizing you now . . . Do you notice that my voice seems rather distant? And after a while you become susceptible to my suggestions, so if I tell you to focus your attention on the tip of your right index finger, which is feeling a little twitchy, well, it's difficult to ignore it.

Here's a question for you . . . Have you considered that every time you watch a movie or get lost in a book, you allow the filmmaker or the author to weave a hypnotic spell and carry you into trance? Perhaps you experience real fear, or even cry real tears. To give a random example, you may feel the stirrings of empathy when you hear of the hardships of a lonely orphan boy. Without even realizing, you have allowed the storyteller to enter your mind. This is the incredible power of suggestion. I could argue that at this very moment you have given permission for me to enter your mind . . . You barely noticed, but Jack has 'hijacked your brain'!

Hello, Jack Morrow calling . . . I'm inside your head . . . Thanks for the invitation. I've had a look about, and apart from a few murky corners, everything seems in pretty good order!

Do you see how it works? And you've probably realized by now that I'm no run-of-the-mill scientist. Although my colleagues in Neurology are clever with the wires and the sensors and the brain scans, the thing they can't seem to grasp is that hypnosis is more of an art than a science. My colleagues are smart – brilliant even – but not one of them has what my ma would call 'The Gift'. She and Da both had it, and the minute I was born they looked at my eyes and said, '*Ah now! Do you see that? The little fellow has it written all across his face, so he has. It'll make him or it'll break him, but little Jack has The Gift . . .*'

That's why they need a fellow like Jack Morrow in

this new university – it's not something you advertise, but I have The Gift, see. Here in the laboratories amongst the dials and the machines, I am employing the ancient skills of my Celtic ancestors. So don't be too surprised if you hear old Jack using the old dreamy-voice technique, which hypnotists have employed since the dawn of time. Don't be at all alarmed if you hear me say that *my voice is the voice of the wind in the trees, or the soft whisper of waves on the shores of Kerry . . . You have nothing to fear because I will be your guide . . . Just let my words settle in your mind as you drift deeper and deeper . . . until you are quite, quite relaxed . . .*

And as I relaxed on the deck of my bungalow on that balmy summer's evening, the never-ending sky above Dead River Farm might have been a metaphor for the endless possibilities I sensed within my work. What I was beginning to understand in the spring of 'sixty-three is that there are truly no limits to the potential of the human mind.

But I was wrong about one thing – I thought that Dead River Farm was a relic of a forgotten age that had nothing to do with me. What I failed to realize was that the bewildered young passenger letting himself so fearfully into the farmhouse was Pip, the extraordinary young fellow who would change my life, and the lives of all he met . . .

And now I'll ask you to keep looking into my eyes . . .

Come with me now as I take you deeper and deeper into the hypnotist's tale . . .

3

Lilybelle

The ragged curtains of the farmhouse were drawn permanently against the sun, so it took a while for Pip to adjust to the gloom within.

A deep silence sat in the house and yet he felt watched. Above his head a motionless fan was festooned with cobwebs, and on a mantelpiece stood a broken clock – the hands stopped at twenty to nine.

At the orphanage, every surface had been scrubbed and polished – 'shipshape', they called it – so the neglected state of Dead River Farm troubled him.

Then Pip noticed the eyes – dozens of black eyes staring down at him. They were the glassy eyes of mounted animal heads. Each dead beast and every object in the room was thick with dust.

In spite of the heat, he felt a shudder run through his body; he caught a movement from a side room and found

Zachery, slumped in exhaustion, in a stifling kitchen where fat flies feasted on unwashed pans. When he saw the boy, the old man rose silently, tossed some cold meat and bread onto the table and handed Pip a mug of creamy milk. They ate side by side and did not speak, although Zachery carried out a noisy ritual of tearing and sucking and gasping. Pip realized that with his mutilated teeth, the old man was unable to chew, and this also accounted for the pile of discarded crusts on his plate.

It was at that moment that Pip heard a sound that brought every hair on his body to attention – a tiny tinkling bell accompanied by a sleepy singsong voice from the back of the house: 'Zat you, Zach? You brung me a bo-oy?'

Zachery reached out and gripped Pip's arm so tightly that he let out a cry and dropped his bread on the floor. The old man pushed his bristly face against Pip's and hissed, 'Ah need ter rest now, boy, y' hear? You go on back and innerduce yerself to Lilybelle. Every taime ye hear that bell ye run t' her saide. You tawk polite an' don't say nothin' 'bout her 'pearance. Go on now, skeedaddle!'

Zachery stumbled out of the kitchen and Pip was alone again. He retrieved the bread from the floor and some of the crusts from Zachery's plate and stuffed them in his pocket for later.

There was that tinkly bell again, and the sweet melodic voice – 'Come an' show y'self.'

Leaving the plates on the table, Pip returned to the living room, where the glass-eyed herd watched over him. He noticed a dark corridor leading to the back of the house, with a row of mismatched doors and walls papered with fading newspaper. From the far end came the sound of laughter from a television or radio.

'Someone there?' she cooed. 'Don' be shaiy now.'

The words floated like sickly incense in the air so Pip could not decide which door to choose. At random he picked a battered wooden door and turned the greasy handle. It was the wrong one. Zachery was standing in a squalid bedroom preparing to rest. He had removed his dungarees and was wearing nothing but a string vest on his skeletal torso and a pair of ancient underpants, exposing the thinnest, whitest legs Pip had ever seen. The old man glared furiously and waved him from the room.

Pip returned hastily to the corridor, hugging the book to his chest. Again he heard the tinkling bell and the teasing saccharine voice. 'Ah hear y' now. Don' ha-ide. Ah'd like t' see yer purty face.'

Pip selected another door – a yellowing plastic panel, which slid sideways on uneven runners. Wrong again. This was a foul-smelling bathroom, with a cracked and filthy toilet. It was clear that no one had bathed in months because the nicotine-coloured tub was piled with unwashed clothes.

'Come 'n faind me now. Ah'm longin' t' see you.'

Two more doors to choose from. The one to his left was unnaturally tall, as if some clumsy carpenter had raised the frame almost to the ceiling. Pip reached out and touched the metal handle. It felt icy to his touch. He pulled and rattled but the door was firmly locked. High above his head Pip noticed a porcelain nameplate screwed to the frame. It was grimy and hard to read in the half-light. Standing on tiptoe, he jumped up and wiped the dirt with his fingertip. It was a child's name plaque from long ago – a souvenir from a fair perhaps, or a visit to the sea. Pip saw a hand-painted image of two honey bears in hats – one in dungarees and one in a flowery dress. They might have made him smile, had it not been for the name painted carefully between: *Erwin*. Pip released the handle like a high-voltage cable.

Tinkle! Tinkle! Tinkle! 'Ah hear y' comin'. You're growin' warm.'

And there was the last door at the very end of the corridor. It was a battered candy-coloured door with a rose china doorknob. On a small table to one side stood a vase of plastic flowers.

He stood before the candy-coloured door for what seemed like hours. He listened to the deep silence broken only by the tinkling laughter of a TV show from behind the door. He felt the sultry heat, and he was, without doubt, the loneliest boy in America.

The silvery siren voice called again, trembly and seductive. 'Why, ah do believe thar's a precious l'il boy standin' raight outsaide mah door. Ah cain't imagine why he won' step insaide an' meet Lilybelle.'

Pip's heart was pumping furiously and he realized he had forgotten to breathe.

'That's raight,' she sang. 'All y' gotta do is turn the purty handle. All y' gotta do is step insaide.'

Before he could change his mind, Pip seized the rose doorknob, feeling the serration of its petals in his palm.

With a gasp of resolution, he swung open the candy-coloured door.

What he saw sent a tide of dread and confusion surging through his exhausted body. The salmon-pink room contained a double bed, so wide that it almost reached the walls on either side. On tables and shelves stood teetering piles of magazines, discarded burger boxes and empty soda bottles. The smell was almost overwhelming – a choking odour of cheap cologne, masking something fetid below. Pip saw a black-and-white TV set, a shabby collection of soft toys – some wrapped in cellophane – a long-handled bedpan, a chugging electric fan and hundreds of pill bottles. The occupant of the room was clearly an amateur artist because there were dozens of gaudy paintings propped on every surface.

On the bed itself, amidst twisted sheets and pastel-pink eiderdowns, lay a fleshy landscape of hills, valleys, gorges and caves. And in the centre of that chaotic vortex of flesh Pip saw an extraordinary face beneath an elaborate beehive hairstyle with a faint pink wash. The face was so heavy with make-up that it resembled a porcelain doll. It was a sweet baby face with slow-blinking lashes, rouged cheeks and cherry lips, and it smiled at Pip as the TV laughed and laughed and laughed.

Slowly Pip began to understand that this was Lilybelle – the landscape was her gargantuan body. Now he made out fat toes, round hands with tiny fingers holding the bell, and the rolls of flesh in a nylon nightie, which were thighs and belly, tumbling from one side of the bed to the other.

'Oh my,' she sang. 'You brought a *book*! What a precious boy you are. Come here, honey chil'. Lemme take a lo-o-ong look at you.'

Pip's legs were made of concrete.

'Aw, he's shaiy. Ain't that cute! Maybe he ain't seen a curvesome lady afore.'

Lilybelle batted her lashes, and Pip realized that although Mr Zachery's wife was indeed larger than any person he had ever seen or imagined, her face was surprisingly pretty and her voice was soft as caramel.

In one tidal wave of emotion, the whole experience of the long journey, the lonely years in the orphanage and the death of his beloved parents erupted from him. He simply could not contain himself. Pip's eyelids melted beneath a torrent of hot tears. He trembled and shuddered and dissolved.

'Oh Lordy!' said the doll's head on the bed. 'Oh, ah declare, don't craiy. Ah cain't stand t' see a boy craiy. C'mon raight over an' sit besaide Lilybelle. Look, there's a li'l place just for you.' She patted a space beside her.

At last Pip's need for human warmth outweighed his fear. He stumbled forward, clutching his book to his heart. Squeezing along the wall, he huddled into a fleshy valley. As he trembled and sobbed, Pip became aware of Lilybelle's huge pink beehive hovering over him, and her hand gently stroking his shoulder. Apart from the occasional clout at the orphanage, this was the first human touch he had received since the death of his parents four years before.

'What's yer name, honey chil'?'

'P-P-Pip . . .'

'Oh! Oh, ain't that ador'ble? P-P-Pip. I laike that name. You come to stay with us, ah understand?'

'No . . . No, I ain't. I gotta leave right now. I gotta go . . . some place. Right now . . . tonight!'

'Bless yo' li'l heart, Pip, ah understand everthang is new to you. Old Zach is a grouchy ol' billy goat, but he don't mean no harm. Also I realize you probably ain't seen a large lady laike me afore. That's OK. I know mah bawdy ain't pleasin' ter the eye. But when we git ter know each other, you'll learn that Lilybelle is beautiful inside. Truly ah am, Pip. Truly ah am.'

A vast heat emanated from Lilybelle, as well as a deep musky odour from within the blankets, like the smell of a bear-cave in winter.

'Ah do b'lieve in beauty, Pip. Ah love to hear beautiful songs on the wah'less. Most 'f awl, I love to make beautiful paintin's. Take a look, Pip. Ah made every one with mah own hands.'

She thrust a pile of decorated cardboard onto his lap. From behind tear-filled eyes, Pip saw naively painted landscapes of beaches and palm trees. Jungles filled with parrots and exotic animals. All lovingly detailed in tropical colours.

'These are all the places ah'd like to go. But now ah cain't wawk no more, ah have t' visit in mah head. Maybe you'd like t' join me? We cin take a vacation together!'

Pip wiped his eyes and listened to Lilybelle's soothing tones.

'Y' know, ah lie here awl day an' awl naight. I make mah paintin's an' ah stare outside. Ah watched a whole street o' new houses goin' up, plank by plank, awl painted white, neat as you please. Can you see, Pip? Look, there's a strange man sits outside with pah-culiar eyes. Ah see him, but he don' see me . . .'

Pip followed her gaze. There was indeed a person sitting on the deck of the bungalow opposite the yard. A curly-haired man of about thirty years, very short in stature; he was working at a portable typewriter placed on a small table. He glanced up as if searching the air for an idea, and although there were some two hundred yards between them, Pip was struck – no, he was *dumbfounded* by those eyes.

For some unaccountable reason Pip found himself drifting momentarily away – out of the window, through the stifling heat of the late afternoon and across the dirt track . . .

And then Lilybelle was tugging at his sleeve and her incessant chatter returned him to the salmon-pink room . . .

'Course, ah got a li'l girl t' look after me, but truth is, she ain't strong 'nuff, Pip. She cain't lift mah bawdy ter . . . you know, clean me 'n everthang. Besaides, she's what you maight call the silent type, so she don't never read t' me. Fact is, Hannah don't say one word from dawn to dusk. She's s'posed to clean too, but truth is, she cain't even care for herself, bless her li'l heart. Only reason ah keep her on is she cooks so good. So y' see, Pip, tha's why ah tol' Zach, bring me back a chil' who can keep me proper company an' read t' me. We cin be friends, Pip. Would y' like that?'

Pip said nothing, but he became aware of a profound exhaustion in every limb of his body.

34

'Sure you would. Now c'mon, don' waste no time. Turn off the TV. Lemme hear you read. Is tha' a storybook in your hand?'

Reluctantly Pip opened the cover. On the inside page, beneath the address of his mama's school, was a neat pencil inscription:

For my darling Pip. May your expectations be great.

Pip could never see those words without recalling the magical day just before Christmas when Mama had first told him about his baby brother or sister, curled so snugly in her belly. They had sat cuddled together, watching the cold world outside, and he had read to her from *Great Expectations*. She said that although she was head teacher and should never say such an unfair thing, Pip was the best reader in the class and maybe in the whole school. And as if she had arranged it just for him, the sky opened its gentle dark eyes and let loose snowflakes, so fat and slow, it was like a dream. And as Pip sat in the windowseat, Mama went over and took a pencil from her school bag. She sharpened it carefully, creating a perfect wooden spiral, and then wrote, slow and neat, that special inscription inside the book. And she said that from that day, her book would be his. And no matter if she ever forgot when the baby came, he was and always would be her precious Pip. She told him then that he could do *anything* with his life. That his future was as big and bright as he dared to dream. 'Yes, indeed, Pip, your expectations are very great indeed.'

Pip did not tell that story to Lilybelle, or show her the

pencilled words, but because she had stroked his shoulder and shared her paintings, he showed her the illustrations that brought the story alive.

As her swollen fingers turned the pages, Pip listened to her laboured breathing, loud and heavy through her nose.

At last Lilybelle pushed the book across to him and said flatly, 'Ah wish ah hadn't seen them pitchers, Pip. Ah wish you'd never let me see. When ah see beaut'ful pitchers laike that, ah wanna toss ma paintins on the stove. That book o' yours makes me feel dumber than a bucket o' hammers.'

She collapsed on the pillows with a heavy sigh. 'Bless yo' li'l heart, Pip. Ah know you didn't mean to cawse no trouble. Now read. Go on, read the story.'

That was when Pip was confronted with an awkward truth. The fact was, he hadn't done much in the way of reading in the orphanage, and now the long words and old-fashioned language of Dickens were too much for him. However, his mother had read the story to the whole class so many times that he knew it almost by heart. With the aid of memory, his stunted literacy skills and the richly detailed line engravings to fire his imagination, Pip began to tell Lilybelle the story in his own way. In that stifling bedroom deep in the South, he conjured up the foggy marshes of Kent, where his namesake, Pip, an orphan just like him, had knelt before his parents' graves. Then, suddenly, 'the most fearsome man you ever seen jumps out the mist. His name is Magwitch, see. He's an escaped convict and that's the name fer a fellah who breaks outta jail. He comes up to Pip an' he says, "You breathe one word an' I'll cut your throat from ear t' ear . . ."'

'Oh mah!' squealed Lilybelle, fanning herself with a magazine. 'That's the most shockin' thing ah ever heard!'

And so the storytelling sessions began. And for those hours, Lilybelle and Pip lost themselves entirely. Pip described the dilapidated mansion belonging to Miss Havisham, a weird and wealthy spinster, dumped at the altar and dressed for ever in her fading wedding dress. Pip was just attempting to bring alive her adopted daughter, Estella, when there was a quiet tap at the door.

The shock of the unexpected sound brought Pip's imagination racing back across the foggy marshes, over the ocean, and through the years to where he sat perched on Lilybelle's bed.

'Ah smell summin' naice!' sang Lilybelle. 'Come on in now. We're gettin' hungry!'

And very slowly, the rose-petal doorknob turned and an enormous tray entered sideways through the doorway, piled high with steaming food. Behind the tray was a girl.

Seeing Pip sitting there, she seemed to panic, and he had barely a moment to take her in before she had shoved the tray on the bed and disappeared. Pip was left with a fleeting vision of a wild, ochre-skinned girl of about his age. Her feet were bare and her clothes were a ragged T-shirt and jeans. It was the gleaming black of her hair and eyes that affected him most. Those angry oval eyes – and to his surprise, Pip realized that she was a Native Indian girl.

Lilybelle barely acknowledged the girl. She was staring happily at the tray, which overflowed with food – fried potatoes, baked beans, charred chicken wings, wodges of thickly buttered cornbread and a bowl of lurid pink blancmange beneath an avalanche of whipped cream, scattered with multicoloured sprinkles.

Pip's head was reeling. The girl had affected him more than he could comprehend – she appeared scruffy and poor and wild, but to Pip's mind, she was disturbingly beautiful. There had been no girls at the orphanage, but this one had agitated parts of his being he never knew existed. Again and again, his thoughts returned to that smooth-skinned copper face with the high cheekbones and complex almond eyes. The girl had made not one sound, and yet those angry eyes had yelled at him, *Whoever you are, you are not welcome! Do not look at me! Do not speak to me! Do not try to know me!*

And now she was gone. And Pip was left rattled and reeling. What was that phrase he had heard? *Love at first sight.* Pip had never understood its meaning – and yet . . .

And yet . . .

And yet . . .

Pip turned to Lilybelle, chewing contentedly on a chicken wing. He whispered, 'I seen a girl . . .'

'Did y' now?' she mumbled. 'An' thar's me thankin' the tray floated in like Aladdin's carpet . . .' She folded a slice of cornbread and dunked it deep in her beans. 'Wal, that was Hannah . . . *Mmm, mm, mmm* . . . Laike ah say, she do the cookin' roun' here. She understand everthang raight enough, but don't 'spect her to say nothin', 'cos Hannah cain't tawk. She's what y' maight call moot. Kinda surly too. Don't pay her no maind.'

Lilybelle prised open Pip's fingers and stuffed his hand with French fries and tender scraps of chicken, which smelled sweeter than life itself.

'*Mmm . . . mmm . . . mwah . . .* You have an except'nal intelligence, Pip. Anyone tell you that? A boy of your age who cin read laike that, why tha's a *remarkable* thang. But see, Pip, Hannah ain't laike you . . . She do what she tol' when she's mainded and she don' make too much trouble, but 'tween you 'n me' – Lilybelle tapped the side of her head – 'she's slow as molasses up hill.

'*Mmm . . . mmm . . .* Now, Pip, ah adore havin' you here an awl, but ah'm sure you're taired after all that travellin'. Also . . . wal, maybe Zach mentioned this, but it may be best if you're settled afore our li'l boy returns. Jes for the first day or two. Erwin's faine if he's in a good mood, but if he's been at the moonshaine . . . wal, he cin git a little *twitchy.*'

Pip closed the book and slid quickly to the floor.

'You gotta kiss fer Lilybelle?'

Well, a thirteen-year-old boy doesn't hand out kisses too freely, so Pip mumbled and muttered awkwardly until Lilybelle hauled him against her vast body and planted a sweet, greasy smacker on his forehead. Then she whispered into his ear, 'Ah've loved havin' you here, Pip. Truly ah have. Come agin tomorrow, y' hear? Promise you won' run away, Pip? Ah couldn't bear to lose another chil' . . .'

Pip turned the rose-petal handle and let himself into the dim corridor. He stepped nervously, alive to every sound, scanning with dread for Erwin and with restless hope for Hannah. He crept past the tall, tall door, then into the living room with the stopped clock, and the eyes like spies. The girl was nowhere to be seen.

Out on the porch, Pip found Zachery, spindly legs stretched in a broken easy chair, with Amigo curled at his feet. The old man was dressed in his long johns, a bottle by his hand, rolling a cigarette, as a peachy sunset filled the sky. Pip stared across the track to the whitewashed bungalow, but there was no sign of the strange man he had seen through Lilybelle's window.

'You an' Lilybelle git 'quainted?' said Zachery, gesturing at a plastic stool near his feet.

'Yes, sir.'

'Her health ain't good, but she's still the gull ah married. Ah'll go 'n tawk to her by and by. Now listen up, boy, ye must be hankerin' fer yer bed. That buildin' thar, that's the tool store – young Hannah sleeps 'bove . . .'

There was her name again . . . there was her name . . .

'Yer bed's directly across the yard 'bove the stable block. Ye'll find a ladder, an' thars mor'n 'nuff blankets t' keep you warm, an' water at the pump.'

'Thank you, sir.'

'That's good, Pip. Y' know ah'd find you a bed in the house if the law permitted. Anyhows, you 'n me gonna git 'long faine. You don' ruffle mah feathers, 'n ah don' ruffle yourn.'

There was a moment of absolute silence, which almost seemed like calm. Pip tried to imagine himself living there, with the hens and the dog and the beautiful silent girl; reading stories to Lilybelle and being fed.

On the other hand, there were no locks on the yard

gates, so presumably he would be free to wander away whenever he felt like it. All he would have to do is tuck his book under his arm and stroll calmly towards those mauve mountains on the horizon . . .

And a faint picture floated into his head in which he and Hannah walked side by side into the setting sun . . .

But as if he were reading Pip's mind, Zachery reached down to his feet and picked up a shotgun. He raised it to his eye and squinted through the sights, then laid it on his lap and fondled its parts as if it were a mewling pussycat. He said, 'By th' way, my neighbour, Cletus, has a pack o' huntin' hounds. Ye wander off without mah permission – yer'll come home in naice thin slaices, y' hear me? Laike bacon rashers, boy.'

Pip shuddered silently on his stool. The orange sky turned violent red and purple like a spreading wound. Then, from far away, the faint drone of an engine stirred the silence. The sound barely entered Pip's consciousness, but in absolute synchronicity, Zachery and Amigo sat bolt upright and stared goggle-eyed at the dirt track leading to the yard.

'It's Erwin!' hissed the old man. 'Move yerself, boy! Go on – git t' bed – skedaddle!'

Pip raced towards the stable block, but the vehicle was approaching at speed and he realized he would never make it in time. The dog was faster – tail between legs, he scuttled into the doghouse. Pip heard the roar of an engine, saw a rapidly approaching dust-storm and, in an instant of blind panic, fell to his knees and scrambled into the kennel after Amigo.

A split second later, a battered olive-green Jeep hurtled

into the yard, engine gunning, brakes squealing. Pip huddled against the dog, who scrambled to the back of his den.

From his hiding place, Pip watched a pair of gargantuan combat boots swing lazily from the vehicle and stride across the yard, more slowly than is normal in a man. Less than three feet from where Pip crouched, the legs halted, like twin tree trunks framed by the arched mouth of the dog-house. Pip clutched his arm tight around Amigo's trembling ribs. Under his knees, he felt the curves and splinters of gnawed knucklebones.

In his short life, Pip had experienced more suffering than is reasonable, but now his terror knew no bounds. He felt a warm trickle seep inside the leg of his pants.

'How y' doin', Erwin?'

There was a long, long pause. Then, from way up near the roof of the farmhouse or the menacing sky above, Pip heard the man's slow, deep, terrible voice. And it said: 'Ah hear you brung a boy?'

'Well, that's true, son. Your ma needs help, an' this boy cin read. You know how your momma love—'

'What kaind of boy?'

'Jes a reg'lar boy. Two arms, two legs an' a heed on top—'

'He ain't a *Negro* boy?'

'Ah'm tryin' to 'splain, Erwin. He was the only one as could read. Besaides, a Whaite boy would'a cost more than ah got. Y' know we ain't worried 'bout that kinda thang at Dead River, Erwin . . . never have been. Way ah see it, don' make no diff'rence if the boy's braight blue. S'long as he cin work, any boy's the same to yer ma 'n me.'

'Zat right? Well, maybe it don' make no diff'rence to you . . . maybe it don' make no diff'rence t' me . . . but lemme tell yer summat, it makes a *big* diff'rence to summa mah freends. Mibbe you should mention that to your . . . *boy*. Y' hear what ah'm sayin', ol' man?'

'Ah hear ye, Erwin. Ah hear ye.'

4
The Night (I)

I had a squatter in the bungalow. A stray cat with ginger tiger rings had taken to turning up on my deck. Sometimes when I came home from the university I found him waiting for me, bathing in a pool of sunshine or licking his wrists and washing his pink nose with his paws. He chose to go without a collar and you could tell he was awful proud of that.

What I like about cats is they couldn't give a damn whether you are there or not – although this fellow wasn't averse to the odd tickle behind the ears when the fancy took him. My da used to say that if you call a dog, he comes; but a cat takes a message and gets back to you!

After a few days we became friendly and the little moggy would hop through an open window and march right into the living room, bold as brass, tail sticking up like a car aerial. Then he'd rub against my legs until I relented and forked some food into a bowl. When he purred in thankfulness, I felt insanely grateful for the favour. I named that pussy Finnegan, to remind myself of home.

It was Finnegan who kept me awake the night the boy arrived. The cat was restless, prowling around the bungalow . . . or maybe I was restless myself. It was awful hot, and out in the night the crickets crackled like static.

Sometime in the wee hours I gave up trying to sleep. I switched on the bedside light, picked up a copy of *Scientific American* and got absorbed in a great little article about the development of computers. The fellow was arguing that within a few decades, every home would have their own computer, which they'd use for everything from ordering shopping, to communicating with friends, to educating the kids. There'd be telephones with moving pictures too. What a world that would be!

That was when I noticed the rumbling. I felt the bed vibrate slightly and it crossed my mind that it might be a small earthquake – not unknown in this part of the world. I got up and walked to the front room in my pyjamas. Under my bare feet I felt the floorboards tremble beneath the carpet. It was an unsettling sensation.

There was an unpleasant buzzing sound in the room and I realized it was the windows rattling in their frames. I pulled back the curtain a little and peered into the night, where ragged clouds dragged at a lemon-slice moon. Then a strange thing happened: my front yard and Dead River Farm became bright with wavering spotlights. A convoy of vehicles was approaching along the track.

The rumbling grew louder and I could make out ten or more slow-moving vehicles. It made me shudder to my bones. I stood well out of sight and counted four large motorbikes, several station wagons, a garage tow truck, two or three hefty customized four-wheel drives with giant tyres, spotlights and grilles on their fenders. I even noticed a couple of police patrol cars.

What were they doing out there? Where were they going?

As they trundled by, I caught glimpses of a crew of heavily built White men, some with caps over eyes, or bandanas and thick muscled necks. I saw beards and tattoos and the occasional flicker of studs and rings and chains. For one terrifying moment I thought those visitors were heading for my door . . . but they kept on rolling, up a steep path by the side of Dead River Farm and into the fields above.

For the rest of the night I lay sleepless, my ears scanning the night. I heard occasional shouts and revving engines far away in the fields, and it was almost light before those vehicles returned, the same way they had come, rumbling slowly past my door.

Being a rational fellow, I searched for some explanation for what a group of men would be doing in the dead of night. A hunting party perhaps? Or maybe they played poker or brewed moonshine together?

Whatever it was, it was not conducive to sleep.

5

The Night (II)

Scritch, scritch, scratch!

Pip was woken by a scratching sound in the deep heat of the night. He didn't know where he was and the room was black as pitch. He thought about going into his parents' room opposite. He knew that his mother would half open one eye, pull him under the blankets and nuzzle him against the warmth of her body. He'd wake in the morning and his father would pretend that he'd discovered a baby bear in the bed – he'd grab Pip and they would play-fight until Mama said he'd be late for school.

Then, to his dismay, Pip recalled that his parents were lying dead in the cold ground. With a feeling of over-whelming loneliness, he remembered that he was in the dormitory of the St Joseph Poor Boys' Orphanage. The scratching sound must be another boy in the darkness beyond.

But that wasn't right either. There had been a long, long journey in a truck and now he was lying . . . where? In a bed made of wooden palletes and straw above a disused stable. There had been a huge woman who had stroked his shoulder; a beautiful silent Indian girl; and a giant of a man who hated him with a fierce violence, although he had never once set eyes upon him.

Pip sat up in bed. He heard a faint drone of engines and a cold slab of light leaped onto the ceiling. The light multiplied and a kaleidoscope of geometrical lights danced about the room.

The engines grew louder, and it became clear to Pip that the lights were the headlights of many approaching vehicles. Then the sound seemed so near, he feared they would enter the room.

Pip dived beneath his blanket and squeezed his palms tightly to his ears. It seemed a long time before the sound subsided and the vehicles passed the farmyard and continued uphill into the fields.

And all that remained was the scratching – *scritch, scritch, scratch!* – of rats in the stable below.

6

The Dreamcatcher

The next day was a Saturday, which was just as well because it was after nine before I stirred. Old Finnegan must have let himself in through the bathroom window and now he was padding about on my bed, demanding to be fed.

As I washed and dressed, the memory of the night returned to me. Again I struggled for some explanation for that slow-moving convoy, but the logic eluded me.

After breakfast I decided to take a stroll in the direction they had gone. Of course, it crossed my mind that I might be trespassing, but what harm could I be doing by taking a little walk beside the fields?

It was another sweltering day as I skirted round the side of the farmyard and up a gentle slope lined with twisted apple trees. There were plenty of tyre marks in the cracked clay beneath my feet, and as the path levelled off in the fields, I saw the first of the high voltage towers about a quarter of a mile ahead. The closer I got, the more aware I became of the awesome scale of those pylons – almost twice the height of the ones at home. Near the base of the steel tower stood a red barn with a rusting corrugated roof, not uncommon in that part of the world. It was a large barn but it appeared dwarfed beneath that huge pyramid. The front of the barn was constructed entirely of two enormous wooden doors in the same oxide red; and in front of the doors was a flat area of cinders and compacted rubble, where twenty vehicles could park with ease.

The path continued past the barn, but from this point it narrowed so that it was barely wide enough for a horse. I concluded that the red barn was where the convoy had stopped. I pulled at the great barn doors, but although they clanked and rattled freely, they would not open.

With the sun scorching the back of my neck, I circled round the barn. Except for a hayloft way up near the roof I could see no other door; just the usual heaps of rusting metal and discarded beer bottles amongst thick weeds.

Almost hidden in a tangle of bushes I found a tiny trail – an animal track perhaps. I fancied a walk and I was curious, so with my jacket slung over one shoulder, I waded through waist-high grass alive with butterflies until the trail led me to a cluster of birch and pine trees. It was ridiculously hot and I reproached myself for coming out without a drink. After ten minutes the trail stopped and I found myself on a ridge looking steeply down into a small canyon or natural bowl. It was a little secret valley, and all along the bottom of the valley, a dry creek or river bed wound like a stony scar. It had been a long time since water flowed here, and the roots of the willows along the banks had something desperate about them, like twisting fingers grasping for moisture in the dry river-bed. And then it dawned on me that, of course, this was the Dead River.

I felt a sudden wave of homesickness as I recalled the lush green countryside of Kerry where my family had spent their holidays. I had a memory of trying to keep up with my six older siblings as they whooped and chased each other down a slope like this, to the welcoming waves at Dingle Bay. But this valley seemed lifeless, inhospitable and even dangerous. I suppose what I was feeling was the ancient dilemma of Irish people all over the globe – we go where the opportunities lie, but our hearts belong to the Emerald Isle.

I was about to turn and head home when, with some alarm, I noticed a figure crouched on the bank of the Dead River below me. It took a moment to comprehend that I had stumbled across the secret hiding place of the black-haired girl I had occasionally seen on old Zachery's farm. She didn't see me because she was lost in a dream, squatting silently between the roots of an ancient willow, her wide face and oval eyes fixed intently on the object in her hands. She was working on some kind of ethnic jewellery, and her slim fingers were expertly weaving and twisting a circular willow hoop around a red net. I had seen these things in souvenir stores and I realized she was making what Native Americans call a 'dreamcatcher'.

There was something indescribably magical about

that feral child working patiently with coloured feathers, beads and scraps of wire and yarn; completely focused on her task in that secret den. I suppose she was at that in-between time – not quite a woman and not quite a girl. With that gleaming hair and grubby white T-shirt, she brought to mind the magpies at home, who are supposed to collect sparkling trinkets for their nests . . . *One for sorrow*, goes the rhyme.

I took one step too far and she heard me. Those vivid eyes seemed to shoot up like arrows and she recoiled with fear and anger like a wildcat in a trap. I called down to her: 'Wait a minute. I won't hurt you. I'd love to talk . . . Won't you show me what you're making there? It's the loveliest thing I've seen in a while.'

But my words were left floating like so much woodsmoke, because the barefoot child had snatched her belongings and set off faster than a deer across her valley. When I looked again she was gone, and all that remained was a turquoise feather hanging in the air.

A strange start to the day, and I was looking forward to a cold beer in the cool of my bungalow. But I only got as far as the dented mailbox which sits on a post in front of Dead River Farm when old man Zachery stumbled towards me with a spanner in one hand and a rag in the other.

I waited on the top step of my deck, with sweat running down my collar, and when he drew close I smiled, as is my way. 'Hello there, Mr Zachery. It's definitely time I introduced myself properly. The name's Jack – Dr Jack Morrow, to use my full moniker.'

'Y' Bridish or summat?'

'Well, Irish actually,' I replied with a wink. 'We're a more evolved species!'

Not a flicker of a smile. And I realized he was doing that thing again – just staring at my face for so long it was embarrassing. Eventually he said, 'Yer maighty sweaty. Thought ah saw ye headin' up to th' barn.'

I said, 'Oh yes. I meant no harm. Just a little stroll. See, back home a fellow is free to wander the countryside so long as he keeps to the paths and closes the gates behind him. As a matter of fact, in Kerry—'

'Zat so? Wal, round here a fellah is free to wander so long as he don't maind a barrel o' buckshot up his ass. Jes' a friendly warnin', maind. See, that barn belong to ma boy, Erwin, an' he don' take kaindly to trespassers.'

And then I made the connection! The extraordinary-looking fellow I saw occasionally in an ex-army Jeep was Zachery's son. If you'll forgive an old Irish expression, he scared the living crap outta me, so he did! The first thing that struck you about Erwin was his height. I mean, there's tall and then there's towering. I never put a tape measure to the fellow, but I reckon there was around seven foot of him from the tips of his combat boots to the top of his shaven head. Now, I'm not one to discriminate against anyone – Tolerance being my middle name – but Erwin was a brutal-looking thug. On one occasion I was working at the typewriter on my deck. He didn't so much look at me, he *glared* at me, with tiny bullet eyes buried deep in his skull. He had a curious way of moving too, like King Kong or some class of prehistoric creature that might rip a small Irishman into a multitude of pieces.

If the barn belonged to Erwin, then the night drivers must be his pals. It was all beginning to make some kind of horrible sense.

Zachery conjured a cigarette from his beard and studied me a while longer. Eventually he spat on the ground, turned and walked away. Just as he reached the gates, he paused as if he'd reached a moment of enlightenment.

'Yer a doctor, huh?'

'Ah no, not a medical doctor . . . more of an academic. I teach at the new university.'

'Ah wus gonna say, if yer a doctor, how come ye don' do summat 'bout them ahs? Makes ye look laike you wus born on crazy creek . . . Snee, hee, hee!'

For the first time, his beard parted in what might have been a grin. All I noticed were the dreadful teeth within, like a desecrated graveyard.

7

Pip Meets Jim Crow

Whenever that sinister Jeep was in the yard, Pip knew that Erwin was home.

On those days the atmosphere was tense at Dead River – the dog skulked in the doghouse and Zachery retreated into a shed. By some unwritten code Erwin never entered Lilybelle's room, although they occasionally shouted brief practicalities to one another through the closed door. At the sound of that terrible voice, Pip would cling to Lilybelle. He knew this game of evasion could not last for ever; sooner or later the dancers would dance.

Fortunately, Erwin was often away for days on end. Pip would see the colossus piling ropes and rucksacks into the Jeep, and as soon as he was gone the house seemed to sigh with relief. Pip lost himself in work. First he used the disciplines he had learned at St Joseph's to bring order to Lilybelle's room. The boy wiped greasy surfaces, threw out bags of garbage and candy wrappers, and brushed the thread-bare carpet, which involved crawling beneath that great bed.

As he rearranged the family of soft toys on the shelves, Lilybelle looked up from her painting and smiled. 'Bless yo' little heart, Pip. Look at 'em awl sittin' in a line. You cin tell they happy now!'

Pip found it a pleasure to answer Lilybelle's tinkling bell. She was easy company – always positive, always full of homespun wisdom. Her attitude was infectious, and with something close to cheerful determination Pip carried in a bucket of soapy water and washed the bedroom windows. It was evident they had never been cleaned before.

'Lawd!' she sang. 'It's laike a fresh new day since you arrived, Pip. Yo' mah precious ray o' sunshaine.'

Before long Pip was caring for her in other ways – she liked him to hold an ornate plastic mirror while she worked on her complicated make-up or backcombed her hair. At her request, he even sprayed her body with the perfume she called *Clone*.

It was clear that a complete lack of exercise had created problems for poor Lilybelle – aching limbs, poor circulation and, most worrying of all, acute attacks of asthma which left her wheezing and gasping for air.

Pip was a kind-hearted boy and he realized the simplest way to be of use was to help Lilybelle to wash. There was no hot water in the bathroom so he had to boil a kettle in the kitchen and fill a bowl and creep as nervously as a fox past that outsized door.

With great patience, Pip washed Lilybelle's hands and

feet, as round and bloated as the udders of Zachery's goats. This simple act provided her with so much pleasure and relief that eventually Pip realized that a full bed bath would be an even greater kindness.

He attempted to ask Zachery how this could be done, but the old man looked appalled. 'Listen, boy, y' got yer chores an' ah got mine. See me askin' ye how ter split wood or fix an engine?'

Eventually Pip raised the subject with Lilybelle herself. Immediately the tears sprang to her eyes. 'Ah know it ain't raight fer a boy t' do these thangs,' she wailed. 'But ah don' know where else t' turn. Hannah's strong but she's awful surly and ah don't much care for her. Ah had two naice boys once – twins, they wus. Ah don' know what happened to them . . . Ah sure hope they's in a happy place. Ah used t' have friends too, but th' bigger ah got, th' less ah see o' 'em. Prej'dice, ah call it, Pip. Oh Lawd, ah made a mess of mah life, an' tha's the whole truth of it!'

Pip watched her sniffling into a tissue and his heart went out to her. He resolved to do what he could, no matter how hard the task. In fact the real problem was not so much the practicalities of bathing Lilybelle, more the sheer embarrassment of the situation. Having been brought up without sisters and having lived so long at the orphanage, Pip knew little about the intimacies of the human body. In particular, the anatomy of the female form was a mystery to him. He recalled a time when, aged six or seven, he and his school friend Foxy Brown had taken it upon themselves to climb inside the square laundry basket in the bathroom at home. It was nothing more than an innocent game, but when Pip's mother had come in for her evening bath, Pip and Foxy had been too slow or too ashamed to give away their hiding place. The boys found themselves watching through the woven wicker in ever-increasing alarm and fascination as Mama removed every item of her clothing. Then she proceeded to soap each part of her gleaming body, and it was only Pip's struggle to cover Foxy's bulging eyes that gave away their refuge.

Pip's mother was a liberated woman and a compulsive teacher, so when she heard a rustling, raised the lid and saw two small boys squirming amongst the dirty linen, she did not scream or punish them as others would; she simply said that a sense of curiosity was a commendable thing and if more young men took the trouble to understand the natural beauty of the female form, there might be a little more respect and lot less stupidity amongst them.

Pip swore that if he and Foxy had not fled the room in embarrassment, his mother might have dragged them through to her classroom and provided them with a full discourse on the female reproductive system, with diagrams to assist.

And that was the full extent of his education on the subject. Now it fell to Pip to remove Lilybelle's grimy nylon nightrobe and do his best to cleanse the uncharted continent of her body. The task was hard and upsetting for them both; hard because the boy had to physically heave and push Lilybelle onto her side – the weight of each leg alone was as much as he could manage, and it took his whole strength standing on the bed to haul her over. Upsetting, because Pip discovered terrible sores, which he tenderly cleaned and dried before smearing them with an antiseptic cream designed for diaper rash on babies.

When the operation was complete and Pip had tugged the filthy sheets from beneath her and somehow forced clean ones on in their place, they collapsed and cried together, both completely exhausted.

What made it all so much easier was Lilybelle's sense of humour. On one occasion as he was washing her, Pip misplaced a bar of soap between the folds of flesh. He searched long and hard to find it . . .

'Oh mah! That tickles!' she hollered. Then she collapsed into hysterical fits of laughter, which sent her whole body wobbling and rippling so that the bar of soap dislodged itself and shot across the bed, leading to further shrieking and wheezing from Lilybelle.

Of course, there were other parts of the job that were almost impossible to bear. Several times a day Pip had to force the long-handled bedpan beneath Lilybelle's body, and the subsequent wiping and cleaning made him recoil in disgust.

As the weeks went by, Lilybelle and the boy found themselves growing closer. When everything was done, they sat together with the hot breeze blowing through the open window, and Pip read to her from his book or from the newspaper. There were plenty of issues to discuss at that time: Pip became aware of race riots, freedom marches, and many alarming stories of people of Colour or immigrants who had disappeared without trace. Lilybelle had an unschooled homespun wisdom about these matters which was surprisingly profound.

On one occasion as she mixed paints on an old plate, she said, 'Ah don' know whay folks cain't git along, Pip. Truly ah don'. People faightin' an' killin' each other 'cos o' the colour of their skin, or they religion or . . . *anythang*! Way ah see it, people is the opposite o' paint.'

'What does that mean, Lilybelle? Opposite of paint?'

'See, when you mix colours, Pip, laike ah'm doin' now, wal, the more colours you mix, the muddier it awl becomes. You git yo'self in a faine ol' mess with dull greys an' browns an' awl that. Ah laike *braight* colours! Tha's wha' makes me feel good. Now, with people, it's the other way round – the more folks mix together, the braighter the world becomes! In fact, Pip, if folks don' mix, they git in awl kainds of trouble. There's a family live up near the mountains name o' Trencher-Feetus and, well, ah don't know how t' put it polite, but ev'ry las' one o' them married they cousin, o' they nephew, and it cawsed no end o' problems. Put it laike this – if brains wus dynamite, ol' Trencher-Feetus ain't got enough to blow his nose.'

Pip may not have understood the full argument, but instinctively he agreed. The question left hanging in the freshly antiseptic air was how a person like Lilybelle could have raised a son like Erwin?

Beyond the candy-coloured door the other occupants of Dead River went about their lives – old Zachery worked wearily on the farm, battling with the infertile soil; feeding, milking and killing sundry animals, before shuffling in to eat, hunched, sucking and tearing at his food in the kitchen. He must have realized that Lilybelle was happy with her new companion because, although Zachery did not go in for praise, he seemed to gruffly accept the boy's presence, like a new dog, or another turkey or chicken in the yard. He never 'rolled him a nickel', but he occasionally surprised him with a gift of a warm egg and, once, a ruffle of his hair, which felt as good to Pip as six months' salary.

Pip avoided Erwin at all costs, but he tried his hardest to bump into Hannah. Once or twice his heart leaped when he saw her at the stove; but the meeting did not go as he hoped – she glared at him with open hostility and Pip found himself launching into a tide of embarrassed babble –

'I beg your pardon, Miss Hannah . . . I should 'a knocked . . . But only a fool knocks on a kitchen door, don' he? I just wanna say, you sure look good . . . ! I mean the *food* . . . ! The food looks good . . . Good enough to eat, ain't it? It's you that smells – *good*, I mean – I mean, the food smells good . . . Oh Lord . . . !'

Then she would stare at Pip like he was crazy to even attempt a conversation, leaving him flushed and crushed by the encounter as she backed silently from the room.

And that was Hannah – the silent ghost-child who seemed to live half her life out in the countryside. She prepared fine meals but never ate with Zachery or Pip. When he was hungry, Pip wandered into the kitchen alone and helped himself to slices of creamy chicken pie with mashed potatoes thick with butter; or salty 'chitlins', which are deep-fried pigs' intestines in a spicy sauce. He discovered these delicacies by their smell, concealed in pans on the stove, or beneath a mesh cover in the pantry. Perhaps it was not the healthiest of diets, but it was exactly what his thin frame required. Although he barely noticed it, the boy put on a little muscle and even grew a fraction taller.

In addition to the three meals a day that Hannah delivered to her door, Lilybelle liked the occasional 'li'l treat' or 'tiny snack', and towards the end of his first month at Dead River, Pip was deemed trustworthy enough to go alone to the burger bar in town. It was a big occasion – Lilybelle gave him a small purse of coins, detailed directions and precise instructions about how to respond to any awkward questions.

'Now, Pip, you know we have real strict Jim Crow laws roun' here. Tha' means Black folks and Whaite folks cain't do nuthin' together – no schoolin', no eatin', no dancin' . . . nuthin' at awl; otherwaise tha's a *felony*, y' hear? Don' even think 'bout usin' th' Whaite folks' drinkin' fountain. Best thang – you don' speak to Whaite folks at awl 'less they speak to you first. Then you say, "Yessah", real polite. You say yo' name's Pip and you're houseboy at Dead River Farm. You tell 'em Mr Zach got all the necessary paperwork.'

Erwin had been absent for four days and Pip felt a new sense of liberation. 'Lilybelle, can I take Amigo?' he asked.

'Wal, sure. Ah don' see why not. Jes' find a piece o' cord to tether him. Go on now, you have a real naice time.'

Amigo did not appreciate the length of cord which Pip tied to his collar out in the yard, but he seemed happy enough to trot at the boy's side, along the dirt track past the white bungalows, with the scent of magnolia in the air. Remembering Lilybelle's warning, Pip did not even glance at the White folk cutting their lawns or polishing their cars, and he seemed utterly invisible to them. Vivid in his mind was the shocking story he'd heard of a Black boy of exactly his age: Emmett Till had come to the Deep South to take a vacation and stay with relatives. The boy had grown up in Chicago, which was another world entirely, with no segregation, and Emmett even attended a mixed-race school. So he was severely warned, just as Pip had been, to avoid any contact with White folk. But Emmett was a playful boy and he had not heeded his mother's advice. He went out one morning with a group of friends, and it was three days before they hauled his swollen body from the Tallahatchie River, weighted down with a seventy-pound cotton-gin tied tight around his neck with barbed wire. One eye had been gouged out and the boy had been shot in the head. His crime? Emmett Till was accused of whistling at a White girl, although those who knew him said that Emmett Till had a lisp and whistled all the time.

Pip and Amigo came to the large copse of poplar trees that Lilybelle had described, and from there it was another fifteen minutes into town. They took their time, because elaborate window displays and interesting odours diverted them. Besides, it felt good to get out of the yard.

Averting his eyes and stepping carefully out of the way of White folk, Pip reached the burger bar. But to his dismay, when he peered through the glass, he could not see one Black face inside. There was the sign on the door:

NO DOGS, NEGROES OR MEXICANS

Crouching on the sidewalk, Pip squeezed Amigo tight against him and whispered, 'Look at the sign, ol' friend. Between the two of us I reck'n we offend on every count.'

65

He turned and ran home at full tilt, flustered and empty-handed, his happy mood and sense of liberation abandoned.

'Aw, honey,' crooned Lilybelle, stroking his cheek. 'Didn' ah tell ya? You have to wawk round th' back. There's a li'l shed there for Coloureds, an' the food is exactly the same. If you turn an' run, fast as you can, you'll git there afore they close.'

Once again, Pip called Amigo from the shade. The dog seemed confused about being trussed again, but he was willing enough. Pip turned and sprinted back along the track with the purse gripped tightly in one hand and the cord leash in the other. When they reached the burger bar for a second time, Pip discovered a small alley leading round the back. There, as Lilybelle had promised, was a short line of Coloured folk in front of an open hatch. He tied Amigo to the fence and joined the line. When the friendly Coloured lady handed him the huge box of hot food, he opened it to check that the order was correct and, as any boy would, tasted a handful of hot fries, tossing one to Amigo. Then they sprinted back as fast as they could, running along the road rather than the busy sidewalk.

As they approached the farmyard, Pip saw the curly-haired stranger sitting on his deck with a striped cat on his knee. The cat bolted inside at the sight of Amigo, but the man called after Pip in a cheerful kind of way. Once again, it was the man's peculiar eyes that struck him, but immediately Pip realized that staring at a White man was the one thing he had been warned against, so he dived through the gates and into the farmhouse.

8
The Tutor

I had a grand day at the university – one of the best! On the drive home, all the details replayed in my mind . . .

It had started a few days earlier with a message from Professor Walter Cerberus, Vice Principal at the university and a very important man.

I hadn't met Cerberus but I knew he was interested in what we got up to in Neurology. The professor was a historian rather than a scientist, but it turned out that he had heard about my lectures and hypnosis demonstrations and wanted to bring along a few VIPs and university benefactors to see me in action!

Of course I felt flattered, and I suppose I was showing off a bit when I decided on a performance to demonstrate the effects of hypnosis on body temperature. The first thing I needed was a volunteer – preferably somebody pretty tough, so I paid a visit to the Sports Department to look for someone suitable. We hypnotists are always on the lookout for what we call 'susceptible subjects' – in layman's terms that means people who are easy to hypnotize. So how do you spot a susceptible subject? Well, there are a number of give-away signs which I'd rather not divulge, but suffice to say, I spotted my man right away – a muscular young hockey pro who was obliging but none too bright. I offered him five dollars for a few hours' work and he seemed more than happy to get involved.

In the meantime some of my students had installed a large glass tank on the stage of the lecture hall and, following my instructions, they filled it right to the top with ice. I'm not averse to a bit of showmanship and I asked to have all the lights dimmed except for a spotlight on the tank and a smaller light projecting upwards from below a lectern with a microphone. I could tell that I'd achieved the right effect because as they filed into their seats, all 225 students were whispering as if they were in church!

While the audience was getting settled, I was at the back of the stage with my volunteer and, as expected, it didn't take long to put him into very deep trance.

At the allotted time I stepped onto the stage, to a very warm welcome, and I was delighted to see Professor Cerberus and his colleagues in the back row nudging each other in anticipation. After a short introduction a couple of my students guided our man onto the stage. He looked a little dazed and he was dressed in swimming trunks and a bath robe.

When the auditorium was absolutely silent, I stood at the lectern, and this is where the spotlight below my face comes in – let's just say that it intensifies the effect of my eyes! Having carried out my pre-induction, all I had to do was whisper a few trigger words and place my hand lightly on my volunteer's forehead before he slumped back into trance, amidst audible gasps from the audience. As I led him across the stage towards the icy tank, I whispered continuously and quietly in his ear, persuading him that, except for his butler, he was alone in a magnificent hotel bathroom and was about to relax in a tub of steaming water.

You should have seen the lovely calm smile on the fellow's face as I helped him out of his robe and into the tank of ice! My assistants had taped thermometers to various parts of his body, and these were projected onto a screen at the back of the stage so that the whole audience could monitor his body temperature. For a bit of fun I handed our fellow a scrubbing brush, and there was a delightful moment when he started singing and washing beneath his arms. Meanwhile the thermometer on the screen showed that his body temperature was plummeting!

After five or ten minutes it was evident that our man was close to hypothermia and a few of my students began to panic! We hauled him out, and although he looked slightly blue, he wasn't even shivering because he truly believed that he had stepped out of a hot bath.

He stood there dripping a pool of icy water onto the stage, but perfectly comfortable. I got him to take a few bows amidst tumultuous applause, and even some foot stamping and whoops from the enthusiastic audience.

For an encore, I informed our man that he was now standing in a desert, and as he hopped from foot to foot on the hot sand, the thermometer showed his temperature rushing upwards until he was approaching heat stroke. All the water evaporated from his body and he began to perspire.

Just a bit of fun! Just a simple demonstration to show the power of hypnotic suggestion. But I must admit that I savoured the delight and amazement on the faces of Professor Cerberus and his visiting VIPs; and the Vice Principal gave me a broad grin and a thumbs-up as I took my bow.

What a day! I couldn't wait to share the story with my family back home. And that's what I was thinking about as I drove up the track and parked the old Spider in front of the bungalow. As I hopped out, I was surprised to see old man Zachery relaxing on the swing seat on my deck, as calm as you please. All that talk about trespassing, and there he was, behaving as if he owned the place!

As I climbed the steps, he waved an envelope in my direction. 'Got mahself a letter from the state authorities. Summat 'bout edoocation an' ob-lig-ation. Truth is, I cain't understan' a dog-darn word they say. Lilybelle say, go show it t' the young fellah yonder.'

'Delighted to help if I can,' I said, dropping my bag and unfolding the letter.

'S' long as they don't want no money, 'cos I ain't got no money.'

'Let me see . . . *Dear Mr Zachery . . . blah, blah . . .* No, they don't want money . . . This is a letter advising you that if you have children under the age of fifteen in your care, you are obliged by state law to provide them with an education.'

'Wal, I ain't got no chil'ren. Erwin's near twenny now.'

'Now, that's not strictly true, Mr Zachery. I've often seen children working in your yard. I bumped into that young girl the other day, and there's a new lad too . . . What's his name?'

'You mean th' orphan boy? Name's Pip. But everyone know ye cain't send Coloured kids ter a Whaite school.'

'Yes, I know about the segregation laws . . . But presumably there's a Coloured school in the district?'

'Wal . . . yeah, thar's a Coloured school out towards th' mountains, but tha's miles away. Ah ain't drivin' thar each day. Wha's th' point o' it, anyways?'

'The point of what?'

'Th' point o' edoocation. Ain't no school teach a boy t' split wood or skin a rabbit. Tha's raight, ain't it, Doc? Pip's a workin' man now. He's gonna learn hisself real skills.'

'Well, you're entitled to your opinion, Mr Zachery, but the law disagrees. The letter clearly says that you are registered as having children at this address and you are obliged to provide them with an education, on pain of legal proceedings.'

'Wha' 'm ah gonna do?'

I recalled the bewildered boy stepping out of the truck with his book. I'd seen him several times since then, running around on errands. And then the startled girl with the dreamcatcher by the dry river-bed. There had been other children too, although I hadn't seen them in a while. I answered almost without thinking, 'Ah, well, send them to me, Mr Zachery. I suppose I could spare an hour or two in the evening. As I told you, I work at the university so I'm not a school teacher, but I could probably help with reading and writing.'

He re-lit his cigarette. 'I ain't payin' nuthin'.'

'No. I didn't expect you would.'

'Could give you a few aigs.'

'Some eggs would be grand.'

'Th' gull cain't tawk. She's dumb.'

'Is she now? That's most interesting. Would you know if she's physically mute or suffering from elective mutism?'

'Wha' . . . ? What th' hell ah know? She don't tawk – 's awl ah know.'

'All right, Mr Zachery. Why don't you send the children over on . . . let's see . . . Wednesday afternoon? We'll give it a try for a few weeks, just to help a neighbour.'

An appropriate response might have been, 'That's very civil of you, Jack.' Or simply, 'Much obliged.' But old man Zachery just shuffled across the track, scratching his buttocks beneath his overalls.

I went into my cool kitchen and took out a beer. I thought about what I had let myself in for. I wasn't a school teacher, so why on earth had I offered to give up my free time to work with those kids? Well, if you want to know the truth, I was a little lonely. Ah, I know what you're thinking: the Head of Neurology at the new university – he probably has invitations to dinner parties every other night of the week. And I did get invitations. The trouble was, when I went along to those barbecues and baseball games, I felt like the odd man out. I'd always had trouble fitting in.

Besides, those youngsters – Pip and Hannah – they intrigued me far more than my clever colleagues. I wanted to know where they came from. There were all kinds of things that didn't stack up: Zachery had said that the girl was mute, and yet on that scorching Saturday when I had intruded on her hiding place by the dry river, I had heard something extraordinary. In the seconds before she ran away, that Indian girl had been singing to herself in a small and beautiful voice.

I heard every haunting note, and the words of that song were so strange and mysterious that I had written them in my notebook . . .

9

Song of the Silent Girl

i am spirit
i am sky
i am eagle
flying high
i am river
i am stream
i am sleep
i am dream
i am ocean
i am earth
i am death
i am birth
i am mountain
i am tree
i am spirit
flying free

10

The Boy Without a Face

Pip loved the smell of paints and the bright colours that Lilybelle squeezed from stubby tubes.

On a rectangle of card cut from a cereal box she was creating a childlike scene: there was Dead River farmhouse beneath a bright blue sky and a sun as yellow as an egg yolk. On the pink cobbles of the yard stood a line of smiling people. The bearded one holding a cockerel was Zachery, with Amigo at his feet. The brown and black ones were Hannah and Pip, side by side, and on a chair beneath a densely fruited apple tree sat Lilybelle herself, nicely plump and smiling too.

'That's th' way it should be,' said Lilybelle. 'Folks livin' together in harmony laike spoons in a drawer.'

She squeezed a line of paint onto her plate and, with a fine brush, sketched in the outline of the final character in her painting – a boy as tall as the apple tree.

Pip watched her struggling with the face of the oversized boy; again and again she tried, but she couldn't get it right.

These days Erwin was around more frequently – driving about in the small hours and sleeping away the days. When Pip thought of Erwin, the image that came to mind was not of a spoon but a long knife – pointed and razor sharp. The kind of knife that could open a throat like a watermelon.

'Lilybelle . . .' Pip began his sentence nervously. 'Lilybelle . . . how come you're so kind an' Erwin is so . . . you know . . . ?'

'*Un*kaind, Pip. Come raight on out an' say it. Erwin's hard as nails an' it breaks mah ol' heart.'

Pip saw a tear roll down her lovely face. She seemed instantly agitated, as if the creative spell had been broken. 'Awl ah wanna do when ah think about it is to eat an' eat, till there's no more room fer sufferin'.'

She tinkled the paintbrush furiously in a jar, and Pip watched a dark typhoon swirl within the glass. Then, with a rag on her fingertip, she wiped away the unsuccessful face of the boy and tried to paint his boots.

'Even when he was a kid, Erwin was tall an' lanky . . . doctors called it Gigantism. Ah had thyroid problems, see, so Erwin had excess growth hormones. Zach and me used t' say a tall boy laike that gonna be a basketbawl star fo' sure . . . 'cept . . . 'cept there was somethin' strange about Erwin – he made th' other kids wary.

'We used t' lie awake at naight frettin' about him. Then one day he says he's signed up t' join th' army.

'Course, he was too young, but he musta lied about his age, and bein' so big 'n awl, ah guess they believed him.

They took ma boy off to a military trainin' camp an' next thing we know he's in some place named Vietnam, me an' Zach ain't never heard of. Ah never learned 'xactly what happened there. All ah know is when he came home to Dead River, me 'n Zach didn't hardly recognize the boy shufflin' up the track laike a zombie. If it weren't for the height o' him, ah'd have thought they sent th' wrong boy home.

'Oh yeah, Pip, ah remember that homecomin' laike it was yesterday. At twenny to naine Erwin walks in the door an' his face was jus' fulla naked hate. Zach noticed somethin' weird – th' clock on th' man'lpiece stopped raight there an' then. Ain't never worked since. It wus laike mah whole laife stopped too.'

Lilybelle was sobbing openly now, honking and snorting into a tissue.

'There wus summat *brutish* got into him, Pip. Erwin used to cuss an' yell an' break thangs, an' kick th' dawg. At naight we heard him shoutin' an screamin'. Only time he found peace was out huntin' with a gun . . . Ah don' wanna tawk 'bout it no more, if it's awl the same t' you. Awl ah know is what ah tol' you – it's best when folks git along.'

'Like spoons in a drawer, Lilybelle.'

'Yeah, Pip, like spoons in a drawer.'

She stared at her unfinished painting and then, very quietly, she said, 'It ain't somethin' a mother say easy, but ah don' know mah son no more. He don't speak more'n twenny words t' me in a year . . . There's somethin' evil in his heed, Pip. Scares me. Erwin scares me bad.'

Even talking about him scared Pip too. He rose to his feet and began gathering an armful of Lilybelle's clothes for washing. These chores were second nature to an orphanage boy.

'Giss who ah'm gonna give mah li'l picture to?'

Lilybelle stroked the top of Pip's head and handed him the painting.

Pip looked at the surreal image. The farmyard characters, the egg-yolk sun, the apple tree, and the giant boy without a face.

When that painting was dry, Pip slipped it between the pages of his book and it stayed there for many years.

Out in the yard he filled a tin tub with water. He carried out saucepans and kettles of boiling water from the kitchen and poured them in too. Then he set about pummelling and scrubbing the clothes until they were clean. It was pleasant enough to be kneeling with the warm sunshine on his back.

'Boy . . . ah say, boy, ah got somethin' to tell ya.' Zachery shuffled over. 'Now listen up – ah fixed fer you 'n Hannah to git an edoocation. Private schoolin' near caust a fortune, but ah figured it were th' right thang to do.'

'Yes, sir, thank you, Mr Zachery, sir. But who gonna teach us?'

'Crazy-eyed feller in the bungalow yonder. Teaches at th' university, he do, an' that's why he's so 'spensive. You start after chores this af'ernoon.'

Then Zachery climbed into the truck and set off to sell a couple of goats.

Lessons at the white bungalow with Hannah? It all seemed very peculiar. Pip puzzled over it as he knelt down at the tub to wring out the last of Lilybelle's clothes.

And it was in that moment that a colossal shadow fell from behind, and all the weeks of dodging and dancing came to an end.

A mighty hand descended from above and Pip found himself catapulted violently into the air, ten feet above Dead River farmyard.

With arms and legs paddling like a helpless swimmer, Pip looked down at Erwin's snarling face – it was infinitely uglier and crueller than he had imagined. Apple-seed eyes buried deep beneath a hulking brow. Knotted red ears projecting like bolts from his shaven cranium, and that terrible jaw – as huge and solid as a tombstone.

'Seems ah caught mahself a li'l black rat!' said the deep, slow, teasing voice. 'I kep' on hearin' it scritchin' 'n scratchin' 'n snuckin' about; but ever' taime ah looks fer it, it turns its li'l black tail and scampers everwhichways.'

Erwin held Pip high above his head as if he weighed no more than a bundle of twigs.

'Now you don' wanna be doin' awl that washin'. That ain't work fer a boy. The li'l dumb gal cin finish that.'

He lowered Pip to the ground and set him on his feet, holding him firmly by the collar so he could not escape. Pip felt giddy and sick with fear. The top of his head reached little higher than Erwin's waist, so that the giant had to bend right over to speak to him – stabbing him repeatedly with a finger as long as a bone.

'We's gonna take a wawk, li'l rat. Jes' you 'n me. Up to th' red barn t' play.'

Pip felt the collar tighten around his neck. He thought fondly of his mother and prepared to die.

11

David and Goliath

I returned from work and swung the silver Spider into my drive.

I hopped onto the deck and was just unlocking the front door when I saw something that disturbed me greatly: in the yard opposite, Zachery's gigantic son Erwin was dragging young Pip along by the scruff of his neck like a fellow with a string puppet. It was clear that the boy was petrified.

I dumped my books on the folding table – and, I admit, I didn't know what to do. I was the outsider, after all, and anyway, you'd have to be a damned fool to take on a monster like Erwin. Common sense told me to go inside. Common sense told me to take a shower and avoid trouble, but my conscience is an undisciplined fellow. It yelled at me to intervene and it simply would not shut up. If there's one thing I cannot stand it is blatant injustice. I had trouble

83

enough with the disgraceful Jim Crow laws in this part of the world, but the appalling abuse of a child by a seven-foot bully could not be tolerated.

With no real plan, I rose to my feet. 'Excuse me!' I called. 'Excuse me! Are you Erwin? Are you Mr Zachery's son? My name's Jack – Dr Jack Morrow, to use my full moniker . . .'

He turned his lantern jaw and leered at me. Once again I noticed the peculiar lumbering quality of his movements, like a creature from a swamp.

'You tawkin' at me?'

'Look, it's none of my business but—'

'Goddam raight it's none 'f yer business, y' puny freak.'

He held the boy with two fingers and stared at me in utter disbelief. The scene was straight out of the Bible – like David and Goliath, except that wee fellow had a slingshot, didn't he? David had been in with a fighting chance.

'Well, in a way it is my business, see, because I'm about to be a kind of tutor to Pip – and to Hannah too – starting this afternoon, as a matter of fact. Look . . . look here, I have all the books and I've bought them a pencil case each – the Flintstones, isn't it? Fred and, er . . . Wilma?'

I rummaged in my bag and dangled two pencil cases in the air. I was babbling. Terrified actually, but just trying to defuse the situation. Erwin seemed so astounded by my effrontery, by the pencil cases, by my Irish tone, that he must have loosened his grip on the boy . . .

In a split second of mayhem, Pip seized his moment, wriggled free of Erwin's grip, darted between those giant legs and bolted – straight across the track towards me.

With a single bound, he vaulted all four steps, dived behind my back and disappeared through the door of my bungalow like a fellow with his hair on fire.

Erwin blinked at his empty hand, like a raptor who has fumbled his prey. Then, slowly, his eyes turned to me. I have never seen a look quite like it. It was a look of unmodified violence. It was the expression of a stone-hearted killer, and it chilled me to the marrow of my bones.

He lumbered slowly out of the yard towards me, arms extended like a vision from a nightmare.

I employed all my training to search for an appropriate way to handle the situation, but all that came to me were rambling prayers from my convent school:

'. . . *Holy Mary and all the saints defend me. Be my protection against all evils of the world below . . . Amen, Amen, Amen.*'

12

In the White Room of Dr Morrow

With heart pounding like a racehorse, Pip dived through the door.

He found himself in a tidy living room, where a stripy cat sprang for cover beneath a table. The room was remarkably white, creating an atmosphere of cool and calm. Pip saw neatly stacked bookshelves and framed photographs of many smiling children, whose resemblance to the man on the deck was obvious.

Although Pip's trust in human nature was pitifully thin, there was no doubt about what had happened: the man who had introduced himself as Jack Morrow had risked his life for him. That strange-eyed man was neither big nor tough – in fact he was shorter even than Pip – but he was braver than anyone he had ever met.

Now Pip stood gasping in the white room and waited for the sounds of violence to begin – splintering wood perhaps, or the shattering of glass as a small Irishman flew through the windowpane. But no sound came, except the steady ticking of a metronome by a large padded couch and the pounding of Pip's heart.

He looked around for an escape route. He noted a glass door at the back of the kitchen with a key in the lock. If necessary he could run into the back yard; but he had to see what was happening on the porch.

Falling to his hands and knees, Pip crawled across the spotless white carpet towards the front window. Very slowly he raised his head and peered above the sill. Jack Morrow was standing with his back to him, looking out at the shambles of Dead River Farm. And there was Erwin, moving slow as a sleepwalker towards them, with a deadly leer on his face.

But still Jack Morrow did not run. In fact, to Pip's amazement, he seemed to be walking across the deck to greet his killer. Jack had his hand extended in a friendly way, and although he was standing high on the deck, Erwin was still a head or more taller.

Transfixed with amazement and dread, Pip was reminded of a photograph in a wildlife book – a tiger approaching a deer; a predator about to disembowel its prey.

And then something extraordinary happened – Jack Morrow reached out and grasped Erwin's hand. He was speaking softly to Erwin all the time, although Pip could not hear the words.

For a moment Erwin appeared puzzled and distressed. His eyes were transfixed by Jack Morrow's and now . . . now he was allowing the small man to help him onto the deck.

With some regret, Pip realized that he would never know his tutor. Because now the killing would begin.

13

Erwin Makes a Friend

One thing to say about Erwin is he speaks his mind.

'Ah'm gonna keel you,' he said as he approached my bungalow. 'Ah'm gonna tear off yer puny leegs laike a fly an' ah'm gonna feed 'em to the dawg.'

I knew he meant it too. But I struggled to compose myself. I waited at the top of the steps.

'I can see why you're feeling a little unsettled,' I said, locking directly onto his tiny eyes. 'Would you like me to help you up to the deck?'

I clasped his hand and was appalled by its size. I felt a surge of panic, but sharply pulled myself together.

'Wha' . . . ? Wha' the hell you doin'? Ah don' need no one's heelp. Wha' you lookin' at me laike that? What 'n tarnation's wrong yer ahs?'

'No, it's fine, Erwin. Everything is fine. You were tired, that's all . . . but as you step onto the deck you begin to feel a little calmer . . . Do you notice it? And now you are starting to relax . . .'

I felt a worm of doubt. Supposing this great clod of a man couldn't be reached? Some people – not many, but a few – are simply not susceptible to induction.

'Ah'm . . . ah'm gonna . . . Yeah . . . ah ah'm kinda tired. Ah don' know whay . . .'

'It's been a long hot day, Erwin . . . a long life . . . We all get tired and that's fine . . . You are safe here with me and your body needs to rest . . . Ah, now this is interesting . . . Do you see the way your hand floats in front of your face . . . ?'

I held Erwin's wrist lightly and his enormous hand began drifting up and down like a leaf on the breeze.

The giant stared at it with fascination. 'Ah gotta . . . ah gotta keel tha' boy.'

'There'll be time for everything later, Erwin, but now you need to rest . . . Look – I'm helping you onto the swing seat . . . and it's so comfortable, so soft . . .'

'Yor ahs . . . !'

'Yes, keep looking at my eyes, Erwin . . . and listen to my voice . . . because my voice is the voice you have always known . . . my voice is the voice of the wind . . .'

'The wind? Goddam it . . .'

'Now this is where we count backwards, Erwin . . . You know how it goes . . . from ten to one . . . You can do that, can't you?'

'Ah laike countin'.'

'Of course you do . . . so let's begin with ten . . .'

'Tin . . . nan . . . aight . . . sivun . . .'

'That's grand, Erwin, and when your eyes can't stay open any longer, it's OK to rest them . . . Just keep counting backwards . . . That's all you need to do . . .'

'Siux . . . faive . . . fower . . . threeah . . .'

'That's good counting, Erwin . . . and as you count, it's like floating slowly downwards in a lovely soft cloud . . . down, down, down . . . and when you reach the very bottom, you'll find me waiting there . . .'

'Twouh . . . wun . . . Ah'm sleepin' real good . . .'

'You are sleeping very well, Erwin . . . just like a tiny child. You feel quite relaxed because this is Erwin's happy place . . .'

'Ah'm gawn . . .'

'The only sound is my voice, deep, deep in your mind . . .'

'Ah thought ah had important thungs t' do . . . Ah gotta keel somebawdy . . .'

'No, there's nothing to do except relax on your cloud and float down, down . . . deeper and deeper and deeper.'

Carefully I placed his limp hand on his lap. I realized Pip had emerged into the doorway.

'Come and watch, Pip. Look, Erwin's taking a nap. He was ever so tired.'

'N-n-no . . . He's gonna kill me . . .'

'It's all right, Pip. He won't hurt you now. I promise.'

'How'd you *do* that? It ain't natural.'

'A little trick, Pip. I can teach you one day.'

'But he's . . .'

'Yes, he's very relaxed, isn't he? Shall we play a game, Pip?'

91

'Wh-what kinda game?'

'We'll have a little fun. I have no idea if this will work, but it would be amusing to try. You watch, Pip . . . Erwin? Erwin? Can you hear me? It's Dr Morrow. I'm talking to your subconscious mind now, way, way down in your happy place . . .'

'Ah hear y'.'

Something about Erwin's military haircut gave me an idea.

'Erwin . . . you can think of me as your commanding officer if you want to . . .'

'Yessir, I wanna be good. I wanna do what ah'm tol'.' His hand floated loosely to the side of his head, like some kind of dreamy salute.

'That's grand, er, soldier . . . In a moment I will awake you . . . and when you awake you will feel calm and very happy . . .'

'Ah'm real happy.'

I felt Pip tugging at my sleeve, whispering desperately.

'Sir, sir, why you wanna wake him? Why don' you jus' leave him lie. He ain't hurting no one.'

'You call me Jack, Pip. And it's all right. Trust me. I've done this before.'

I crouched down and took hold of Erwin's cherry-red ear in my fingertips. Then I whispered, 'Erwin . . . Erwin . . . listen to me . . . You won't remember anything that has happened this evening, but here's a funny thing . . . whenever you see that lovely fellow, Pip, it will make you calm and happy all over again. It will take you right back to your happy place. You will want Pip to be your friend . . . your best friend in the world.'

'Pip's mah freend . . . He makes me happy . . .'

'That's right, Erwin . . . Pip's your best friend and he will be your friend for a long, long time. Now I'm counting, and when I reach ten, you will awaken . . . One, two, three . . . gradually awakening . . . four, five, six . . . opening your eyes . . .'

We watched a huge pumpkin smile spread across Erwin's face. He yawned so deeply, we saw the gap between his front teeth, and his tonsils swinging in his cavernous mouth. Then he stretched his long, long lazy arms above his head, knocking my books from the folding table. As the sleeping giant awoke, I saw his eyelids flicker; but before they fully opened Pip was off like a rabbit – down the steps and across the track.

I called out, 'Pip, don't forget our first lesson! Five o'clock sharp. Oh, and be sure to bring Hannah, won't you?'

14
The Lesson

To use a phrase of Zachery's, Pip was as nervous as a long-tailed cat in a room full of rocking chairs.

After the strange events of the morning he had spent the day holed up in Lilybelle's bedroom. He did not emerge until he heard the sound of the Jeep leaving the yard. Erwin had gone, though for how long he had no idea.

And now Jack Morrow was welcoming him warmly, and for the second time that day Pip found himself standing awkwardly in the white living room. The Irishman behaved as if nothing unusual had occurred. In fact he was chatting enthusiastically about the book under Pip's arm. 'Ah, I've seen you with this before and I wondered what you were reading.'

Reluctantly Pip allowed his new tutor to take the large volume. Jack placed it on a table and studied the illustrations with delight. But when Pip saw Jack reading his mother's inscription in the front and even running his finger down the neatly written address of the schoolhouse, he could stand it no longer. He closed the book and snatched it away.

'I'm sorry, Pip. I didn't mean to pry; but can you really read this? I mean, it's pretty heavy going in places . . . I've always loved the scene where Pip— Now, wait a minute – you wouldn't . . . I mean, you wouldn't be named after young Pip in the story, would you?'

Pip admitted that he was. Then Jack Morrow rushed to his bookshelf and, after a few moments of searching, pulled out a shiny new copy of *The Complete Works of Dickens*, with illustrations in full colour.

'It's something we have in common. I've always loved Dickens too. What larks we'll have, Pip! What larks! That's a quote, isn't it? Now, come and sit yourself down . . . No sign of Hannah, then?'

Pip had done his best to tell Hannah about the lessons, but she had glared at him in her usual hostile way.

'Well, let's not worry for now, eh, Pip? Why don't we begin by talking about the wonderful names Dickens uses? Ebenezer Scrooge is my favourite. But there's also Silas Wegg, Uriah Heep, Mr Sloppy, Polly Toodle, and how about the teacher, Wackford Squeers?'

Pip could tell the man was trying to be kind. He was making some sort of joke, but it made little sense to him. He found himself staring absently about the room. Everything was stylishly modern, except for a curious sepia photograph in a frame on a shelf. It showed a happy couple from long ago, with arms entwined. There was something odd and familiar about the man. And then Pip realized that the man in the photograph had the same peculiar eyes as his tutor. It had to be Jack's parents.

His thoughts were broken by a movement on the porch. With a jolt of excitement, Pip saw that Hannah had appeared like a beautiful spirit, and here she was, holding Jack's cat in her arms. The cat's head was hanging backwards in the most relaxed fashion possible and Hannah was rubbing his ears against her cheek. A small part of Pip longed for that attention.

Jack went to the door, moving slowly as if he might frighten her away, and as he waited at the table, Pip could hear him talking softly to Hannah in his lilting Irish accent.

'Well now, Hannah, I'm glad you could join us. I see you met Finnegan. He's a wild thing, a bit like yourself. Would you like to bring him in and join us?'

Her oval eyes darted about at the countryside. Pip sensed that she would rather be running, leaping and free. But as Jack stood patiently with one hand holding the door, she slipped under his arm and entered the white room, the cat purring in her arms. She shot a warning glance at Pip and settled herself at the far side of the table.

'Good. Now we're all together. I feel I should ring a school bell or something, but it's not like that here. A warm welcome to you both. My name is Jack – Dr Jack Morrow to use— But never mind all that, I want you to call me Jack. I want us all to be friends.'

Pip felt restless. This lesson did not feel like the lessons his mama had taught, in which all the children had felt comfortable because they knew who was in charge. The other thing was that Pip kept thinking of Erwin in that dreamy state out on the deck. Surely the spell would be broken by now and he would be angrier than ever. All the time Jack talked, Pip was constantly alert for the returning Jeep on the track outside.

'Now, Hannah, Pip and I were talking about a writer named Charles Dickens. I don't suppose you've heard of him. That's fine. Dickens was an English writer and . . .'

Jack Morrow told them a little about Dickens; how he had grown up in terrible poverty and worked in a factory as a small boy. All the while, Jack showed them pictures from his book. But the illustrations in Jack's book were not right – all the characters were White people with rosy cheeks; even Pip was a White boy!

Then, in a blinding moment, Pip realized that all these years he had been mistaken – the beautiful illustrations in his mother's book were black-and-white line engravings and he had always assumed they were Black folks . . . especially Pip, because Pip was him, wasn't he?

'. . . and the amazing thing is that our Pip, sitting right here, was named after the hero of this story. Did you know that, Hannah? I think it's something you should be very proud of, Pip.'

Pip did not feel proud. He felt foolish. He felt betrayed.

'All right, Pip and Hannah. Here's a question for you – why do you think Dickens chose that particular name – Pip – for his young hero? Any thoughts at all?'

Pip was thinking about all the books in the world and

wondering if every last one of them was filled with White people.

'Pip . . . The name . . . Why would Dickens . . . ?'

'Dunno, sir. Guess he had to call him somethin'.'

'Well, first of all, I'd like you to call me Jack, if it's all the same to you. I don't like being called Sir. The next thing is that there was nothing random about Dickens – everything he did was for a reason. So let's have a little think. What was the significance of the name? What about you, Hannah? Any ideas? Let's see . . . How are we going to do this? If I ask you questions, you'll nod or shake your head, I suppose?'

Pip came out of his daze. 'Give her a pencil, mister – er, Jack, an' she'll write for you.' He had seen Hannah do it for Lilybelle.

'Really? Hannah, is that correct?'

Hannah nodded shyly and accepted a pencil and an exercise book.

'So, Hannah. Why do you think the writer, Dickens, would call his character Pip? Why might that be a good name?'

Hannah thought for a long time; then, with the pencil gripped awkwardly in her fist and the other arm shielding the page, she began to write – very slowly, with a great deal of rubbing out. As Pip watched Hannah, he felt something like pride and satisfaction at her efforts. After several moments she handed the exercise book to Jack. Their tutor stared blankly at the abstract scrawl, which looked more like hieroglyphics than letters.

a pip is reel smol

With a sudden flash of frustration, Pip seized the exercise book and said, 'I can read that. It says *a pip is real small*, don' it, Hannah?'

She glowered at him. Then Jack studied the page again, and slowly a look of comprehension spread across his face.

'Oh goodness! Yes, Hannah, a pip is small, isn't it? That's excellent . . . excellent! "Pip" is a small word too. This is grand. Now, I wonder, can you tell me something else about a pip?'

Hannah deliberated again. The cat grew bored and jumped off her lap. At last she resumed the laborious act of writing. When she had finished, Pip studied the words she had written:

it gros

'Hannah says, *it grows!*' he announced. 'A pip grows, don't it, Hannah?'

She nodded reluctantly. Jack was visibly excited. 'My goodness! You are a clever girl. A pip is small, but it grows. See, that's the whole point of the story – Pip is a small boy, but he has great expectations and he grows. It couldn't be a more perfect name. And I suppose another thing is that poor old Dickens would have had to write the name hundreds of times by hand; and readers like us have to read it too, again and again, so a nice simple name like Pip is agreeable for everyone, if you take my meaning.'

Pip noticed a tiny smile flicker on Hannah's face. And Jack seemed suddenly animated.

'Ah now, this is marvellous! Now we're away . . . And I've

thought of something else. Ha, ha, yes! There's another clever thing about Pip's name . . . and – guess what? – your name is clever in exactly the same way, Hannah! Look. Let's write your names side by side: PIP and HANNAH.'

The children stared at the words. Pip leaned a little too close and Hannah elbowed him firmly away; but their concentration was intense.

In a flash the answer came to him. It was as if Pip's brain was awakening after years of hibernation, and he recalled the sensation of pleasing his mother with his clever answers.

'The names are the same forward an' backward – ain't that right, Jack?'

Jack leaped up with excitement, practically knocking his chair to the floor.

'Oh my goodness! The man's got it! I don't believe it! Oh, you are clever people! Now, would you look at this, Hannah? The names are the same forwards and backwards! Try it: HANNAH and PIP. Each name works the same from the front and from the back. It's what we call a palindrome, see? I used to love palindromes – *are we not drawn onward to new era*; that's another long one – but I won't bother you with that now . . .'

He told them he'd fetch them a treat, and soon he was banging cupboard doors and clanking plates in the kitchen.

Hannah and Pip sat opposite each other at the table. Pip's doubts about the lesson had evaporated. He had enjoyed himself and he had loved the opportunity to show off his ability to Hannah. He was smart – Mama had said so, Lilybelle said it, and now Jack said it too.

Hannah examined the eraser at the end of her pencil. Pip fidgeted with the laces on his boots – for days now his boots hadn't felt right. Either the boots were shrinking or his feet were growing. He noticed Hannah's bare feet swinging under her chair, perfectly small and caramel brown.

He grinned at her, and for the very first time since he had arrived at Dead River she did not look away.

Jack returned with mugs of sweet tea and a tub of blueberry ice cream. As they licked happily at their spoons, a warm feeling of mutual trust settled in the room. Jack said, 'I think I'm going to enjoy working with you two, I really do.'

Jack gave Pip an exercise book too, then asked them to write their names and ages on the cover. As Pip wrote his age, he realized that it was only two weeks until his fourteenth birthday. Then he would be almost a man. Hannah wrote her name, but Pip was astonished to discover that she had no idea what date or year she was born. How was that possible?

In the following hour Jack set about assessing their educational ability and Pip was keen to prove himself. He wrote some sentences in his best handwriting, completed a few elementary sums, and read aloud to Jack. All the while Jack made notes in his notebook, and finally told them that, in his estimation, they were both exceptionally bright, although it was clear that Hannah had received little formal education and Pip, whose early tuition had been outstanding, seemed to have fallen well behind in recent years.

While they worked, Hannah and Pip exchanged glances – submissive and puppy-like from Pip; wary and irritable from Hannah. At last Jack seemed to realize that their concentration had reached its limit and he began to close the books and collect the pencils and pens.

Then Pip said, 'You said you was gonna teach that trick, Mr Jack, sir. The one you done with Erwin.'

'Ah, well, it wasn't a trick exactly, Pip. It's certainly something I'd be glad to talk about on another occasion, but—'

'You shoulda seen it, Hannah! Erwin was set to kill me . . . then he . . . kinda fell asleep.'

'Well, in a manner of speaking he did fall asleep, although he could hear what I was saying, couldn't he? What happened with Erwin was a little thing we call *hypnosis*. You've heard of it, right? Well, it's what I do. Hypnosis is my trade. It's a funny sort of job, I'll grant you.'

'Show me how t' do it, Jack. I wanna know so I can make folks do what I tell 'em, 'stead of always doing what they say.'

'Well, some people can't be hypnotized no matter how you try. Erwin was pretty resistant, wasn't he? I had a struggle to win him round. But other people are easier to hypnotize. They're what we call *susceptible*.'

'Am I sissyball?'

'Well, you know, Pip, from the moment I saw you I thought there was something about you. I said to myself, "Jack Morrow, if ever there was a fellow who was susceptible, then I'm looking right at him." I'll tell you what – you've both done extremely well today, so I suppose there'd be no harm in finding out for sure. We'll try a little game, shall we? Clasp your hands together, Pip – and you too, Hannah, if you'd like to play. That's right, just interlink the fingers of each hand as if you were praying, and squeeze the fingers together good and tight. That's it – now cross the thumbs right in front of your face.'

Pip and Hannah sat at the table, hands clasped tightly in front of their eyes, as if in prayer.

'Now just raise the index finger of each hand – that's your pointing fingers, Hannah. Good. Get the two fingers up nice and straight as if you were pointing at the ceiling. It's a steeple on a church, if you like. But keep the fingertips apart, see – don't let them touch. Now I need you to stare hard at the tips of those two fingers . . . and as you relax, you stare right at them . . . but keep them separate. Now . . . listen to my voice . . . and imagine for a moment that you have a tiny magnet in each fingertip . . . Can you feel the magnets? Your fingertips feel like they are pulling together, but you keep them apart . . . You keep staring at the fingertips . . . and keep your hands praying nice and tight . . .'

Pip's fingertips began oscillating violently.

'You just stare at your fingers . . . with the magnets inside . . . and although you want to keep them apart, the magnets are very, very strong and . . .'

Pip was gone! It was as if Jack Morrow's voice had carried him away into a lovely warm and comfortable world. He stared at his index fingers, and it felt like they were firmly glued at the tips.

Whether Hannah felt the same or not he could not tell, but Pip was vaguely aware of Jack gently lifting one of his eyelids with a huge fingertip. And then, somewhere far away, he saw Jack leaning towards him to shine a small flashlight into the pupil of his eye. When Jack spoke – it was as if his voice came from many miles away across the fields – he asked Pip to follow his finger with his eyes, and Pip found he had no choice but to stare transfixed at the mountainous finger, which swung slowly from side to side.

After a very long time he heard that distant voice counting again, and slowly Pip felt himself rise up through a warm ocean of treacle, until he submerged into the white room, where Jack was making notes.

Pip stared about in amazement. The air seemed unnaturally bright and clear. He had been somewhere else entirely, though exactly where and for how long he could not say. When he was sure that his mouth would work, Pip said, 'Wal, what you say, Mr Jack? Am I sissyball?'

Jack was obviously excited. 'Pip, you are extraordinarily sissyball! You are perhaps the most naturally susceptible subject I have ever met. But, look – my task here is to teach you writing, reading and arithmetic! Hypnosis was never part of the job description.'

'I wanna do it, Jack. I don't know why, but I want you to hyp'tize me properly like you done with Erwin.'

'I'll think about it, Pip. But you've had enough of people exploiting you in your life – you both have – so I don't want to take advantage in any way. However, you're absolutely right – hypnosis can be like a martial art. When I was young, bullies often picked on me and I've lost track of the number of times hypnosis saved my skin.'

'But how did *you* learn it, Jack? Someone musta taught you.'

A distant look came across his face. 'My parents taught

me when I was very small, and their parents taught them . . .'

Pip rose to his feet and picked up the sepia photograph in the frame. 'Is this them, Jack, sir? Is this your ma 'n pa?'

'Yes, that's them . . . Well, all right. If you want to know a little about me, I suppose there's no harm. It's a lovely evening, so why don't we all sit out on the deck and I'll tell you something about Jack Morrow? I'll tell you about the Voice of the Wind . . .'

15

The Voice of the Wind

Hannah and Pip sit side by side on the swing seat with Finnegan across their laps. I realize that the children are the first real visitors I've had at the bungalow.

Hannah seems more than a little irritable about having the boy so close, but Pip pulls off his old boots and settles in like he's swinging in heaven.

I love the early evenings in this part of the world – when the heat of the day has softened but it's still warm enough to sit in your shirtsleeves and listen to the song of the crickets and smell the blossom in the air.

The two of them rock backwards and forwards, forwards and back, and when they are quite settled I begin my story. I take them right back to the Old Country where I was born . . . 'It's a colourful tale,' I tell them, 'and the way my parents met was more than a little romantic . . .

'See, between the wars my father worked in the

107

theatres of Dublin. He had his own show three nights a week and people flocked to see him. He worked under the name "Morrow the Mesmerist".'

'What's a mesmerist, Jack?' asks Pip.

'Well, Pip, a mesmerist is another name for a hypnotist, and my father was the best in the business. He never had a night without a full house. At one time Morrow the Mesmerist was the most famous stage hypnotist in Ireland – maybe in the whole world.

'My da specialized in fast techniques of hypnosis such as his incredible "handshake induction". Here's the way it works – maybe you can picture this, Hannah . . . There's five hundred or a thousand people in a gorgeous theatre on a Saturday night. When everyone is settled, the house lights go down and my father enters the stage in almost total darkness. He was a small fellow, but good-looking – like me! – and with a colossal stage presence. He stands in the dark with nothing but a few candles below his face. Now, my da had the same thing with the eyes as me, so you can imagine the effect. He says absolutely nothing at all, and after a few moments everyone stops chattering and the whole theatre falls silent, and there's not one person in the room who isn't staring at him.

' "I'd like a willing volunteer," he says, ever so quietly. Loads of people raise their hands. Then a spotlight plays slowly around the audience and my father is selecting "his man", or "his lady". Exactly what qualities he's searching for I'm not about to reveal, but what he's not looking for is the drunk fellow who wants to show off to his friends, or the shy girl who's being pushed forward by her girlfriends. It's like I told you, there are certain people who are naturally susceptible to hypnosis—'

'Like me!' says Pip.

'Like you, Pip . . . and my father and I can spot them a mile away. When I was a nipper, we used to play a game down Drumcondra road. "Is that one, Da?" I used to say. "Is that one there?"

'In the theatre Morrow the Mesmerist picks out his "mark". Let's say it's a quiet but confident lady in her thirties. Well, right from the start Da has blocked out the rest of the audience and he's fixed straight onto her eyes. She comes forward down the aisle and the audience are making a hell of a din, but there's not one second when he hasn't got those startling eyes locked right onto hers. She approaches the steps in front of the stage, and – this is important – my father reaches out his hand to help her up . . . It's an invitation, see! As far as anyone can tell he's helping her up the steps, but what's he's actually doing is asking permission to control her mind . . . Are you with me, so far?'

Their wide eyes tell me they are.

'Now, what you have to understand is that by accepting his hand and stepping onto his territory, the subject has given her consent. In the few seconds it takes her to climb the steps, my father begins whispering to her – he's imparting a whole series of what we call "subliminal commands", so that by the time she stands on the stage, the transaction is complete and our quiet but confident lady is in a deeply hypnotic state—'

'Jack! Jack – that's what you done with Erwin!'

'Exactly, Pip. It was the same thing. I used the old "handshake induction". I invited him up here on the deck, and when he took my hand, he was actually giving me permission to put him into trance.'

'He was lying right here,' says Pip. 'Exactly where we're sittin' now. You shoulda seen it, Hannah!'

'In the theatre two dramatic spotlights pop on – one on my father, and the other on the lady, who looks for all the world like a dummy in a shop window. By now, you could hear a pin drop in the auditorium.

'There are plenty of stage hypnotists who'll do all manner of foolish things to entertain their audience – they'll get their subject to bark like a dog, or take their clothes off, or cluck about the stage like Zachery's hens! But Morrow the Mesmerist never lowered himself to that. He was a professional! He was a genius! My father would never humiliate people – on the contrary, the point of the show was to reveal the hidden talents we all carry inside. Why, I have seen the shyest of people belting out opera tunes in front of a crowded theatre, or speaking in languages they didn't know they had. The most extraordinary feat of all was what my da called *regression*. Regression is where a subject is taken back through the years to their childhood and even – so my father believed – into past lives!'

Hannah and Pip swing their bare toes in unison, backwards and forwards, forwards and back, and I see they are right with me in the foggy gaslit streets of old Dublin . . .

'Well, the story goes that one evening, long before my

six siblings and I were even a glimmer in those amazing eyes, Morrow the Mesmerist heard that a rival hypnotist had set up another show in a theatre not two streets away. He was more than a little irritated because people were forever copying his ideas. So my da decides to investigate – he buys a ticket, and on his next night off he pops round the corner to see a performer calling herself "The Voice of the Wind".

'Well, all I can tell you is his annoyance quickly changed to delight – in fact he was literally entranced by what he saw! As I'm sure you'll have guessed, The Voice of the Wind was the wonderful woman who became my mother.

'Ma was a performer through and through. She loved to dress in fancy clothes, bless her! She adored veils and bangles and exotic costumes with backdrops of pyramids and whatnot. The long and the short of it was that, for the first time in his life, Morrow the Mesmerist fell under a woman's spell!

'See, my mother had developed a truly sensational act in which she hypnotized not just a couple of volunteers . . . Ah no! My mother hypnotized the entire audience! I witnessed the act many times, and I can tell you it was something to behold! Every night of her life the punters would leave slapping their heads and rubbing their eyes with disbelief. What's more, it was the real thing – no tricks; no illusions. The thing I'm trying to tell you is that both my ma and my da possessed that rare thing we call The Gift. In Ireland it's sometimes known as "The Charm" or "The Cure", but we Morrows always called it The Gift.

'My mother was a star all right, but more than anything, it was that voice! I can hear it now – *My voice is the voice of the wind . . . My voice is the voice you have always known . . . the gentle whisper of the trees and the soft roll of the waves on the shores of Kerry . . . My voice will accompany you deep into trance . . .* and so on. My father adored it, and from the moment I was born, so did I.

'After the show my father managed to charm his way into her dressing room. He stood a head shorter than her, but she knew the reputation of his act. Within a month they had combined their talents, and for many years to come "Morrow and The Voice of the Wind" performed to capacity crowds in famous theatres in London and Paris and all over the world. I have a photo of the two of them entertaining wealthy passengers aboard a famous ship called the *Queen Mary*.

'And that's how they met. And for their next act they conjured up seven healthy, happy babbies, of which I, Jack Morrow, was the last! As soon as we were old enough to totter, my parents began to teach their children every secret they knew. But it was only the seventh of those seven children who truly had The Gift.

'However, as I grew up, I realized that I did not want to be a performer. I was a bookish lad and, to be honest with you, I suffered from terrible stage fright. Although I never told my parents, I was being bullied at school on account of my eyes and diminutive height, and that didn't help my confidence. As I got older and found my way in science, I became more self-assured, but the theatre was never for me. After school I got a place at Trinity College to study Psychology and set out on my lifetime's work of combining scientific study with the mysterious art of hypnosis.

'After university I had my own hypnotherapy practice in a cosy little office in Lower Baggot Street with a magnificent chestnut tree outside the window. As a therapist, I was able to help half the population of Dublin with their eczema, their smoking, their fear of flying or public speaking. You name it, Jack Morrow sorted them out. And I often used the old regression technique, to unravel the source of their suffering.

'But I always felt I was capable of more. And then, one day, I was sitting on the top deck of a bus, browsing through a magazine called *Scientific American* – which I had sent over each month from New York at great expense – when I came across a great little article about a state-of-the-art Neurology Department they were constructing in a new university down here in the Southern states of America. That very day I sent them a letter, and to my utter joy I was invited for interview and accepted as Head of Department.

'And that's how I ended up sitting in front of you in the evening sunshine on this very deck. It's a grand job and the people I've met are some of the kindest I've known. But there are things I don't like here . . . You'll know what I'm talking about, both of you . . . The Jim Crow Laws and all that.'

'Ain't they got that back home, Jack?'

'It's a good question, Pip, and sad to say there's prejudice all over the world. Like a lot of Irish people, most of my sisters and brothers emigrated to England in the fifties to look for work, and they suffered terrible prejudice there. There's even a special word for it: Hibernophobia, which means prejudice against the Irish. Believe it or not, advertisements for jobs and flats in London often say *No Irish need apply*. Every Irishman knows about prejudice, and that's why my heart goes out to you and all the oppressed people in this cruel world. The American Constitution says that all people are created equal, and that's what I believe. If you keep coming to my little lessons, I'll teach you about a very great fighter for equality named Martin Luther King Junior . . .

'But Dr King will have wait for another day because right now Hannah looks like she's falling asleep. So there we have it – that was the tale of The Voice of the Wind, and that's the end of school for today. Before you go, I have a little something for you . . .'

I give them each a satchel. Inside are the Flintstones pencil cases, a pen, a bottle of ink, and a couple of children's books borrowed from the library. I can't tell you how much I enjoy seeing their faces beam with pleasure, and more so when Pip finds that his *Great Expectations* fits inside, as snug as you please.

'Don't ever forget,' I tell them, 'your names are linked. Pip and Hannah – palindromes, see. You stick together forwards and backwards. You keep an eye on each other and I'll keep an eye out for you.'

Then Hannah begins writing something in her new exercise book:

tank yu mista funi is

It takes a moment, but by now I am getting the hang of it. '*Thank you, Mr Funny Eyes?* Is that what you're saying? Well, thank you too, Hannah. And you've got lovely, magical eyes. Now be on your way, you rascals.'

I watch them cross the dirt track in the evening light, just as school pupils do all across the world. And I see Hannah do something that I had done myself as a small kid – she puts the strap of her satchel around her forehead, with the bag slung across her back, and she balances it just like a Chinese water carrier. Pip watches her and it is clear that he simply cannot contain his admiration and delight at every last thing she does. The boy is in love – it is written all over his face!

Long after they have gone I sit buzzing with excitement. If hypnosis isn't your thing, you may not quite understand what I have witnessed – I'm talking about the susceptibility tests on Pip. To put it in perspective, it is the equivalent of, say, a sports coach spotting a future Olympian athlete in their team; a music teacher discovering a child prodigy; or an art teacher who finds a young Picasso at the classroom easel.

That boy, Pip, simply has it – that thing my da and I were always searching for on the streets of Dublin. I knew it from the moment I saw him, but now it was confirmed. I had promised that I would consider putting him into trance, but in truth there had never been a moment's doubt. I couldn't wait to see where his mind would lead.

As I cook my evening meal, with Finnegan twirling

around my legs, I feel optimistic about the world. I had enjoyed my first lesson with Hannah and Pip more than I expected. I had received a message from Professor Cerberus telling me how much he had enjoyed my little show with the ice bath. It seems that Cerberus wants to talk with me in his office – that's exciting, isn't it? I'm thinking promotion . . . I'm thinking pay rise . . . I'm thinking of phoning home and having a little brag!

But sadly nothing in this life is perfect. Late that night, an unpleasant sound rumbles into my dreams. Still half asleep, I feel as if my bed and the whole bungalow are vibrating with the drone of approaching engines.

And sinister headlights dance on the walls.

16

Hannah Sings

i have no voice
like a dry river-bed
silence is my choice
but i sing in my head

in glimmering moonlight
a dreamcatcher gleams
if you weave it right
you capture dreams

i peep behind eyes
like a magic charm
of each sleeper who lies
at dead river farm

old man zachery
dreams wild and weird
his breathing is crackly
behind his white beard

old lady lilybelle
dreams she is thinner
rings on a handbell
cries for her dinner

dog in the doghouse
chasing a cat
and a frog and a fieldmouse
a bat and a rat

new boy pip
dreaming of sea
his bed is a ship
he floats there with me

strange-eye jack
troubled in sleep
hears a rumble on the track
and the grumble of a jeep

dreamcatcher bright
as the web of a spider
captures the lights
of the nighttime riders

who are these strangers
where do they go
what kind of dangers
only hannah knows

wish i could yell
but my tongue dry as dust
which dreamer can i tell
who will hannah trust

17

Red Barn, White Knights

Pip sat frozen in bed.

A far-off sound had wrenched him from sleep – the moaning of motorbikes, the trundle of trucks, the coughing of cars. Just like his first night at Dead River Farm.

But there was another sound too – and this noise was closer and even more terrifying. Somewhere deep below his bed, Pip heard the sharp click of the latch and the scraping of the ill-fitting half-door as it was pulled across the concrete floor. Someone had entered the disused stable below!

Heart leaping and ears straining, Pip pictured the huge form of Erwin making his way through the blackness towards the ladder which led to his bed.

And then the dreaded sounds came – the creak of ladder rungs and somebody breathing.

Pip fumbled for a weapon – anything would do. His hands grasped nothing but night. Slowly, slowly, the footfalls approached. With every nerve straining, Pip sensed that the intruder had reached the top step, and now the assassin was here in his room . . .

He stretched out, fumbled in the blackness and found an arm. He heard a quiet gasp. But this wrist felt small and thin. How could this be Erwin's wrist? Unless he was holding just one finger . . .

In that moment the convoy of vehicles roared past the farm, and the room was thrown into a chaos of lights. Now Pip could see the face of his assassin – but rather than the terrible jaw of Erwin, he saw the apricot softness of Hannah's face. Fully dressed and wide-eyed . . . Beautiful, crazy Hannah!

'Wh-wh-what you wan', Hannah? You scared me half to death. You can see I'm fast asleep.'

In answer, she shook his shoulder violently.

'You wan' me to follow? That it? But they're out there, Hannah! You can hear, can't you? They're drivin' about, and whoever they are, I don' wanna meet 'em.'

She glared at him, seeing deep down into his cowardice. Then she seized his shirtsleeve and tried to haul him from his bed.

Whenever he was with her, Pip felt nothing but confusion. Now half of him yearned for sleep and the safety of his bed, but the other half longed to be with the feral girl – he would follow her anywhere.

And follow her he did. He tugged on his too-small clothing and ill-fitting boots, and clambered down into the yard, where she stood waiting and alert, breathing in the crystal night air like a wild animal searching for a scent. Pip wanted to talk – he wanted to beg her to stay – but Hannah had already turned, and now she was gliding barefoot across the moonlit cobbles to the back gate, which led out of the yard and up towards the silver fields.

As Pip followed in fear and dismay, he felt the comforting brush of something soft against his legs, and there was Amigo, trotting happily at his side.

'You can come, but don' make a sound, you hear?'

The one thing Amigo had learned from various swinging boots was to restrain his barking. In fact the dog rarely made a noise, except an affectionate snuffling or a kind of cough from years of passive smoking in Zachery's truck.

So Pip and Amigo ran in silence. Pip thought of himself as a fast runner, but he struggled to catch up with that flying girl. She moved as if she was born running, pausing repeatedly to hurry him along, stamping her feet, eyes impatient and demanding. And although Pip's stomach was knotted with anxiety, he could not take his gaze off her face and the sheen of her hair in the moonlight. It made him long to reach out and touch her.

The truth is, there is no one more foolish than a young man with the first stirrings of love in his heart; no matter what insane danger awaited him in that diabolic night, some part of him rejoiced to be running with that fiery girl at his side.

The three of them bounded up the clay path, the twisted silhouettes of apple trees like vile hags on each side. At the top of the hill Pip saw lights and, near the vast steel skeleton of a high-voltage tower, the shape of a barn – red and hulking like an ocean liner.

There were sounds too – the slamming of car doors and deep male voices baying and bellowing like beasts before heading inside the barn.

Pip had no notion of what this was about – all he knew was that it had nothing to do with him. Whatever courage he had was gone. Then, for the first time, Hannah seized his hand, and the touch of her fingers was enough to carry him forward.

In the moonlight and the light from the barn, Pip felt dangerously exposed; but he followed Hannah, silently zigzagging between the vehicles. Pip noticed the distinctive black and white of a police patrol car, but this only added to his sense of alarm – the law didn't side with boys like him.

As they approached the mouth of the barn, they dropped down onto their hands and knees and scrambled from one car to the next. At last Hannah stopped, and they rested, panting, against the huge wheel of a customized truck. Now they could see directly into the brilliantly lit barn.

Pip's first instinct was that he was dreaming. One Christmas his parents had taken him to the theatre and he had been awestruck by the dazzling spectacle of costumed characters. Now he witnessed something equally out of this world: inside the barn a surreal pageant was taking place. Thirty or more ghosts were gathered. Each figure was dressed entirely in white robes with a flaming torch in his right hand. Many of the creatures had ropes around their waists and long-armed white gloves, and over each heart was the symbol of a white cross in a red circle, with a single drop of blood at its centre.

But what made Pip's skin crawl was that where their heads should be, each ghost-man wore an unfeasibly tall pointed hood with black sockets, like the gaping eyes of a skull.

Pip gasped for breath and, without thinking, reached out and slipped his arm round Hannah's waist.

One of the spooks was speaking. His voice sailed out through the still night so they could clearly hear each word.

'Ah wanna thank every las' one o' you for comin' out tonight. The Exalted Cyclops will be joinin' us real soon, so while we waitin' we gonna go raight ahead and take the oath. Klansmen, when you ready now.'

Each man extended his left arm in salute, and with each call and response they slowly raised their torches.

'For God!'

'FOR GOD!'

'For Country!'

'FOR COUNTRY!'

'For Race!'

'FOR RACE!'

'For the Klan!'

'FOR TH' KLAN!'

The smell of burning paraffin reached Pip's nostrils. And as he and Hannah stared transfixed at the bizarre scene, an even more sinister figure emerged from the shadows at the back of the barn. The white followers turned respectfully as he emerged, and formed a circle around him. The leader was taller than the others and his robe was red as blood.

With one voice, their shouts echoed into the night. 'WE GREET YOU, EXALTED CYCLOPS!'

The red leader raised his burning torch high above his conical head.

'Klansmen, I greet you, 'an ah 'pologize for the delay. You know ah travel all around, state to state, organizin' trainin' camps and suchlaike; workin' tairelessly for th' Invisible Empire.'

There were murmurs of appreciation and approval.

'Now, y'all know why we're here. We're here to defend our country 'gainst the invasion o' Negroes, Mexies, Injuns, Jews an' all them . . . *non-Whaites* who's tryin' t' steal it from our hainds.'

'That's raight!'

'You tell 'em, Cyclops!'

'Raight now there's fellahs laike that Martin Luther King claimin' Black folks is the equal o' honest Whaite men. You know that ain't raight!'

'It's a lie!'

'String 'em up.'

'All across 'merica, Negroes, Jews 'n homosexuals have been workin' t' take control of the teevee, the schools, noospapers, banks . . .'

'We seen it!'

'But we faightin' back now! Now the Klan is gittin' *STRONG* again. Yessir, RACIAL PURITY IS 'MERICA'S SECURITY! We got brothers raight here from the pol-eece – we got judges – we got teachers! You know wha' that means? It means we got the law on our saide. It means we got edoocation on our saide . . . and thars summat else we got too: we got GUNS on our saide!'

'Tell it, Exalted Titan!'

'Whaite Power!'

'Tonaight, mah brothers, is the Gatherin' of the Klans. Every Klavern fer miles is out huntin'. I understan' some o' our knight brothers will be ridin' over to show solidarity wi' the Dead River Klan.'

There was thunderous applause and shouting.

'Raight now, we gonna step outsaide fer th' Illumination. Knights of the Dead River Klan, raise the cross!'

Hannah and Pip huddled against each other in the shadow of the huge vehicle. They stared wide-eyed as ten or more hooded men bent down and raised a huge wooden cross to their shoulders. The cross was the length of a mature tree, wrapped tightly in sacks and sheets, bound with baling wire. Carrying the cross as ceremoniously as a coffin, the ghosts stepped into the night.

Pip felt weak with horror, but even in that hellish moment he rejoiced at the warmth of Hannah's body against his.

He turned and whispered fiercely into her ear. 'Hannah, we gotta leave this minute! Why you wanna be here? C'mon now, let's run 'afore they find us.'

But Hannah just pushed Amigo a little further under the truck and stared at the strange torchlit procession winding into the fields.

At the brow of the hill the ghosts laid down the enormous cross. Now two of them stepped forward with gasoline cans and doused the fabric around it. There must have been a ready-dug hole, because the band of ghouls inserted the foot of the cross into the ground and, slowly and majestically, hauled it upright.

From their perspective, three hundred yards down

the slope, the children saw the strange shapes in silhouette – the conical men and the huge crucifix against the endless sequined sky.

'Klansmen, salute the crauss!'

The men formed a circle around the cross, arms spread wide, flaming torches in every right hand.

'Klansmen, do you accept the laight?'

'YES! WE ACCEPT THE LAIGHT!'

'Klansmen, approach the crauss.'

At the order of the red leader, the white army glided forward.

'May th' laight of the crauss shaine down . . . ON THE MIGHTY KU KLUX KLAN!'

Simultaneously, the ghost-men hurled their torches at the cross, which erupted into flames, leaping and licking into the sky.

The sight of the blazing cross, along with the whoops and howls of those masked spectres, was more than Pip could bear. He seized Hannah's hand and dragged her to her feet.

'Hannah, I seen what you wanted me to see. Now it's your turn to listen, you understand? I read about these people – the Ku Klux Klan, ain't they? These are evil people, Hannah. They ain't got nothing to do with you an' me. We gonna turn round and head back.'

Pip spoke with such desperation and conviction that Hannah did not resist, and at last she followed him meekly down the hill.

It was exactly the wrong time to leave! At that moment Pip felt a rhythmic pounding beneath his feet and, to his absolute horror, saw a dozen horsemen thundering towards them. The faceless riders were like medieval knights in their streaming white robes; even their horses were hooded. They carried banners, flags and guns.

'Run, Hannah! Run!' he screamed.

But it was too late. The leading rider had spotted the children and turned his horse so sharply that it whinnied and reared on its hind legs. Leaving his fellow Klansmen, he thundered towards them.

In an instant Hannah had set off down the hillside, with Amigo close behind. But Pip knew that even Hannah could not outrun a racing stallion. In that wild moment he turned towards the galloping horseman, spread his arms and legs and waited for the explosion to come.

In every cell he anticipated the impact of that huge flying beast and the sensation of his skull being smashed to bloody fragments by iron-clad hooves. But at the last second the immense horse reared up, almost throwing its rider to the ground.

The knight was a skilful horseman: he brought his animal under control while simultaneously leaping from the saddle. Pip felt the colossal weight of the man crash upon him and tumbled breathless to the ground.

Lost in a confusion of flailing white sheets and strong grappling arms, Pip glimpsed Hannah and the dog pause and turn as if to help.

'RUN!' he screamed. '*Run, run, run!*'

The urgency in his voice must have convinced her. With a look of despair at his plight, Hannah and Amigo disappeared like phantoms in the night.

'Wal, lookee here!' panted the Klansman, forcing Pip's head against the ground. 'We been out huntin' all over the damned country, and jes' when ah thunk every snake an' possum is hidin' in its hole, I catch mahself a rabbit!'

Another horseman galloped over. 'The li'l Injun gal jes' disappeared into thin air, Lyle.'

'No matter. Lookee here! Git a sheet 'n some cord outta ma saddlebag. He's a slippy devil – best truss him up real taight. Make a special offering fer Exalted Cyclops.'

The Klansman sat on Pip's chest, and in spite of his terror, the boy bit and spat and kicked and scratched. But the ghost-rider only laughed. He had more strength in one arm than Pip had in his entire body.

'Boy, you fight like a bobcat . . . Guess ah'll have t' truss yer mouth up too.'

Perhaps the rider was used to working with cattle or sheep, because, with expert skill, he wrapped Pip tightly in a robe and encircled him from head to foot with rope, rolling him about and tugging on ropes until Pip lay bound as tight as an Egyptian mummy, barely able to breathe, let alone see or speak.

Despite the heat of the night, his blood had turned to ice. Now he was hauled upright and tossed across the strong man's shoulder like a rolled-up carpet. As he was carried up the hill towards the burning cross, Pip heard the Klansman mutter, 'Ah got some freends ah want you t' meet. Summa them laike t' practise their skills on li'l black rabbits. Kinda sport, ah guess . . . an' ever'one needs a li'l sport in their laives . . .'

Pip heard the crackle of flames. He smelled burning wood. He heard the cruel shouts and laughter grow.

'That you, Klansman Lyle? What you got there? Looks laike the biggest maggot ah evah dun see!'

'Hee, hee, hee!'

'Lyle caught hisself a li'l critter. You bringin' him up t' the fire?'

'Damn raight ah am. Ah'm goin' cook him till he's tender.'

The stench of burning gasoline stuck in Pip's throat. Amidst howls of laughter he was thrown down on the hard ground like a log. Then he heard a cry.

'Y'all gotta noose? Who brung a noose?'

Blindfolded and unable to move, Pip smelled the earth beneath his face, and for a moment the world seemed to turn below him.

In the blackness he heard his kidnapper, Lyle, call out, 'Klansmen, I greet you! Exalted Cyclops, I brung you a li'l gift to celebrate the Gatherin' of the Klans.'

'KIGY, Klansman Lyle. Glad y'all could join us. You gonna unpackage that thang or am ah gonna toss it straight on the fire?'

Strong hands grabbed Pip and he was hauled upright. He felt the cords bite into his limbs, until knots were loosened and the white sheet removed from his face. He stood blinking in the firelight, and for a moment he struggled to find his balance; then he managed to kick free of the tangle of ropes and robes around his feet.

Standing on the hilltop, trembling with fear, Pip had never felt smaller than he did now, beside those huge robed men, the towering cross and the vast steel pylon that stretched up to the sky.

Further out in the shadows, white-clad horses grazed on silver grass without a care in the world. There must have been sixty or more robed Klansmen around the blazing cross, and ten feet away, the crimson leader stood infinitely taller than the others; Pip had the strong impression of eyes staring at him from the vacant sockets of that mask. Two knights seized Pip's arms and dragged him before their leader. And now they forced him, shivering, to kneel before the towering figure of the Exalted Cyclops.

'You wanna noose, Cyclops? Or you gotta another plan?'

For a long time the Exalted Cyclops studied the boy. And then, very slowly and very quietly, he said, 'That's Pip! You brung me Pip!'

The men began to mutter in confusion.

'Jus' a Negro boy, Exalted Cyclops. Ah reck'n he was spyin' on us. The Injun girl got away . . .'

'No. No, you ain't *listening* . . . You brung me Pip . . . He's mah freend.'

'Your *freend*?'

'Did Cyclops say the Negro wus his freend?'

'What's Cyclops say?'

'He say the boy is his *freend*!'

'That's raight, Klansmen! Awl o' you listen, an' listen real good. Ah wan' you t' meet Pip. Ah love this boy. Don' y'all wanna squeeze him taight?'

Pip stared upwards in astonishment as the red giant raised his hood to reveal Erwin's lantern face, illuminated by flames and spread in that weird pumpkin grin.

The meeting disintegrated into confusion.

'Cyclops, we ain't hearin' yer. We brung you a boy – a Coloured boy, see?'

'Ah'll say it one last taime – This is *Pip* . . . He's mah freend.'

'Ha! Ah reck'n ol' Cyclops is havin' a joke, boys!'

There was awkward laughter, but Pip sensed that Exalted Cyclops was not known for his jokes. One of the bravest of the men stepped forward.

'Wal, joke or no joke, this here's a Negro boy, bin spyin' on the Klavern. Tonaight's the meetin' of the Klans an' we got a reputation to uphold. Ah'm real sorry, Cyclops – but wi' awl doo respec', ah'm gonna take this boy an' string 'im up. Tha's mah sworn duty, an' yours too, if ah may be so bold.'

Erwin seemed baffled. His head was twitching in grotesque convulsions, as if caught in some inner battle.

'Ah seed . . . Ah seed, Pip is mah freend. Any o' you touch him, you gotta settle wi' me.'

There was a long, awkward rumble of muttering. On his knees, Pip felt cold sweat streaming down his forehead.

It was clear that Erwin was still under the influence of Jack's hypnotic suggestions, but the spell seemed fragile. Erwin was a natural killer – a man who took life as easily as taking salt at the table . . . Could he really be restrained by *a thought*?

Another man stepped forward, holding something in white-gloved hands. With a terrible shudder, Pip realized that it was a neatly fashioned noose.

'Cyclops, you know ah serve you every way ah can. Ah carried out many difficult orders, 'cos ah respict you. But tonaight, Cyclops, ah feel you ain't well. Yo' sickenin' or summat. You 'member what you tawt us? Hate, hate, hate! Keel, keel, keel! Don' think, act!'

'HATE, HATE, HATE!' went up the cry. 'KEEL, KEEL, KEEL!'

The man stepped forward and, seizing Pip by the neck, hauled him to his feet. 'As second in command, ah'm takin' it 'pon mahself to deal with this boy in the 'propriate manner as you trained us t' do.'

He was a huge, powerful man who reeked of sweat and alcohol. Now he forced Pip under his arm, so that his neck was twisted in an unnatural, painful manner.

He heard a general shout of approval, and then Pip understood that Jack had been wrong. The hypnotist had overestimated the power of the mind against brute force and evil. To his horror, he felt the noose slip about his neck. The sensation of that cool cord was uniquely chilling, and his breathing changed to short desperate gasps as the knot slowly tightened.

A crowd of Klansmen had gathered. In his robes, with hood hanging from one gloved hand, Erwin towered over them, but still his head was jerking with indecision. Pip was close enough to hear his strange mumbling words.

'Hate . . . hate . . . love . . . Wait a minute, hate . . . keel . . . love . . . !'

And then, choking from asphyxiation and desperation, Pip found his voice and cried, 'Erwin . . . Erwin, I'm your friend. You love me, remember? I'm your best friend in the whole world, an' I make you happy, don' I? You remember your happy place. You wanna be a good soldier, don't you . . . ?'

It was a crude attempt to imitate Jack's hypnotic tricks. But something got through – Pip saw the weird smile return to Erwin's face and his hand floated vacantly to the side of his head in that same dreamy salute.

'Yes, sir. Ah wanna be good, sir.'

The man with the noose had seen enough. He slapped a gloved hand over Pip's mouth and dragged him towards the barn. Pip sensed that he had one last squeal at life. With all his might he bit the man's fingers, and when he swore with pain, Pip managed to wail, 'Erwin, Erwin, these people are tryin' to hurt your friend Pip *right now*! That's wrong, ain't it? You know that ain't right . . .'

Erwin walked slowly towards them. 'You hurtin' mah freend . . . He maked me happy . . . Ah love Pip . . .'

His captor swung Pip round, so that he was placed between him and Erwin. And then, as easily as a man might toss a bundle of twigs, Erwin grabbed the man by his robes, lifted him above his head, and hurled him to the ground.

Then Erwin was hugging Pip so hard it almost forced the breath from his body. The giant planted a cold wet kiss on his forehead and, gently patting his back, sent him on his way down the hillside.

Pip did not wait for further debate. He ran as fast as his shaking legs would carry him; and all the while, to his horror and disgust, he felt the tight noose around his neck, its end trailing like some foul umbilical cord in the night.

Fighting back nausea, heart convulsing, bloodstream churning, he stumbled towards the path. At the same time his fingers fumbled to release that appalling knot. At last he managed to haul the hateful thing over his head and fling it to the ground.

He turned once to make sure he was not followed, and saw Erwin one more time against the skyline, a great conical red shape, pointed hood in hand, scratching the side of his face in bewilderment.

Propelled by fear, Pip hurtled past the twisted apple trees. He was beaten, terrified and abused . . . But he was alive!

On that starlit night, and still in his thirteenth year, Pip joined the most elite society in the world – those who feel the hangman's noose, but live to tell the tale.

What he did not see was that, far away, behind the line of high-voltage towers, another cross burned on a hilltop. And beyond that another. And all across the countryside, as far as the mauve mountains, a chain of flaming crosses stretched far into the stifling night.

18

Summer Insomnia

Do you know the feeling when your sleep is so troubled
that you are glad when something wakes you?

That something was a quiet but urgent tapping on my
front door.

The girl, Hannah, was standing on the porch, wearing
her usual grubby T-shirt and ragged jeans, with bare feet
below; but her expression was wild with alarm.

I grabbed her wiry arm and pulled her into the living
room, locking the door firmly. As I did so, I recalled the
sounds that had disturbed my dreams – the engines and
the shouting. I remembered that throughout the night I
had half woken again and again. There had been all kinds
of shenanigans up at the barn – some sort of devilish party,
it sounded like . . . But surely it wasn't possible that
Hannah had been caught up in that madness!

'What's going on, Hannah?'

She stared at me.

'Oh, for goodness' sake . . . I suppose I'll have to find pen and paper . . .'

I fumbled around searching for a notepad and pencil, realizing that it could take the rest of the night for her to write the story. When I returned she was standing by the window, gazing into the moonlight.

One of the fascinating things about people who have been mute for many years – either physically or electively mute, as I knew Hannah to be – is that their faces become incredibly expressive. Before she had written a word I understood that Pip was out there and he was in profound danger.

In a civilized society a fellow would get straight on the phone and call the police. But with a feeling of absolute dismay, I recalled the patrol cars amongst the night convoy.

I threw down the notepad and grabbed a coat. 'Hannah, now listen. You're going to wait here and I'm going to take a walk and see if I can spot him. Is that all right?'

She turned towards me, and I read her thoughts again as if she were shouting in my face: *There's nothing you can do out there alone!*

I sat her at the table and gently placed a cardigan around her shoulders. Then I went to the kitchen to make her a warm drink, and all the time my mind was whirling as I struggled to formulate a plan . . .

And that's when I heard it!

I stood at the door with a mug in each hand – and simply froze in my tracks. At first I thought it was the radio or a voice outside, but then I saw her head bent sadly and realized that Hannah was singing again – quietly and tremulously in that beautiful, natural voice.

It was a song called 'Strange Fruit', which they were playing a lot on the radio those days. 'Strange Fruit' was a protest song, but it wasn't an angry song. Oh no. What made it so disturbing was that it was sung softly like a sad, sleepy lullaby. Every time I heard it, it made my skin crawl. And it happened again that night as I heard Hannah sing. Because, you see, 'Strange Fruit' is a lullaby about lynching. Go and listen to it sometime . . . listen carefully to the words and maybe you'll shudder like me when you realize that the strange fruits in the poplar trees are nothing less than lynched Black bodies with bulging eyes and twisted mouths, swaying gently amidst the sweet fragrance of magnolia.

I restrained myself from moving until the last pure notes had died away, then I walked quietly to her side and placed a mug in her hand.

'Ah, that's a wonderful song, Hannah. One of my favourites. Was it Billie Holiday?'

She nodded, and I was completely taken aback when she whispered, 'Don' tell no one, Jack.' Her voice was cracked and hoarse.

'Hannah, I won't tell a living soul. Not until you're ready. But I loved hearing you. It's a gorgeous voice you have there.'

It was a precious moment, as we sat side by side watching the timid rays of morning creeping into the room.

At one point I asked her a question, but I was pretty sure I knew the answer. 'It's the Klan, isn't it, Hannah? It's the bloody Ku Klux Klan!'

She nodded and wiped her eyes with the back of her hand. Of course, I knew a little about the KKK. Who didn't know something? The papers were full of their despicable lynchings and beatings and the unexplained 'disappearances'. In segregated states like this, Black people were not allowed to serve on juries, so on the few occasions when Klansmen were brought to justice they were released within hours, and TV footage sometimes showed them smoking cigars and laughing arrogantly with police officers outside the courts. So if a Black orphan like Pip went missing . . . well, it would barely get a mention in the barber shop on a Saturday morning.

My mind was in turmoil and, although I hate myself for admitting it, there was fear too. It was not the same fear as when Erwin had confronted me; this was something far darker and more sinister. It was the realization that the world I thought I knew did not exist at all – the word 'justice' had been torn from the dictionary. There was nowhere to turn and no one to complain to. Perhaps this was the same feeling of overwhelming helplessness that decent law-abiding Jewish families felt when the Nazis came to power.

This must be the world that Pip and his family had always known. How could anyone sleep safely in their bed in this stifling climate of dread?

And what about Hannah? Where were her family? Where was her tribe? On my way to the university I had often seen those dispossessed Native American people sitting sadly and silently on benches around the town, with an empty expression or an empty bottle.

That's why Hannah is here in the hypnotist's tale. This mute girl represents those proud and noble indigenous people who hunted these mauve mountains long before it was taken from them.

As I was thinking these sad thoughts, the boy appeared quietly on the deck, staring in at us with eyes aflame. He looked taller and older than the last time I had seen him, and a little more harrowed.

Hannah ran to the door and fumbled with the key. I saw his shoulders drop with exhaustion as she smothered him in her embrace. The relief I felt was like a loosening of every muscle in my body and a warmth flowing through my veins.

It was 5.30 a.m., and the glow of the moon was melting into daylight. I left the children huddled beneath a blanket on the swing seat. Something had changed between them; Hannah now rested her head affectionately on Pip's shoulder.

I washed and dressed and prepared eggs and bagels and muffins. I saw Finnegan return from his night's hunting and crawl onto Hannah's lap. I carried out the food and we ate together on the veranda, like three washed-up refugees.

In brief sentences Pip told me the incredible story of what had taken place. I must admit that at various times I wondered if the story was a little far-fetched but, as if to chasten me for my doubts, we heard the familiar drone of engines coming down from the fields. A look of dread spread across Pip's face, and we had the sickening experience of watching that slow-moving convoy roll down the dirt track by Dead River Farm. They filed past my bungalow – the pickup trucks, the customized four-wheel drives, the farmers' vehicles, the patrol cars, the Harley Davidsons, two or three Cadillacs, a Thunderbird . . . As they passed, every head of every driver and every passenger turned and stared directly at me as I sat with my two young friends. A patrol car slowed. The stony-faced cop leaned his head out of the window – he touched his eyes with two fingers then rotated his hand and pointed them aggressively at me. I understood what it meant all right – 'I see you, fellah . . . I see you.'

When the last vehicle had gone I stood up, my heart belting, my body aching with fatigue. I looked at Pip and Hannah curled up beneath the blanket, and suddenly my thoughts came into focus. 'Pip . . . Hannah . . . Did you ever go on holiday?'

They stirred a little and stared at me blankly.

'A vacation, I mean. You know what? I've got a feeling we'd all benefit from getting away from this infernal place. And I've an interesting destination in mind. Call it Jack Morrow's Mystery Tour if you like!'

19

Love Is Something To Steal

if you aint got nothing
you cant lose nothing
thats always been my plan

been running round this world
like the old lone wolf
catch me if you can

well theres nothing to lose
when you aint got shoes
theres nothing they can take

so why should i care
when my heart is bare
theres nothing there to break

if you dont love no one
you cant lose no one
is that so hard to explain

but

along comes this boy
chains my heart with joy
now all i feel is pain

cos when you got something
you can sure lose something
love is something to steal

if they take him from me
and swing him from a tree
i aint never gonna heal

20

Down by the River (I)

How Pip survived the following days he would never know. Wherever he went — along the dark corridor in the farmhouse, reading aloud at Lilybelle's bedside, or lying in his makeshift bed above the stable — his fingertips would rise of their own accord to touch his throat, and he would feel once more the tightening of that evil noose.

The events of that night seemed like a strange dream or a terrible nightmare and, after the affection she had shown him, Hannah seemed distant again; sitting alone beneath a tree working on her mysterious dreamcatchers, or wandering the countryside. It hurt Pip more than he could say.

In spite of his anxiety, Pip's sense of duty to Lilybelle remained. It never crossed his mind that he should not turn up at her bedside each morning.

He saw Erwin fleetingly. On the first occasion Pip emerged from the stable block and had the fright of his life.

There was the man they had called the Exalted Cyclops, relaxing in a broken easy chair on the farmhouse porch, dressed in a camouflaged hunting jacket and cleaning a gun – and this was not a shotgun like Zachery's, it was a blood-chilling assault rifle constructed from the same grey-green metal as his Jeep. Erwin raised the weapon and stared, one-eyed, in Pip's direction. Pip prepared to have his head blown from his body, but incredibly, Erwin lowered the gun and waved vigorously with his huge hand, like an infant waving to its mother at the school gates.

'Lookee thar. It's mah freend! That's li'l Pip. Awww, he makes me reel happy! Come here, Pip. Ah wanna hug ya reel taight.'

During the following days Pip did everything he could to avoid the maniac. And whenever they met, the encounter was the same – the gap-toothed grin, the childlike wave, and the disturbingly friendly greeting. 'Hey there! Hey . . . ah see you. That's Pip. That's mah freend. Ah jes' wanna say, ah truly love you, Pip . . .'

To Pip this was more terrifying than violent hostility; so the boy was mighty relieved when one afternoon, concealed behind a shed, he watched Erwin load up the Jeep with tents, ropes, shovels and military equipment before driving out of the yard.

Once the Jeep had passed the row of white bungalows, turned left at the end of the track and disappeared from view in the direction of the mountains, Pip emerged from his hiding place and stood there for a while, savouring the relief of Erwin's absence. He heard the faint tinkle of Lilybelle's handbell from the farmhouse, and he was about to see what she wanted when his foot kicked something metallic on the ground where the Jeep had stood a moment before. It clanked and scuttled across the cobbles, and Pip thought it must be a nail or a tent peg. But what he found lying between two stones was an old-fashioned key, unusually long and cold to the touch.

Holding the heavy key between finger and thumb, Pip wandered into the farmhouse, beneath the glass-eyed animals and down the corridor towards Lilybelle's room. As he passed the huge door to Erwin's room, some instinct guided his hand towards the keyhole, and the key slid into place as easily as a murderer's blade slips between a man's ribs.

Pip felt a wave of panic, but he knew that Erwin was far away, and something compelled him to see behind that colossal door.

'I'll be right with you, Lilybelle,' he called weakly.

Pip turned the ice-cold steel handle and eased the door ajar. He put his head inside, and then his shoulders, and when he was sure that no living being was waiting there to seize him, he slipped slowly into Erwin's bedroom.

Pip found himself in a long, narrow room which felt cold and lifeless even on that baking summer's day. On the shabby greying walls were many pictures torn from magazines – of wars and helicopters and battle scenes in jungles, and grinning soldiers, and overturned Jeeps and dying men and weeping children.

Along the full length of one wall lay Erwin's long, long bed, and Pip saw that it had been built from two regular single beds, nailed end to end. He noticed that even the grey army blankets were made of two regular blankets sewn untidily end to end. With a shudder, Pip realized that the bedside table, which was covered with empty bottles and weeping candles, was nothing more than a moss-coloured ammunition case turned on its end.

Instead of the cheerful shelves of books he had seen in Jack's room, one entire wall was hung with racks bristling with rifles and ammunition. And instead of a curtain, the single window was covered by a large flag, printed with the same emblem he had seen that fateful night – a white cross on a red circle, with a single drop of blood at its centre.

Unable to stop himself, Pip slid open drawers and discovered foul torture devices – knives, pistols, knuckledusters and swastikas.

With stomach churning and head spinning, Pip stepped out of the huge door, turning the key in the lock behind him. Then he went into the kitchen to fill a bowl for Lilybelle's bed bath. As the kettle boiled, Pip placed the key on the kitchen table where Erwin would be sure to find it when he returned.

Lilybelle seemed blissfully unaware of the horror chamber along the corridor. These days she painted more and more, and Pip was surprised to find her sitting almost upright in bed with a contented expression on her doll-like face as she worked on another imaginary scene.

Later that day, Hannah, Pip and Jack met for the first time since the dreadful events at the barn. The atmosphere in Jack's bungalow was more subdued than before, and although Jack had devised all kinds of lessons to interest them, Pip felt tired and Hannah seemed more withdrawn than ever.

Jack tried to cheer them by reminding them about the mystery tour he was planning. Although Pip didn't want to seem ungrateful, he wasn't interested in a vacation – all he could think about was escaping Dead River for good; a fantasy which even the howling dogs of his imagination had never quite chased away.

The afternoon light was fading when Jack brought the class to an end. As he tidied the table, he put a hand on Pip's shoulder. 'Pip, I'll be honest with you, old fellow, I'm a little worried about you. You know I'm not a medical doctor but I am a qualified hypnotherapist. I've used trance to help lots of people with all kinds of difficulties and I think you said you were keen to give it a try. How would you feel about that? It'll do you no harm and it might help you to move on from all the terrible things you've experienced . . .'

Pip looked up at Jack. He was growing to trust this unusual man. 'I'll do it if Hannah stays with me.'

'That's fair enough,' said Jack. 'What do you say, Hannah?'

Of course, Hannah said nothing, but she nodded a little and the agreement was made.

As if it were the most everyday thing in the world, Jack began making preparations. He closed the curtains in the living room and switched on a small reading light draped with a cotton scarf, so that a soft light filled the room.

Then he placed two kitchen chairs beside the leather couch by the bookcase. When he was satisfied, he invited Pip to remove his boots and settle himself on the couch. Hannah sat at Pip's feet and Jack took his place by Pip's head.

Pip had no idea what he was in for, but he was ready for anything that might settle the anxiety he felt these days. Besides, hypnosis seemed like an incredible adventure to him – the closest thing to magic he had ever seen. Strangely, even as he lay on that old battered couch, he began to relax.

What encouraged him more than anything was a small signal from Hannah, which made his heart soar. It was only a wave – not even that; she just raised her fingertips slightly – but it was enough to reassure him as the hypnotist began to talk in a soft and rhythmic tone.

'Now, Pip, we'll start with light trance and see how we get along . . . I promise you'll be in safe hands. Did you know, that's my very favourite couch you're lying on? I had it shipped all the way from Dublin, and it's where I like to relax with a book of an evening . . .

'Now, what I am about to do is teach you how to find a wonderful safe place in your mind. Once you've been there, you'll be able to visit whenever you choose; so it'll be a nice relaxing game – like a lovely dream, if you like, only much more real.'

'I don't want Erwin to be there, nor them ghost-men.'

'No indeed, we'll make sure of that, Pip. It will be your own special place and you don't have to take anybody you don't want to. You are completely in charge. So think hard for a moment and tell me about a time when you felt absolutely happy and at peace.'

'Fishin' with Pa.'

'Ah, now, that sounds grand! So you used to fish together when you were younger? Let's see if we can find that place, shall we? All you need to do is turn your head towards me – that's right, you can look deep into my eyes – and I can tell you are beginning to relax . . . So now you might like to count backwards from ten to one . . .'

. . . nine . . . eight . . . seven . . .

And from that moment Pip began to lose all sense of time, so he couldn't say whether the counting lasted an hour, or a day, or maybe a month. All he knew was that a warm fog had settled in his mind, which was not unpleasant at all. And although he did not understand how it could be, the fog seemed to emanate from Jack's soft voice and those marvellous eyes which shone down like the twin moons of some faraway planet.

The twin moons seemed to be telling Pip that he was sliding back through the years, and to Pip's surprise he found that this was not a hard thing to do. In fact it was as easy as floating down a slide at the fair. Pretty soon he found himself far away from the white room, and there was no one there – except his father, of course, who was frying pancakes on the stove. And as he cooked those pancakes, Papa kept humming and breaking into little dance moves, which pleased Pip enormously.

Papa told him that he had the fishing bags all set, and when Mama came in, Pip begged her to join them on their expedition. But she just kissed him and said that no, this was Pop an' Pip time, and besides, she'd be no use at keeping up with two strong men fuelled up with pancakes and maple syrup. Besides, her belly was so swollen, she might as well have been up all night eating pancakes herself.

But just when Pip was feeling quite happy and safe,

something terrible happened that spoiled everything . . . A huge roaring train was coming at colossal speed, and Pip was screaming at the top of his lungs, '*LOOK OUT, MAMA! The train's comin'!*' He needed Papa to turn the car right round, but there wasn't time – the train was coming too fast – and the brakes were screaming and Mama was screaming and Pip was screaming—!

And Pip was yelling and thrashing with fear until the twin moons guided him swiftly back up the slide, and Pip realized that Jack was by his side, and Hannah seemed to have forgotten her indifference because she was squeezing his hand and looking so concerned and lovely that all his fear vanished. Pip sat up on the couch, shaking and blinking and trying to figure out where he was, but Jack was always steady. He said that everything was fine, and just as soon as Pip was ready, they were going right back down the slide to his happy place in *ten . . . nine . . . eight . . .*

And there they were – Pop and Pip, marching along the road in front of the schoolhouse, with all the rainbow-coloured washing dancing on the lines, and some folks were calling out to Papa and waving, and Pip was carrying his fishing rod so proudly, it might have been a spear for fighting dragons in the hills.

And those hills were as soft and green as a dream. As they left the village, Pip couldn't stop chattering about all the fish he was going to catch and how big Mama's eyes would be when the fish come tumbling onto the table, all white-eyed and silvery and fat.

They kept on strolling through the patchwork country-side, heading towards the river. The bees were humming and the butterflies were flitting and everything was astonishingly bright and clear. Pip kept saying, 'Hurry up, Papa!' but Papa wouldn't hurry; he was just taking his time and singing, so Pip ran ahead to the top of the hill until he could see right down to the beautiful twisting blue river below, all clean and bright and full of bubbles and fishes . . .

And from way up in the clear blue sky, Jack said, 'Well, that sounds grand, old fellow. And how are you feeling now?'

And Pip told him, 'I'm feeling much better, thank you, Jack Morrow, sir, because the sun is warm and Papa's by my side. Look, I can reach right out and touch his hand!'

And the twin moons shone down from above, and they said, 'Tell me what you see now, Pip – tell me what you see . . .'

So Pip described how he and Papa were settling into their usual fishing spot, in the shade of the old stone bridge. Papa had brought lemonade, and now he was taking off his boots and rolling up the legs on his pants so he could stand the bottle in the shallow water to keep it cool.

Then they threw out their lines to the deep place where all the fishes sleep, and then it was important to sit very still. 'Gotta be patient, see . . .'

'Ah, patience is everything,' said the moons. 'Now, you just relax there, young Pip, for as long as you want. You're as safe as houses and the day is long . . .'

'Papa says . . . Papa says . . .'

'What does he say, Pip? What does he say, old fellow?'

'Papa says I mustn't ever forget. Not ever . . .'

'Mustn't forget what, Pip?' asked the moons.

'But I *did* forget, Papa!'

'What did you forget, Pip? You can remember everything now if you try . . .'

'Papa says, "Don't never forget, Pip. But you don' tell no one."'

'Well, if it's a secret, you don't have to tell us,' said the moons.

'Papa says, "You know I don't trust banks, Pip. The White banks ain't no good for folks like us. Me an' your mama made our money by the sweat of our brows – ain't no bankman gonna take it from us." And then Papa's standing up and laying the rods on the ground. He's taking my hand and leading me under the bridge . . .'

'What's under the bridge, Pip? Can you see?'

'Sure I can see. I see it plain as day. Can't you see it? Papa is counting stones in the wall. There are hundreds of stones, but Papa knows exactly which one he's lookin' for. He starts countin' . . . five, six, seven stones up off the ground . . . seventeen, eighteen, nineteen stones from the right . . . "That's the one!" he says. And he's pointing at a big blue-grey stone. Now he gets hold of the stone in his hands. He's trying to wiggle it, but it's jammed real tight. He says, "Pip, fetch ma blade from the bag." So I'm going over to Papa's bag and I'm getting the old jack-knife and I'm handing it to Papa. Now Papa jams it in beside the blue-grey stone, and I'm scared he's gonna bust the blade. Then, real slow, the stone starts easin' out a little, and Papa gets his strong fingers round it, and suddenly it leaps out and darn near drops on his toes. We're laughing and he's hopping about, and inside the hole where the blue-grey stone was – that's

154

where I see it. "You won't ever forget where it's hid, Pip?"
"No, sir. I'll *never* forget where it's hid . . ."'

'Where what's hid, Pip?' ask the moons way up in the blue, blue sky. 'What's behind the stone under the bridge?'

'Why, the cookie jar of course! The jar fits real neat in the hole. Ain't no one ever gonna find that jar if they don' know where to look.'

'But what's in the cookie jar?' wonders the moons.

'Well, you can see, can't you, Mr Moons? It's plain as day.'

'Tell us, Pip. Tell us what you see, old fellow.'

'Papa twists open the lid, and inside the cookie jar is a canvas flour bag. Papa pulls out the bag and drops it right into my hands. It smells of old canvas and underground places. And there's something heavy inside. I'm opening the strings on the top of the bag and peeking inside . . . "Whoo-ee!" I say. "WHOO-EEE, sir!"'

'What is it, Pip? What is it, old fellow?'

'"Why, that's my great expectations!" That's what Papa says. He says there's only one kind of bank a man can trust – and that's a riverbank! That's Papa's joke, see. Then he helps me stuff the flour bag back in the cookie jar and we push it back deep inside the hole. Now we pick up the heavy blue-grey stone and wiggle it in place.

'Papa shows me how to cram soil into the cracks around the stone, so it's hidden from every peepin' eye. Then he gathers a fistful of moss to smear over the scratch marks on the rock. And all the time, the river whispers and whispers like it knows the secret too.

'And when the job is done, Papa and me stand back, and

we can't even see which was the special blue-grey stone . . .'

Then the twin moons let Pip sit by the river a while longer. The moons tell him that Papa loves him very, very much. They let Pip catch a fish if he wants to – the biggest, fattest, wettest fish that ever swam.

And at last the moons are counting back from one to ten, and the river is rushing and rushing, louder and louder, and when Pip looks up, he sees that the twin moons are the kindly eyes on Jack Morrow's face, and there's Hannah smiling at him, with eyes as round as buttons.

21

The Man with Six Fingers

It was the easiest induction I'd ever performed.

I timed it on my watch, and later, when I checked my notebook, I found it had taken less than three minutes to put Pip under. There was a tricky moment when he seemed to be reliving some awful event. He started screaming and shaking so violently, I thought he must be back with the Klan at the red barn . . . But no, it was the train crash he was re-living. The terrible accident that had torn his world apart. Regression is a subtle business and not for the inexperienced – I pulled him back very quickly, but I made a note that there was extensive work to be done.

What an imagination that boy had! I could tell that he was smelling every smell and experiencing every texture and colour in his trance world. I wasn't exactly sure what he thought he had discovered in the cookie jar concealed beneath the bridge, but when he emerged from trance he was like a different fellow – relaxed, and happy and confident.

Now, before you say anything, I want to assure you that I thought very carefully about performing an induction on a lad of Pip's age. It's not something I would normally do without parental consent, but I had seen how anxious the boy was and I'd noticed the nervous habit he had developed of repeatedly touching the tender skin of his neck.

When I was sure he was steady on his feet, I sent Pip and Hannah on their way, and as I watched them walking calmly across the track to Dead River Farm I was pleased to see that they were holding hands. No one can prevent suffering in this world, but how much easier it can be with a friend at your side.

I was certainly mindful of the risk Erwin presented to Pip. I'd dealt with all kinds in my work, I can tell you, and I know that humans are not killers by nature. Most of us do not wish death or pain on even our worst enemy. But then again, there is a tiny number who have something wonky with their wiring. These people have no empathy at all. As few as one per cent of the population may be psychopaths, but an infinitesimally smaller number will simply kill for fun. I was beginning to suspect that Erwin was one of these.

In spite of that, I was fairly confident from what Pip had told me about their recent encounters that my hypnotic commands were holding and Erwin would not harm the boy . . . What I had foolishly failed to consider was the threat he presented to Hannah.

That evening I went to talk to Zachery. Checking first that Erwin's Jeep was not in the yard, I wandered around until I discovered a stream of engine oil and curses oozing from beneath the brown truck.

I called out, 'Mr Zachery, it's Jack – Jack Morrow. I'd like a word.'

I stood and waited until several tools were tossed out and Zachery emerged. With much coughing and swearing, he hauled himself upright, wiping his oily hands on his overalls. He spat on the ground and relit his cigarette. 'Wassa matter? Ye growed taired o' teachin'?'

'No. Not at all. I love our lessons. And I don't know if you've noticed how much their language skills are improving . . .'

'Oh yeah, the gull don' never quit tawkin' . . .'

'No, she's not talking, that's true. But have you seen her written work? I think she may be really musical too. And Pip is a very bright fellow. I reckon he's now almost where he would be if he had stayed in school . . .'

'Waste o' taime, laike ah seed.'

'Well, you're entitled to your opinion and I hope you'll respect mine. Anyway, I'm here to ask your permission for something. You remember the letter you received from the education authorities about your obligation to provide an education . . . ?'

'Th' one ah used t' waipe mah ass?'

'Well, if you'd read it, you'd have learned that every child is entitled to a certain amount of holiday too. A little break from time to time. It's a legal requirement.'

'Oh yeah, ah'll get raight on an' book their vacation in Florida . . . Li'l hotel wi' a swimmin' pool . . .'

'That's not what I meant.'

'A cuppla weeks croosin' on an ocean liner, suit 'em jes' faine.'

'Of course not. It won't cost a cent. My idea is that I would take them away for a few days. I'll act as their guardian and take full responsibility. What do you say now?'

'Ah say no.'

'Well, in that case you shouldn't be surprised if you get a visit from the state authorities . . .'

'Listen, Doc – Jock – whatever yer thunderin' name is. Who in tarnation's gonna cook mah meals an' look after Lilybelle while you *spoilin'* them kids? Who gonna *spoil* me?'

'I'm sure you can manage for a while . . .'

Zachery slammed the bonnet of his truck and discharged a jet of mucus from one nostril, which I took to be a sign of agreement.

Our expedition was becoming a reality, and as I drove to my appointment with Professor Cerberus at the university the following day, I reminded myself to mention that I was owed some holiday time, and I planned to see a little more of this huge and beautiful country.

I entered the campus between water sprinklers hissing on the grassy hill and parked the Spider. As I strolled beside the glass windows of the labs, I could see my students engaged in all kinds of fascinating experiments.

It was indeed a new dawn in psychology, and I began to think about finding new lodgings away from all that madness, so that I could focus on my work and the bright opportunities the university offered me. Surely the Klan belonged to ancient history like Dead River Farm itself.

I rode the lift to the second floor and marched along the air-conditioned corridors. As I approached the Vice Principal's office, I heard the familiar woodpecker sound of dozens of busy typewriters. You people of today take computers for granted, but at that time every institution employed a pool of typists, shorthand secretaries and clerks to maintain the complex paper filing systems. Everything was done by hand.

The proud inscription on the door read:

PROFESSOR W. M. CERBERUS JR., PH. D

VICE PRINCIPAL

I knocked and waited, and I was conscious of dozens of pairs of heavily mascaraed eyes watching me. I knew I was still something of a curiosity.

Walter Cerberus flung the door wide, grinning at me in a slightly superior way. He was a small man of about my height; around fifty, I would guess, with a little round belly, a yellow bow tie and suede shoes.

'Ah, Dr Morrow . . . Jack, if I may. We meet at last. Step right on in. Welcome to Mission Control!'

His handshake was warm enough, but there was something a little irregular about his grip, which I couldn't quite identify.

'What can I get you, Jack? Brandy? Coffee?'

'A coffee would be grand.'

He went to his huge desk and flicked a switch on the intercom. Then I realized what was odd about his handshake – the man had an extra digit on his right hand. How very peculiar! Walter Cerberus had six fingers – so that was why the students called him Professor Pinkie!

'Can we get two coffees, Marian?'

'Right away, Professor,' answered the machine.

He was one of those fellows who shouts rather than talks. He waved me towards an over-designed chair and I glanced somewhat enviously around the big modern office – impressive bookshelves, a set of golf clubs in a corner, huge windows overlooking the campus and expensive modern art on the walls.

'Now, Jack, would you like me to tell you how delighted I am, out of ten?'

'Well . . .'

'Ten, Jack – no, wait, *fifteen*! That's how delighted! Your little hypnosis show was Out. Of. This. World!'

'I'm glad you were happy, Professor.'

'Happy? Jack, the show was Broadway Gold! The spotlights, the dreamy voice, the guy in the ice tub – that boy should get an Oscar! The part where he thinks he's in a desert and starts perspiring . . . Oh my Lord! Let me tell you, Jack, every person in that theatre was fooled!'

'Well, now, there was no acting—'

'Sure, Jack! You keep your magic tricks to yourself! Who can blame you? All I can say is that my group of VIPs couldn't stop talking about it all day long . . . Classic, Jack!

162

Classic! Ah, here's the coffee – just set it right here, Marian.'

His secretary placed a tray on a low table, smiling dazzlingly all the while. Cerberus's eyes followed her slim legs out of the door.

'Now, I'm hearing a lot of good things about your department, Jack. You folks in Neurology are teaching us all some interesting lessons . . . Sugar? Cream?'

'Er, just a little milk. That's plenty . . . Well, we couldn't do it without your support, Professor.'

'Call me Walter.'

The professor strolled to the window and gazed like a little fat god at the campus below.

'We all enjoy having you here, Jack. It's no secret that I've got your name in my PPP file – that's Possible Promotion People! If we can tick a few final boxes, we'll be moving ahead with that before the new semester. Now, my wife Doreen and I are involved in all kinds of charitable work in the town. Doreen is forever organizing barbecues and fund-raising events and we'd like to have you along. Spread a little of the old Celtic charm!'

'Well, that's awfully kind of you, Professor.'

'Walter. Think nothing of it. Some of the events are real family affairs, and then there's golf and other activities which are . . . kinda men only! Doreen and I have always felt it's healthy to separate some parts of our lives and . . . well, Jack, there's only so many Tupperware parties a man can stand!'

'Ha! I'm sure that's true.'

Cerberus handed me a cup and saucer.

'In the meantime I have a favour to ask – a university matter – and that's why I invited you here this morning . . . By the way, did I mention that Doreen and I took our honeymoon in Ireland back in 'forty-nine? Didn't stop raining for a month.'

'Ah, yes, that's why they call it the Emerald Isle—'

'Here's the situation, Jack – I have to go away for a few days to a conference in North Carolina and I need a reliable man to take the helm.'

'Well, I—'

'I want you to move right here into my office, Jack, so you can keep an eye on things. You'll have Marian and the whole team at your disposal.'

'That's an incredible honour, Professor . . . Walter.'

'No problem. That's the way it works here, Jack. Like I said before – we stick together . . . look out for one another – you know what I'm saying? You'll be my deputy sheriff for a few days! Could lead on to *big* things.'

I pictured myself in that oak-panelled office, with the bookshelves and the modern art. Maybe I'd have a little knock about with the office golf set, and I'm ashamed to tell you, I imagined calling home from behind the big desk – Ma would never believe it!

'Thank you, Walter. I'd be absolutely delighted!'

'Well, that's wonderful!' he shouted and whacked me so hard on the back that my coffee went flying.

'Oh, my! I'm sorry 'bout that, Jack! Just got carried away. Here, let me . . . No – look, the restroom is right through there – why don't you wipe that before it stains?'

Professor Cerberus had a bathroom attached to his

office, exactly as you'd imagine – lots of white marble and gleaming sanitary ware. I dabbed at the stain on my shirt as best I could, then reached for what I took for a towel hanging on the back of the door. What I saw made my blood run cold! It was not a towel – it was the lynched body of a man!

No. No, that's not correct. It was not a corpse hanging on the back of the door, but it might as well have been. What I saw hanging from a hook in the Vice Principal's bathroom was a pointed hood and white robe, embroidered with the distinctive blood-drop cross of the Ku Klux Klan! There was even a pair of long white gloves folded neatly on a hanger. With a shudder, I realized that the gloves had been specially made with an extra finger on one hand.

It was a full five minutes before I ceased trembling and my heartbeat returned to near normal. I washed and dried my face and flushed the toilet. There was no other way out – I turned the handle and stepped back into his office.

'Thought y'all had got stuck down the john! Your coffee's cold now, Jack. I'll send for some more. Wait a minute – you don't look too good. Man, you look like you seen a ghost! Oh . . . Oh, OK I get it. Did you see something hanging on my bathroom door, Jack?'

'Professor, I have to leave now. I have a seminar to attend—'

'Wait a minute. Sit down, Jack . . .'

'Thank you, sir, I'd like to stay but—'

'*Sit down.* That's an order. OK, you saw the robes. As a matter of fact this is one of the things I wanted to speak to you about. My guess is you've picked up a lot of liberal

165

civil rights propaganda about the Klan. I'd like to redress the balance a little. See, the Klan is a very old institution here in America. All the VIPs who came with me to your lecture were Klansmen. We do a lot of charity work and we give big donations to the church. It's a kind of fund-raising group, if you like, and we have a lot of fun in the process.'

I was seething with fear and fury.

'Professor Cerberus, let's not beat about the bush. The KKK is a racist organization that has been clearly linked to some outrageous crimes.'

'Oh, I get it. You've been talking to the student union and you've been taken in by all their Commie hooey. Listen, I'm an educated man, Jack, same as you. But I'm a History Major, so maybe I know a little more about this than you do. It may surprise you to know that the Klan started as a kind of university fraternity. It has a long and noble tradition. Why, the very name Ku Klux Klan comes from the Greek *kuklos*, which means a circle or band. Look at me, Jack. Do I look like a thug? Do you think I would get involved in breaking the law? The law is on our side – we *are* the law. The Klan is not racist – we're not anti-Black, no siree, we're just *pro-White*. Do you see the difference? I have fought to have Black students enrolled right here at the university. Many of them are excellent sportsmen. The conference I'm headed to in North Carolina will be exclusively for Klan academics, and I can assure you that many of them share my belief that some Coloured folk have nearly the same intellectual ability—'

'Professor! There is not one Black student amongst

nearly a thousand Caucasian students at this university. The only non-Whites are cleaners and kitchen staff.'

'Not yet, Jack. Not yet. But things are changing. I'm all for change, but it don't happen overnight. I mean, there's this whole Women's Lib thing going on too, and we are trying to accommodate that. We have many women in senior positions. Take a look at Marian – she don't just make coffee, you know.'

'I'm sorry, Professor—'

'Walter, call me Walter.'

'I'm sorry, Walter, but I find the KKK very, very disturbing—'

'Ignorance, Jack. That's just ignorance. You're a man of science, so it surprises me that you jump to conclusions without getting your facts straight. A lot of people fear what they don't know. My father was a Klansman, and his father before him, so I grew up with it. It's a family affair. We have good old barbecues and musical evenings. Why, we even have women members now, and kids – you wouldn't believe how cute they look in their little robes! Sure there has been some bad press – a few loose cannons maybe – but I tell you, the Klan is a force for good. It's a place for young people to feel they belong. You're young and you have a great deal of potential, Jack, so if you play your cards right, who knows where you might end up down the line. I'll give you an example: right now the Klan has the youngest County Leader in our history – just nineteen years of age and he's got a very strong following indeed. This boy ain't educated like you and me, Jack, but he was amongst the first of our boys in 'Nam. Believe me,

167

he picked up some very valuable skills out there, and a flair for leadership – I mean, zeal and fervour. I personally checked him out thoroughly, and I recognized a young man with potential . . . just like you, Jack. So the Brotherhood got behind him, and now, well, there's no stopping him . . . Lives up your end of town, I believe. Dead River – ain't that where you reside?'

Grotesque nausea rolled in my stomach.

'See, you choose to live in our country, Jack, and you gotta learn to do things the way we do. When in Rome and all that. I'd like y'all to come along to just one meeting – meet a few of the boys and have a nice homey evening. If you don't like it, well, no one can say you didn't try, and you can go home to Ireland saying you had a new experience and broadened your mind. If you do like it – well, I promise there are people here who can help you *leap* up the promotion ladder . . . like Jack up the Beanstalk, ha, ha, ha! We can really make things happen for you. You understand what I'm saying?'

'You're saying that if I don't agree to join the Klan, my job is in jeopardy?'

'Well, I wouldn't put it quite like that. You make it sound almost like blackmail. But let's agree on a compromise: you take the helm while I'm in North Carolina, just like we said. That will give y'all time to think things over. I've got some Klan literature right here in my desk that I'd like you to digest. See, here's some pamphlets, and this book is what we call the Kloran – it's our bible of abiding principles. Ain't nothing to frighten the horses, Jack. When I return, we'll have another leisurely chat, and if you have any queries,

I'll be glad to answer them for you. How's that sound?'

'I . . . I'll think it all over. But . . . but I wanted to ask you . . . to tell you . . . I'm due some leave, so I plan to get away . . .'

'Sure. Take a few days' vacation and get yourself set to take over the Big Desk when you return. And if you need anything, you just click the intercom and one of my little genies will appear at your side.'

'Thank you.'

'Come on, let me see that Irish smile . . . *Oh, Danny boy . . .*'

I forced a sickly smile onto my face and backed towards the door. I felt a migraine coming on and this loathsome man just wouldn't stop babbling.

'Hey, y'all need to get that shirt dry-cleaned, pardner. Tell you what, charge it to the university – how's that?'

I groped blindly for the exit. He winked at me confidentially.

'One last thing, Jack – the Klan is pretty modest about the charity work we do; that's why we call ourselves the Invisible Empire. We like to keep things hush-hush – you know what I'm saying? Keep it in the family. So you won't feel the need to share our conversation, will you, Jack?'

I felt exactly as I had done at school when the bullies had been working on me all day and I went home knowing I couldn't tell a soul.

As he opened the door, the professor clapped me once more on the back and shook my hand. Although my senses were reeling, I could focus on only one thing – that strange extra pinkie on Walter Cerberus's hand.

22

Hannah's Secrets, One to Ten

hannahs secret number 1

hannah has a secret valley
a grassy place where no one goes
a mossy lair beneath the tree trunks
where the river used to flow

hannahs secret number 2

hannah has a secret treasure
a transistor radio from her dad
keeps it stashed beneath a tree root
wrapped inside a plastic bag

hannahs secret number 3

hannah has a secret story
as she was born her mother died
and her mother was a singer
the finest singer of her tribe

hannahs secret number 4

hannah has a secret daddy
abandoned her one winters day
hannahs dad became a junkie
gave her a radio gave her away

hannahs secret number 5

hannah has a secret pleasure
holds the radio to her ear
then she hears her mother calling
in a voice thats sweet and clear

hannahs secret number 6

hannah has a secret talent
when she hears those lovely songs
making sure no one is spying
hannah loves to sing along

hannahs secret number 7

hannah has a secret admirer
with hands as big as dinner plates

erwin gropes her in the kitchen
leaves her with a bitter hate

hannahs secret number 8

hannah takes a secret vengeance
when hes gone all buttoned up
hannah spits into his dinner
pisses in his coffee cup

hannahs secret number 9

hannah makes a secret promise
if he comes up to her bed
hannahs silence will be over
she will kill that monster dead

hannahs secret number 10

hannah has a secret dream
like a mighty roaring sea
one day the world will hear her singing
one day hannah will be free

23

Summer of Love

Shonk! Ker-r-ack! Thwack!

On the morning of his fourteenth birthday Pip woke to the pleasant rhythm of logs being split in the yard.

It would be a good day. The signs were plain to see – no Jeep parked below his window; instead, old man Zachery cheerfully chopping wood on a perfect summer's day.

Shonk! Ker-r-ack! Thwack!

Of course, 'cheerfully' for Zachery did not mean whistling or breaking into dance moves as Pip's papa used to do, but Pip had learned to read Zachery's mood by the position of the dog: when the old man was calm, Amigo would sleep nearby in a splash of shade. When Zachery was surly and snappy, the dog would make himself scarce entirely.

As he looked out on that sparkling morning, Pip noticed something he had never seen – Zachery had tossed his old jacket on the ground and Amigo was curled peacefully upon it, not three feet from where his master was swinging a sharpened axe.

Shonk! Ker-r-ack! Thwack!

Pip pulled on his clothes, slid down the ladder and stepped outside.

'Morning, Mr Zachery,' he said, snapping open the tobacco tin to fix the old man a cigarette.

'Ye know how t' split wood, son?'

'No, sir,' said Pip, lighting the cigarette and handing it to him as he had been instructed. To a teenage boy there are few things as alluring as a pile of wood and a gleaming axe, and Pip eyed them greedily.

There was indeed something different about that day because, to the boy's amazement, Zachery began to teach him patiently how to swing the long-handled axe.

'Slaide yer hand back to th' end, see. Naice an' long. Then the axe do th' work, not you. Git it raight an' ye c'n split it in one. If yer don', jes' raise the log on the axe an' bring it down ag'in.'

Pip raised the axe and the old man stood behind him, almost like a kindly grandfather, showing him how to place his hands on the hickory handle.

'Keep yer feet back, darn it, or th' dawg'll be pickin' up yer toes.'

Within ten minutes Pip had the hang of it, and as he worked his way through the pile, Zachery sat smoking on the throne of an upturned bucket.

'Hoo-aah! Now y' got it, boy!'

The satisfaction of the leaping logs and the splicing

blade was hard to beat. On top of that, in recent months Pip had discovered brand-new muscles and sinews in his back and shoulders which loved to work. Now he felt them stir and grow. He was taller and stronger, like the man his father had been.

Seeing that he knew what he was about, Zachery wandered away. His parting words – 'Tha's faine. Jes' stack 'em there when yer done, boy . . .' – felt as good as any heartfelt praise Pip had ever received.

As the sun rose above the wind turbine, the pile of neatly chopped logs grew and the boy gloried in the sensation of his labour.

Shonk! Ker-r-ack! Thwack!

Noticing that his shirt was growing damp, Pip stripped to the waist. There was no one about, and in any case, the feeling of the sunshine on his torso intensified the feeling of liberation.

The screen door of the farmhouse opened and Hannah stepped out; shyly, furtively.

In one hand she carried a mug of coffee and in the other a wooden plate. On the plate lay two slabs of homemade cornbread, smeared with creamy butter, and between those slices a rasher of bacon, still sizzling from the pan, and an egg, yellow and round as the sun itself.

In an ideal world Hannah would have sat beside him in the sunshine and shared that meal, and they would have talked – at least, Pip to her – and maybe her sweet toes might have inched towards his working man's boots . . . but that was just a foolish daydream brought on by his loneliness, because in reality Pip had barely thanked her before she was gone.

But since the night he had saved her from the horseman and the time she held his hand while he was in trance, Pip was sure she no longer despised him. And now her absence was compensated for by the pleasure of that food. Indeed, Pip had never tasted anything so good as that simple birthday breakfast.

When he had drained the last sweet drop of coffee and wiped the faintest glaze of egg yolk from his plate, he completed the task that Zachery had given him and washed himself at the pump.

Then he heard Jack calling as he walked across the track. 'Pip, I've got a little something for you! It's not much, but I couldn't let a birthday pass without a gift . . .'

'Jack! How did you know? I didn't tell no one!'

'I'm a hypnotist, Pip – I know everything!'

'Really, Jack . . .'

'You wrote your date of birth on your exercise book. Now, here you are – I hope it's something you'll like.'

And Jack presented him with a cardboard box. When Pip lifted the lid, he found a layer of tissue paper, and when he unwrapped the tissue paper . . . there they were! A squeaky pair of white sneakers.

Pip was overwhelmed with gratitude. But that was only the beginning of that wonderful day. When he presented himself at Lilybelle's bedside, he found her painting happily; the curtain was open, the window was wide, and Lilybelle seemed brighter and calmer than ever before.

'Oh mah, Pip! Where in th' world you get them fancy shoes? It's laike you *bounced* in here!'

And when Pip confessed that it was his birthday and the

shoes were a gift from his tutor, Lilybelle was mortified that she didn't have a present for him too.

'But thar's one thang ah can give you, Pip, an' tha's a day free from chores. You get in th' kitchen an' pack yerself a picnic . . . Ah don' wanna set ahs on ye till you've had a day in the sunshaine! Take Amigo too, and Hannah if she's mainded.'

'Thank you, Lilybelle, I would like that very much. But you know I ain't going no place till I've read to you . . . Now where did we get to?'

'You are a precious boy,' said Lilybelle. 'Come an' sit by ma saide.'

So Pip snuggled against her and opened his book, but just as he was about to begin, the door opened softly, and there was Hannah with Lilybelle's morning snack. She set down the tray and was about to leave when Lilybelle said, 'Hannah, 'less ah'm mistaken, Pip would enjoy your comp'ny on his birthday too! Ain't that raight? You come an' hear th' tale – boy reads laike he was born wi' a book in his hands. It's maighty sweet on th' ear.'

Although Pip squirmed with embarrassment, he was overjoyed when Hannah settled attentively by his side. Then, to his surprise, she pulled out one of her dreamcatchers, and her agile fingers began weaving the web as she listened to the story.

Pip's weeks of practice had paid off because now his reading was clear and confident; and strangely, the antiquated language of *Great Expectations* seemed to mirror the situation in the pink bedroom and express the words that he could never say . . .

'*"Estella," said I, turning to her now, and trying to command my trembling voice, "you know I love you. You know that I have loved you long and dearly."* She raised her eyes to my face, on being thus addressed, and her fingers plied their work, and she looked at me with an unmoved countenance . . . "I am ignorant what may become of me very soon, how poor I may be, or where I may go. Still, I love you. I have loved you ever since I first saw you in this house . . . You have been in every line I have ever read since I first came here, the rough common boy whose poor heart you wounded even then . . ."'*

Pip heard a sobbing, and when he raised his gaze from the page, he was astonished to see tears streaming down Lilybelle's face and Hannah staring in wonder as he warmed to the part.

'*In what ecstasy of unhappiness I got these broken words out of myself, I don't know. The rhapsody welled up within me, like blood from an inward wound, and gushed out. I held her hand to my lips some lingering moments, and so I left her . . .*'

'NO!' cried Lilybelle. 'He ain't gonna leave her, Pip! He cain't do that!'

But Pip read on, his voice growing louder. He even acted the parts of the different characters, giving Miss Havisham an old and croaky tone.

'*"Love her, love her, love her! If she favours you, love her. If she wounds you, love her. If she tears your heart to pieces – and as it gets older and stronger, it will tear deeper – love her, love her, love her!"*'

'Oh mah!' sobbed Lilybelle at last. 'Ah cain't take no more! Go on, you two – run free – leave me now – skedaddle!'

180

* * *

Within ten minutes Pip and Hannah were running out of the farmhouse and through the back gate, with Amigo flying at their feet. They dawdled to pick apples on the hillside, and wandered through the wispy wavering grass that was alive with bees and birds and crickets.

Pip felt as if he had left all his troubles behind and his heart would burst with happiness – until he saw the huge pyramid of the electricity tower and the menacing shape of the red barn, and he was overwhelmed with terrifying memories.

'Where we going, Hannah? I didn't wanna come this way.'

But it was clear that the wild child had a plan, and that she knew every inch of the countryside. She grabbed Pip's hand and led him round the back of the barn where a hidden trail lay. The trail was so narrow they had to walk in single file, but after a few minutes they came to a dancing copse of birch trees at the top of a ridge and, looking down, Pip saw a secret valley spread below, filled with sunshine like a bowl of gold. He followed Hannah, slipping and sliding down the snaking track until they reached a dry river-bed. Then, to his amazement, she reached into the roots of a willow tree and produced a transistor radio wrapped in polythene. Clearly this was her hideaway – a mossy animal's lair with bars of sunlight streaming through the leafy roof.

When you are young, a summer day can go on for ever, and as they lay side by side, music poured from that radio which seemed so sweet, Pip would spend a lifetime searching for those songs. Above them, in a sweeping curve around the valley edge, leaves rustled and whispered like waves around a shore and the sky was a turquoise ocean, through which swallows swooped like flying fish.

They lay lost in the music until Pip turned on one arm and looked down at Hannah's face, as smooth and brown as nutmeg, and her shining raven hair. Summoning his courage, he lifted her hand as Pip had lifted Estella's, and kissed each fingertip in turn. He half expected Hannah to glare at him and rush away, but no – she just closed her eyes and sighed. And then, to Pip's astonishment, she stretched up that hand and clutched the ringlets at the back of his head. She pulled him firmly towards her and kissed his lips. Pip lost himself in that kiss, which seemed as deep as any trance, and he found himself trembling uncontrollably at the sensation of her soft mouth and breath as sweet as apples.

To Pip, the girl seemed to be part of Nature herself – a flawless part of the sunshine and the breeze and the birdsong of that sublime summer's day. He could find nothing about her that was not perfect – her delicate collarbone, the silkiness of her limbs, even the moons on her nails and the smallest pink scar on one shoulder . . .

On his fourteenth birthday Pip would almost have endured the hardships and fears of his life all over again, just to lie with Hannah in that soft grassy valley, where he fell . . .

down,
    down,
        down . . .

            He fell so deeply in love.

24

What I Should Have Said

You'll have to forgive my mood.

Normally I love to prepare for a holiday. Normally I love to pack my bags and check my maps, but since the meeting with the professor I've been feeling a little out of sorts. I can only apologize. I'm sure I'll feel better when we hit the road and get as far away as possible from Dead River Farm and Erwin and Professor Bloody Walter Cerberus.

A summer holiday should be the best time of the year, don't you think? When we were kids, Ma and Da would borrow a big old van, and the whole Morrow clan, plus Granny and Granda and a few cousins, would spin along the mountain roads to County Kerry. Sadly Da's eyesight had deterioriated by then and he was prone to dreadful migranes, which also trouble me from time to time; so my older brothers did the driving. We rented the same holiday cottage each year, high above Dingle Bay. There were never enough bedrooms to go round, so my older siblings would set up tents on the lawn and light campfires and giggle and sing into the wee hours. How I longed to join them, but I was the babby of the family so I had to sleep inside with the grown-ups!

Now, as I check the oil and the brakes on the Spider, all I feel is frustration. I can hardly contain my fury. Up until the meeting in Cerberus's office, I thought of the university as a sanctuary – a vision of a bright tolerant future – but now it seems like a dinosaur stuck in the past; an elite world for privileged White kids.

But more than anything, I feel mad with myself. I could kick myself for my gutless response to the professor's 'history lesson'. As I clean the windscreen and adjust the mirrors, I think of all the clever things I should have said when Professor Pinkie asked me to join his 'homey' organization. The man claims to be a historian, but perhaps he needs a little education about the three thousand innocent folk who have been strung up by the mob which is sometimes given the chilling name of 'Judge Lynch'. After I left Cerberus I went straight to the library, where I got myself in a right stew reading all about the Great Migration. I can't believe they didn't teach me this at school! The simple fact is that six million African Americans were forced to flee the lynchings and the prejudice in the rural Southern United States. Six million innocent folk driven right out of their homes, hoping for fairer treatment in the North. Well, in my book, that's ethnic cleansing – an exodus of biblical proportions!

I expect 'Call me Walter' Cerberus and his White Supremacist friends would say that it's for the best if minority groups 'go back where they came from'! We hear that all the time, right! But the walloping great contradiction is that most African Americans – like Pip, for example – are direct descendants of slaves who were forcibly uprooted from where they originated and dragged to this part of the world by the likes of Cerberus's ancestors!

Here's another steaming, stinking lump of hypocrisy: this gorgeous land which Walter and Erwin and his cronies defend so aggressively was stolen in the first place! Of course it was! It was taken by force from the indigenous tribes of America – that is, Hannah and her people.

And now Mexicans and other immigrant people are referred to as 'illegals'! Think it through, Professor . . . we are *all* illegals! I mean, the native people invited none of us here.

As I furiously stacked my bags in the back of the Spider, it came to me that what I should have said in plain simple language was that I believe in the equality of *all* people. I believe in tolerance and compassion and fairness, and if you don't believe in these things, Professor, then I want nothing to do with you or your university, and especially I want nothing to do with your pathetic boys' club with the pointy white hats and the poisonous White views.

But I had said none of these things. I had listened in disbelief as he talked proudly about the County Klan Leader – 'just nineteen years of age, with a very strong

185

following indeed'. He told me that the boy had returned from Vietnam with valuable military skills and a flair for leadership – 'real zeal and fervour' were his words. I thought of Pip and Hannah, and realized that they would never be safe in their beds while Erwin was alive. It was my responsibility to look after them.

When I went to buy my road maps, I noticed that every bookshop and petrol station stocked the same distinctive travel guide. I picked up a copy and was horrified to read the title: *The Negro Traveler's Green Book*. The book contained a comprehensive list of lodgings and gas stations which would serve Black people. The purpose was to 'give the Negro traveler information that will keep him from running into difficulties, embarrassments and to make his trip more enjoyable'.

There was no mention of what to do when people of different races set out together.

25

What Hannah Like

what hannah like about the boy is his mind
clever honest kind

what hannah hate about the boy is his fear
fear is slavery but I see it turn to bravery
whenever I am near

what hannah like is the body of the boy
see his muscles hustle
fill my heart with joy

what hannah hate about the boy is he has no mother
and no dad hes sad like hannah
we carry emptiness like one another

what hannah like about the boy is his smile
that smile make everything worthwhile
id run a mile for that sunny smile

what hannah hate about the boy is that he live here
    at dead river farm
where there is no key
and no alarm
but he does not flee
and that is also like me

what hannah like about the boy is that he cares
for lilybelle the dog as well
even shares
his love with hannah

what i enjoy about the boy
is that he has stirred something sweet and strong
which i had all along and never knew it
make me squeeze my knees in the night
and lo-o-o-ng for him
i know that boy is right

what i like
is the boy to kiss my lips
and linger
on each finger
dont forget each fingertip
pip

26

Mystery Tour (I)

They set off early one morning at the end of August, and it was a brand-new sensation for Pip and Hannah to be rumbling and bumping and flying along the road, with the sunroof down and their hair streaming behind.

There wasn't much room in the car – a Spider, Jack called it – so Pip and Hannah squeezed together in the passenger seat, which Pip was more than glad to do. They carried little luggage, except for Pip's book in his satchel and a couple of bags in the trunk. With every mile they put between them and Dead River, Pip felt more and more relaxed, and when Jack tuned in to the Jazz channel, the world seemed a kinder place to be.

Shortly after dawn, when Pip and Hannah had arrived at the white bungalow, they had found Jack fussing about how Finnegan would manage while they were away. Zachery was certainly not one of life's natural cat-sitters, and besides, the old man hadn't stopped grumbling about having to care for Lilybelle while they were gone. In the end Jack had simply piled up a couple of bowls of food and left a window ajar at the back of the bungalow. After all, Finnegan was a very independent kind of cat.

The seats in Jack's car were set very low, so it felt almost like flying on a magic carpet, just a few inches above the ground. This kind of travelling felt ten times faster than the old brown truck in which Pip had arrived at Dead River, and on top of that, there was the excitement of a mystery destination.

'Jack, Jack, why won't you tell us where we're goin'?' he pleaded for the hundredth time.

But Jack would say nothing except that it was a surprise, and that Morrow's Mystery Tour would be something to remember. The only other thing he told them was that it would be a long journey. 'So we'll stay in motels for a night or two. Now, just relax and enjoy the ride. You all right, Hannah?'

She nodded, and for a moment she seemed awfully young to Pip. He found himself wondering how often she had ridden in a car – or perhaps this was the very first time.

When they left the town, Jack opened the throttle and the engine roared. All around them lay America in its glory, with mountains and swamps and forests and plains.

'I'll tell you this!' shouted Jack. 'To an Irishman, your country is a huge and beautiful place! All right, hold tight, everybody . . .'

They zipped down the highway, the little car eating up the miles like a hungry tiger, and by mid-morning they had forgotten their cares, as if Erwin and his ghost-men and the orphanage and all those terrible things had been discarded on the roadside somewhere far, far behind. Hannah and Pip were jiggling to the music and for the first time Pip heard Hannah laugh; it was the sweetest, wildest sound he had ever heard.

He noticed her response to the radio with fascination. The wild girl seemed attuned to every note, especially the powerful voices of female blues singers like Nina Simone and Billie Holiday, and she mimed silently to every lyric, with a look of absolute bliss on her face.

The three travellers rolled on past pine forests and breathtaking waterfalls that leaped from crazy crags. When they stopped to stretch their legs, Jack studied his maps while Hannah and Pip ran along animal tracks, whooping and shrieking with joy.

But Jack would not let the journey hinder their studies – in fact he took the opportunity of having his pupils confined at his side to launch into long discourses on every theme imaginable, from literature to psychology to music and movies, and more than anything, he held forth on politics and issues relating to human rights. Pip was particularly stirred by the powerful story of Rosa Parks, a brave Black woman who had been arrested for refusing to give up her seat to a White man on a segregated bus; he pictured the woman as his own mother, silent and proud in the face of indignity. Pip noticed that, over the months, the manner of Jack's teaching had changed: he no longer talked to them as if they were kids; now he treated them like students in their own mini university, and if Pip didn't understand every word, it did not matter – his mind was hungry to expand.

There was only one unusual incident on that first stage of the journey. On an endless stretch of deserted highway Jack told them that a state trooper was following them on a motorcycle. Pip looked in the wing mirror and saw him too, hovering steadily behind, faceless behind white helmet and dark glasses. Jack warned Pip and Hannah that the police in that part of the world were notoriously authoritarian, especially to people of Colour. In fact, Jack said, he had heard that non-White drivers were continually harassed for dubious traffic violations, and the ironic phrase used to describe these offences was 'driving while Black or Brown'.

For fifteen minutes Jack took the greatest care to control his speed. But the presence of the sinister figure on their tail created a feeling of deep unease – Pip had grown up with the knowledge that the law was not there for people like him and Hannah.

Mile after mile, the cop buzzed like a fly on their tail. At last Jack became so irritated that he slowed the vehicle to a crawl. At this point the cop shot past, stabbing the air with his leather gauntlet to indicate that Jack should pull over.

The officer kicked out the stand on his bike and removed his helmet. Then he slouched arrogantly, chewing gum and waiting for Jack to join him. Jack had told Pip that the police seldom carried guns where he came from, but this fellow had an armoury strapped to his waist – a nightstick, handcuffs and a large revolver, as well as a rifle on the side of the bike.

Huddled side by side in the low-slung seat, Pip and Hannah watched Jack walk towards the man. The cop was built like a bulldog, with a neck as thick as a tree trunk, which made the Irishman appear smaller than ever. In the silent afternoon Pip could hear every word.

'Y'all new round here?'

'Just passing through, Officer.'

'See your licence . . .'

Jack handed over the document. The cop glanced at it and stared at Jack through reflective lenses.

'Ah been watchin' fer some taime, an' it seems yo' carryin' aliens in that vehicle.'

'Aliens?'

'Them kids ain't *yo'* kids. You got persons o' Colour in your car an' that sets me wondrin' . . .'

'I'm their tutor . . . their guardian.'

'Lemme git this straight. You're a Whaite male – a foreigner too 'less ah'm mistaken – an' you the guardian o' these minors? Summat don't stack up, mister. Jes' don't feel raight. Y' know ah'd be failin' in my duties if ah didn't take you in.'

'Officer, we've done nothing wrong and we're trying to get to—'

'The town up ahead is a Sundown Town, y' know that?'

'A Sundown Town?'

'Tha's raight. You know wha' that means, don'cha?'

'I'm sorry, the term is unfamiliar—'

'Oh, *the term is unfamiliar*, is it? Wal, it's real simple – a Sundown Town is an all-Whaite neighbourhood. That means decent folks 'preciate law an' order. People o' Colour ain't permitted after dark. That ain't so hard, is it?'

In his head Pip pleaded with Jack not to argue. He knew this cop had the power to do anything he pleased. Pip felt sure he would love an excuse to pull his gun, and a terrible picture came to him of Jack sprawled bleeding on the roadside.

'I appreciate your advice, Officer, but I can assure you we have no intention of stopping in your "Sundown Town". We'll drive right through and out the other side—'

'Let's git somethin' straight – ah don' like you; ah don' like yo' car; ah don' like the fact that you got Negro children in yo' car. Mos' of all, ah don' like yer goddam eyes. An' tha's why ah'm arrestin' you right here an' now.' He reached for his cuffs.

'My eyes? You can't arrest someone because of their eyes – but now that you mention it . . . I've got something in my eye, Officer – an insect or something – would you mind just looking for me?'

'Insect? Yo' ahs? Wha' . . . Ah ain't . . .'

'Thank you . . . It's in there somewhere – would you mind if I just raised your sunglasses . . . ?'

'Tha's a . . . it's a goddam violation . . . Ah mean, thar's a law . . .'

'There's no law against the wind, is there . . . ? You see, my voice is the voice of the wind in the trees . . . I don't know if you've noticed, but you're feeling a little tired . . . a little drowsy and confused . . . Maybe it's the heat . . .'

'Ah . . . ah am taired – how d'you know that, mister? Who the hell are you anyway?'

'The name's Jack – Dr Jack Morrow, to use my full moniker. But you won't remember that . . . People call me the Hypnotist . . . I wonder if you can guess why . . .'

As they pulled away, Pip turned in his seat and was

amazed to see the state trooper curled like a child with his thumb in his mouth, sleeping sweetly by his motorcycle at the roadside.

Pip had a thousand questions about what had just taken place, but Jack would not talk about it. He simply cranked up the volume on the radio and pushed his foot to the floor.

Although they had done nothing that day but stare at the countless miles of asphalt and the patchwork countryside, Hannah and Pip felt exhausted by the journey.

In the late afternoon, Jack pulled over at a sign saying: '*KOZY KABINS MOTEL. Children welcome. Pets allowed.*' They purred up a tree-lined drive, beside neat lawns, towards the reception office. From his low seat, Pip watched happy White families playing tennis or easing away the fatigue of their journey in a glistening turquoise pool. He felt like an interloper. He knew this place was not for him.

As Jack fastened the folding roof of the Spider, Pip said, 'Jack, we can't stay here. You know that. Hannah an' me gonna sleep right here in the car. You go on ahead an' get a bed . . .'

Jack ignored him. He strode purposefully past the NO COLORED sign and in through the office door. Pip watched the little man's silhouette inside. There was a brief discussion; then the receptionist reached behind and handed over some keys.

When he returned, Jack was smiling in that mysterious way he had. All he would say was that the gentleman had seemed a little fatigued, but he realized that Pip and Hannah were such important guests that he had given them three of his best rooms at the quiet end of the site. They were the 'Kwality Kabins', he was informed.

Carrying his bag, Pip scuttled nervously after Jack and the moment the door was unlocked, he darted furtively inside.

But this place was amazing! This place was a wonderland! These cabins were tiny palaces, with smoothly whirring fans and iceboxes crammed with soda. For half an hour, the children ran back and forth excitedly comparing their rooms. They threw themselves onto the soft beds, inhaling freshly laundered linen; they ran into the en-suite bathrooms and blasted steaming jets of water. Then they found the greatest wonder of all – individual television sets on rotating shelves in front of each bed. And unlike Lilybelle's snowstorm TV, the children discovered a whizzing world of crazy colours!

But suddenly Pip was shocked back to reality – as he charged towards Hannah's cabin, he ran headlong into a heavily freckled young woman of about seventeen. 'Pardon me, miss,' he said.

The snub-nosed girl barely glanced at him. 'Boy, my daddy needs fresh towels right this instant, y'hear?'

After she had gone they retreated to the safety of Pip's room, where they lay side by side on the bed, chins resting on arms, wide-eyed in front of frenetic cartoons. A little later, when Jack returned from the on-site diner, carrying pizzas and apple pies, he found the children exactly as he had left them, mesmerised by the TV.

Later that evening, when Pip was alone, he took the first hot shower of his life, then collapsed into a luxurious sleep.

He woke once, bewildered by the neon glow of the 'Kwality Kabins' sign outside and the chattering of television sets from all around. His door opened quietly and Hannah slipped inside. She crept across to where he lay; her lovely face bright with excitement about the whole adventure.

All she did was smile at him in the half-light. All she did was kiss him gently on his forehead before melting into the night.

Then Pip slept peacefully until dawn.

27

I Have a Dream

I planned an early night myself. There was nothing on the television except the usual race riots and civil unrest. I watched in utter dismay as people of Colour were beaten by batons and snarled at by police dogs. I saw powerful firehoses turned on sobbing Black schoolchildren and I wondered what kind of a world we were living in.

I was about to switch the damned thing off, when the Brylcreemed news anchor started talking about an extraordinary event that had taken place that very day in Washington DC. I began to realize that, as Pip and Hannah and I had been bowling blissfully along the highway, history had been happening in the capital of this great and troubled land.

Now I sat upright in my bed and stared in wonder at this event they were calling 'The March on Washington for Jobs and Freedom'. On this hot, heaving, historic day of 28th August 1963, a quarter of a million people of every race, creed and colour had streamed out of buses and coaches to follow marching bands towards the Lincoln Memorial.

Now sleep seemed a distant thing as I watched this march for equality. I saw a colossal crowd chanting and waving banners and flags – the young, the poor and the educated; even representatives of Native Americans Indians were there. I watched the weathered faces of old Coloured folk, who had suffered lifetimes of indignity and oppression. These were the people who had been used and abused to build this mighty industrial nation, and now, like Rosa Parks on the segregated bus, the day had dawned when they were saying, 'Enough!'

As hundreds of policemen waited nervously at the sidelines, I waited for the whole thing to erupt into violence. But it never did. Perhaps the slow train of change was coming at last.

A stage had been assembled in front of the great marble statue of Abraham Lincoln – the president who had overseen the abolishment of slavery one hundred years before. The steps to the memorial bristled with microphones and cameras and I saw many celebrities waiting to speak – all my heroes were there: Marlon Brando, Sammy Davis Jr, Sidney Poitier, Joan Baez . . . I swear to you I saw Bob Dylan himself, fresh-faced, with a mop of unruly hair and guitar in hand.

But the final speaker was in a different league. The final speaker was none other than the Reverend Martin Luther King Jr himself and I cannot describe the effect that electric speech had upon me. Visibly shaking with emotion, the great man gave a sermon like I have never heard before – a poem almost, that summoned up the poor Black children of America who had suffered so long, for no reason other than the colour of their skins. He evoked the mountains, plains and rivers of that great country – the hills of prejudice, which would be laid low by the mighty voice of Justice.

I had the weird impression that the fellow was speaking directly to me – to Jack Morrow from Dublin, Ireland. Wide-awake in my Kozy Kabin, as hot tears of hope sprang from my eyes.

Then Dr King raised his hands to the heavens like the great preacher he was – 'I have a dream,' he proclaimed, 'that a day will come in which the children and grand–children of slaves will sit together with the children and grandchildren of slave owners at the table of Equality'.

Shaking his finger with rapture and rage, his words vibrated through the booming speakers, across Washington and out into the world . . . *Oh, my brothers and sisters, I have a dream!*

At long last, when I stirred myself to switch off the TV, I was surprised to catch the murmuring of the same programme from next door. Could it be that someone else was sharing this moment of history? Could it be that Hannah had watched it too?

Before I slept, I wondered if it had touched that deep-thinking girl as powerfully as it had affected me.

28

Hannah See a Flow of People

hannah see a flow of people
blackface whiteface share the dream
crying freedom freedom freedom
and the flow become a stream

hannah hear a solemn promise
which our nation must deliver
give us freedom freedom freedom
and the stream become a river

hannah see some native people
sisterbrothers share her blood
crying freedom freedom freedom
and the river is a flood

hannah hear a loud commotion
sisters we will all be free
yelling freedom freedom free-ee-eeedom
and the flood become an ocean
and the flood become a sea

29
Mystery Tour (II)

Jack woke Pip at dawn. The three of them slipped out of Kozy Kabins like fugitives in the fog, watched only by two Hispanic gardeners raking leaves by the pool.

For two hours they spun along the freeway. Already the day was hot, so Jack pulled over to open the sunroof and study his maps, while they ate bagels spread with cream cheese. After a while Jack turned down a minor road and soon they were rolling along twisted wooded lanes, deep in lush countryside, where the air was fresh as spring water.

As the world awoke, Pip felt a peculiar sensation which he did not fully understand – something about that landscape unsettled him. As they lurched over hilltops, or spun round shady corners, he felt weird moments of déjà vu like half-forgotten dreams.

By lunchtime Jack seemed a little lost. The lane turned

sharply, and they saw a pretty village below them. Pip felt his stomach knot with alarm.

The village seemed poor but it had a folksy atmosphere, with a small stream running lazily beside the main street, dogs sleeping on the grass and colourful washing dancing on lines like upside-down families. Jack told them he would buy provisions for a picnic and ask for directions, and he pulled up outside a cheerful wooden store with a green corrugated roof.

Huddled silently in the passenger seat, Pip battled with emotions that had no names.

Jack watched him with unease. 'What is it, old fellow? Are you sick?'

And then Pip turned to Jack with a look of absolute desolation across his face. For the first time since they had met, he yelled at him –

'Why d'you do it? I can't believe you'd do such a thing. Why d'you do it, Jack? I thought you was my friend!'

30

Down by the River (II)

'Why'd you do it, Jack? I thought you was my friend!'

I can't tell you how those words stung me. I hadn't intended to upset the boy. It was the last thing I wanted to do. But my plans had all gone astray. See, I thought we had another ten or twenty miles to go and I intended to prepare him gently for what lay ahead. But when I saw that awful expression on his face, I realized that we were already here – what seemed like a charming village to me was alive with the ghosts of his childhood.

In an instant, I regretted the whole plan. The idea of returning to his childhood home had come to me after the induction – the hypnotic time spent with his father had clearly brought him so much happiness, it seemed obvious to physically bring the lad here. All I wanted was to set him free of the past. It was done with the best of intentions.

'How . . . how'd you find this place?' he said, tears streaming down his cheeks. 'How did you know?'

'I'm so sorry, Pip. I thought it would help you to . . . you know, move on . . .'

'Yeah, but how?'

'Ah, it wasn't so hard. The address of your ma's school is written in the front of your book. I saw it that first time you came for a lesson.'

'This was . . . this was Pa's store,' he muttered.

'I feel like an eejit.'

'But he ain't here no more. Someone else owns the store. See – all the signs and the paint is different. It don't look right.'

'I can't apologize enough . . .'

'I feel kinda sick.'

'Of course you do, you poor fellow. Look, I think we should move on – this place has too many memories. But you haven't eaten since breakfast so I'm going to pick up a few things and we'll be on our way in five minutes.'

I stumbled into the store where a bell clanged loudly behind the door. As I selected bread and apples, butter and cheese, chocolate bars and a large bottle of lemonade, I was shaking with self-loathing – we therapists are so self-righteous in our desire to tidy up the past that we sometimes forget the most fundamental tools of all – simple compassion and respect for others. As the lady behind the counter stacked everything in a paper bag, I asked her if she had known the previous owner, but she only glanced suspiciously at my eyes and said, 'No, sir, I only work here. I don' know nothing . . .'

When I came out with my bags, the car was empty. I felt a moment's panic and ran into the empty street. I looked in the direction from which we had entered the village, but there was no one in sight except a heavily pregnant dog lumbering up the hill. I looked the other way, and there they were – Pip wandering into the distance like a dreaming man, with Hannah following anxiously behind. Paper bag in hand, I sprinted after them.

'That was where old Foxy lived . . .' Pip was mumbling. 'And right here, two old ladies used to sit on that porch . . . What was their names, now?'

And then I saw the thing I half dreaded and half expected. It was a lovely old schoolhouse behind a broken picket fence. I say a lovely old schoolhouse, but when I got close I saw that it was in a sad state of repair – broken windows, missing roof tiles, graffiti on the walls and piles of garbage amongst the weeds. Pip had wandered round the back to an abandoned play area, littered with smashed glass and empty bottles. There was a dwelling at the rear of the school, and before I could prevent him, Pip had wrenched open a broken door and found his way into a large classroom.

Hannah came to my side with a look of desperate concern on her face. I peered through a broken window and saw the boy standing in the classroom, his face a mess of grief. I saw a torn map and a tattered Stars and Stripes on the wall behind him, a huge pile of broken desks, more broken bottles on the wooden floor and a small heap of cold black ashes where a lonely intruder had once built a fire. I watched him examining a long mahogany pole with a brass hook on the end, which his mother must have used to open the high classroom windows.

I was about to go in after Pip when he emerged unsteadily through the door. He staggered towards a clump of bushes where, to my dismay, he was violently sick.

I said, 'Ah, Jesus, Pip, I could kick myself! Come over and have a drink.'

He looked up at me, and the anger had been replaced by a hollow sorrow in his eyes.

'I'm OK now. Thank you. Thank you both. It was our school, see. And our home . . .'

'I know it was, fellah. I thought you were ready . . .'

'I – I apologize for yelling at you, Jack – I know you was trying to help . . .'

I gave the lad a warm hug and a cool drink of lemonade, and then I whispered long, slow affirmative words to him and I knew they went deep. I told him that he was strong. I told him that the past was done and his future lay ahead. I told him that his mama and papa lived on within him and that they would want him to live his life to the full. To live a double life, in fact, for the sibling he had lost. We stood clutching each other, and after a long while he shook his head like a pony, and forced a weak smile onto his face. 'We was so happy together, Jack. So very happy.'

'I know, old man. I know you were.'

As Pip and Hannah embraced, I felt an overwhelming wave of tenderness for these exceptional young people.

I said, 'Well, I'll say it one last time – I'm sorry for the pain I caused. I thought we had a few miles before we got here. I intended it all to be different. I'm an eejit so I am, and that's all there is to it. Anyway, let's walk now, Pip. There's nothing for you here.'

We set off up the little lane into the countryside beyond. I glanced back one last time and I sensed that a fragment of the boy's heart was left hanging on the broken fence of his mother's school.

Up ahead, Pip and Hannah were holding hands and I followed behind, carrying the paper bag, like the foolish fellow I was. We continued in this awkward fashion for some twenty minutes, and then I called out, 'Pip! Pip, is there somewhere we could sit to eat and talk a while?'

They waited for me to catch up, and I was relieved to see that a little brightness had returned to Pip's face.

'Up this way, Jack. It's been a long time, but you don't never forget the places you used to go. Come on – there's some things I wanna show you.'

He slipped an arm round my shoulder, and I felt absolved.

With the trauma behind us, I began to notice our surroundings. The countryside was exceptionally lovely, with grassy hillocks and fruit trees. Something about it reminded me of the countryside around Kerry, where I had spent so many happy days.

In the sunshine, Pip seemed re-animated. I watched as he and Hannah found sticks and wandered amongst the trees. I marvelled at how resilient young people can be. Their natural residency is in the present moment.

Their instinct is to release the past and their fears for the future. When we are young, the days go on for ever and the sky is always blue. Who needs the crashing burden of reality?

We walked a long way in the mint-clear air, and there was something about the place that lifted a fellow's spirits. I watched the barefoot girl run up a hilltop with Pip at her side – she moved so lightly she could have been flying. I struggled to keep up, and by the time I reached the top they were already racing down the other side, with the wild flowers and long grass whipping at their legs, as birds rose from their hiding places and zigzagged around them.

The river was winding and blue. White waves bubbled over gleaming boulders and long fish dreamed in deep secret pools. It was a happy, wild place, with not another soul in sight, and the thought came to me that it was as different as anywhere could be from Dead River. I searched for somewhere to eat; there was only one natural spot – Pip and I pulled off our shoes and the three of us dangled our bare toes in the cool water by the stone bridge.

I took the bottle of lemonade and propped it carefully amongst the rocks in the shallows. Pip washed his face vigorously with handfuls of clear water. Then we ate together, the three of us, with dragonflies darting around, and it was almost as if the river moved on our behalf – winding, babbling and whispering – so that we could remain still; utterly suspended in time.

Hannah lay on her back and soaked up the sunshine as Pip rose to his feet. He seemed fully restored now, wandering about in a childlike daze. I watched him head under the arch of the bridge, gazing at the large stones around him. Speaking quietly so as not to rouse Hannah, he said, 'Jack, this may sound crazy, but can you recall what I said when you hyp'tized me?'

I said, 'Yes, I think I remember, Pip . . . One of the stones was special. You called it the blue-grey stone.'

'The blue-grey stone . . . ? Yeah, I kinda remember – except all the stones are blue-grey, Jack. There's hundreds of them – we can't pull them all out!'

'Well, there was a lot of counting . . .'

Pip looked sad. I said, 'Listen, Pip . . . dear old Pip, trance is a magical thing, but it's not real life exactly. When I hypnotized you, you were imagining what you'd *like* to happen . . . like a lovely dream, old fellow! It wasn't real. This is only a stone bridge. There's nothing hidden here . . .'

The boy seemed downcast. I think it was dawning on him that the world is even tougher than he imagined, and that's not a nice thing to see on a young man's face, especially one who had been betrayed so many times. Worst of all, it was almost as though his own father had let him down.

I got up and began to gather my belongings. For better or worse, it was time to head back to Dead River.

And that was when Hannah opened her eyes. I'd thought she was asleep, but of course she'd heard every word. She's not much of a speaker, young Hannah, but she's one hell of a listener. She came over to where I was standing and started rummaging through my jacket pockets. I couldn't figure out what she was after, but at last that crazy girl found what she was looking for – my notebook and cartridge pen.

She crouched on the ground and began doing that writing thing – with the pen in her fist and the other elbow raised to hide her work. I thought we'd have to wait all night, but she had learned to write a little faster.

At last she stood up and handed me the notebook, and as a teacher I felt proud – I mean, I'd have preferred a little punctuation, and a few capital letters wouldn't go amiss, but her handwriting had come on leaps and bounds. There were no spelling mistakes either, even on the long words. To cap it all, the girl had come up with a simple rhyme, as neat as you please.

I stared at what she had written, that funny girl, and it was like a little song, so it was, or a poem . . .

31

Hannah Writes

seven high and nineteen right
pips expectations sure look bright

32

Great Expectations

It is Pip who begins the counting: five, six, seven stones up from the ground, then seventeen, eighteen, nineteen stones from the end of the wall.

'That's the one!' he says in a matter-of-fact way. He is pointing at a blue-grey slab, just like all the other stones in that bridge. Now Hannah comes to his side and they take hold of the stone, trying to wiggle it free from the wall. But the stone is jammed tight, as if it's been there since the beginning of time. So Hannah runs off, and a moment later she returns with a short stick in her hand. Now she's using the end of the stick to pick out the soil and moss and crumbling mortar from around the stone. While she's working, Pip rushes back to the river and returns with cupped hands full of water, which he tosses against the stone to loosen the dirt.

Pip and Hannah dig their fingers into the joints and, very slowly, the dripping stone begins to shift.

Now Jack is there, and he's just in time to see the blue-grey stone stir and shift and budge. He can feel their excitement, and suddenly, like a child being born, the stone loosens . . . leaps forward . . . and tumbles to the ground, almost crushing Pip's toes.

For the second time in his life Pip hears Hannah laugh out loud. It's as if her voice has shifted and broken free with the stone – and the silver sound echoes under the bridge like Lilybelle's tinkling bell.

They stare wide-eyed at the gaping hole where the blue-grey stone has been. At last Pip rolls up one sleeve, and with trembling hands he reaches inside.

'What is it, Pip, old fellow? What's inside the hole?' asks Jack, struggling to keep his voice steady.

And Hannah is there, and maybe it's the excitement, but she seems to have forgotten that she can't speak, because she repeats Jack's words. 'What is it, Pip, old fellow? What's inside the hole?'

Her voice seems so sweet and funny to Pip, because it is her voice and her voice alone.

He reaches deep into the dark cold hole beneath the bridge, and his fingers wriggle back and back and back. His nostrils fill with the secret underground smell of wet earth and moss and worms. And then his fingertips touch some-thing smooth and cold.

If only his hands would behave. If only they would stop shaking and dancing like Papa's funny shuffle-dance. And Pip doesn't know if he's shaking because he chucked up his breakfast, or because this crazy thing that is going on is like the world's weirdest Lucky Dip.

And very slowly he eases it out of the hole just like he did when he was a small kid with Papa at his side.

'What is it, Pip? What have you found?'

'Why, the cookie jar, of course!'

'But what's in the cookie jar, Pip?' asks Jack.

And the peculiar thing is, Pip knows. He knows exactly what he will find inside the familiar jar, which was sealed so expertly behind the blue-grey stone.

Now Hannah and Jack kneel beside him with staring eyes, as if Pip is a great explorer about to open some Egyptian tomb. Very slowly Pip twists the lid, and prises open the cookie jar.

'But what's in the cookie jar, Pip?' repeats Hannah, with her tongue tied around the words in the cutest way imaginable.

Why, the flour bag, of course; the brown canvas flour bag, tied at the top with yarn.

Pip lays the bag carefully on the ground, and all the time the river whispers and whispers, like it knew the secret all along.

'But what's in the flour bag, Pip?' asks Jack.

And the peculiar thing is, Pip knows this too. He knows exactly what he will find inside the brown canvas flour bag. He's fumbling with the drawstring and pulling open the flour bag.

'But what's in the flour bag, Pip?' repeats Hannah. And she's laughing at the whole crazy adventure and this brand-new toy called a voice.

Then Pip peeks inside. And he tips the bag out. And he's saying, 'Whoo-ee! Take a look at all the money, Hannah!

Just look at all that money, Jack! All the dollar bills, and twenties and fifties, that Mama and Papa been saving all them years.'

All those dollar bills rolled up tight in a big bundle with a bootlace round it, as fat as a bullfrog, and neat as you please. Just like Papa says – the only safe bank is a riverbank.

'That's my great expectations, that is!' says Pip. 'Yes, siree! Yes indeed!'

33

I'd Like to Talk to You About a Sensible Investment Plan

On the return journey I tried to have a sensible discussion about finances, which I saw as part of my responsibility as Pip's tutor.

I talked at some length about budgeting and making wise investments for the future. I may even have raised the issues of Inheritance Tax and various fiscal obligations. But the young lovers on the seat beside me were not giving these issues the attention they deserved.

We had counted the bundle of notes by the riverside and, to my amazement, found a little over $28,000. In 1963, that would have comfortably bought a fine house and left enough to cover a college education besides. By any standards it was an awful lot of dollars for a young fellow who had walked out of an orphanage with nothing in his pockets but holes!

You can understand why I was a little anxious about

driving around with a cookie jar stuffed with banknotes. Pip was more than a little discombobulated, and I had visions of him pulling open the lid and all those banknotes fluttering and flapping about on the highway. Then there was the possibility of getting stopped by the law and having to explain why I was travelling with two 'aliens' plus the kind of cash you'd expect from a mid-range bank heist.

In the end I had stuffed the jar deep into my suitcase and pushed it as far as I could into the boot of the Spider.

I couldn't get Pip interested in the topic of pension schemes either, but the one thing he comprehended well enough was that someone like Erwin could rob him of his money, in the same way as his father's store and the schoolhouse had been taken from him after his parents died. I managed to convince him that he shouldn't tell a soul about his good fortune – not even Lilybelle or Zachery.

'Pip, this money can change your life or it can wreck your life,' I told him gravely. 'That's your future in that cookie jar! Your parents left it for you. They loved you very much and they would want you to be wise, now, wouldn't they? Tell me, Pip, what would they want you to do with the money?'

'Get an education,' he said sheepishly.

'Exactly right.'

'An' a house with a swimmin' pool . . . an' a car like this one . . . an' a sharp suit like Smokey Robinson . . . an' a pair of Ray-Bans . . . an' a stereo player . . .'

'Now, wait . . . wait! This money could run through your fingers like sand; and think how hard your parents worked to save it. Listen, Pip, the best thing you could do is to put the money somewhere very safe, then invest some of it so it grows . . . like a little pip or a seed – you understand that, don't you?'

'I want you to hold it, Jack. I don't trust no one else.'

'I'm flattered that you trust me, Pip. I'll hold onto the cookie jar until you decide where to keep it, but . . . well, I won't be around for ever. The money is yours and you must take your future in your own hands.'

For a moment Pip looked terribly vulnerable. 'I don't ever want you to go, Jack,' he said. I'd told him nothing about my troubles at the university or my thoughts of returning home.

'Ah, now, don't look so sad!' I replied. 'What has happened is more than wonderful! You realize you'll be able to leave Dead River and go to school or college? Soon you'll be able to rent your own room and—'

I heard a peculiar noise and realized that Hannah was sobbing again. We had reached the outskirts of a scruffy town with old men playing chess outside cafés, groups of laughing Latinos and street kids leaning against cars. I pulled over to the pavement.

'Hannah, what is it?' asked Pip gently.

We had stopped outside a music store with shining instruments in the window and the deep bass notes of Blues and Soul drifting from the doorway.

In a fragile voice, Hannah said, 'Jack's gonna go. Pip's gonna go. I ain't got nothing – not a mama or a daddy . . . I ain't even got a birthday! I reckon Hannah's gonna die at Dead River Farm.'

Pip was kissing the tears from her face. 'Hannah, I swear to you – everything I got belongs to you too. I ain't going nowhere without you. You're my girl, Hannah, and always will be. You hear me, Hannah? You hear me?'

But she would not be comforted. At last Pip said, 'Listen, I got an idea . . .'

He asked if I would wait a while as he had a surprise for Hannah. I told him I gladly would, but I was less keen when he opened the boot and pulled out a bundle of banknotes, which he stuffed into his pocket, his head bobbing about like a turkey to make sure no one was watching. Pip had no understanding of money and I was worried about what he had in mind; on the other hand, the cash belonged to him – there was no arguing with that.

I waited in the car on the busy pavement, listening to the rolling rhythms from the music store. Someone was playing that record again – that eerie, haunting song called 'Strange Fruit', which I'd heard Hannah singing so beautifully on that moonlit night. Then I must have drifted off, because it was a long time before I heard their voices again . . .

Hannah wasn't crying any more. In fact she was laughing with delight, and when I looked up I barely recognized the handsome young adults with their arms around each other's waists. Pip had bought himself a new shirt and jeans and a red fedora hat with a little feather in the band, and to my amazement he'd bought an identical one for me. I couldn't believe how grown up he seemed now that he had money in his pocket. But it was Hannah who surprised me most – I had never seen her in anything but an old T-shirt, but now she stood in front of the car in a beautiful yellow dress with a wildflower pattern, a pair of stylish leather boots on her feet, and she was holding something large and heavy in one hand.

I was still half asleep, but Pip was saying, 'See, Jack, I told Hannah she was lucky she didn't have a birthday – cos that means she can choose any day she wants! So I said, why not today? 30th August, ain't it? That's a good day for a birthday! And if it's Hannah's birthday, why, she has to have presents, don't she, Jack? That's what you told me . . .'

Then I realized what the young woman in the wildflower dress was holding: it was not a bag, it was not a suitcase. Hannah was holding a guitar case, with a brand-new guitar inside.

34

The Sweet Guitar

hear my mama far away
from a distant star
and her singing is as soft
as a sweet guitar

walking through some crazy town
thought i heard pip say
you never had a birthday girl
so i think that days today

he choose a yellow dress for me
we head back to the car
someplace in a music store
i hear a sweet guitar

listen to the music pip
dont it make you sigh
one day when im famous pip
a guitar is what ill buy

pip say im a patient boy
but I cant wait that far
he walk right in the music store
and buys that sweet guitar

inside the case he put a book
called learn and sing along
practise carefully every day
and you cant go wrong

i hear my mama whispering
one day youll be a star
the world will come to hear you play
on your sweet guitar

i always been a tongue tied girl
and words are kinda new
but three words slip out easily
the words are
i
love
you

35
Pilgrims Return

The first signs that they were approaching Dead River were the wilting crops in the countryside.

Behind the mauve mountains, the scorching ball of the sun was lowering itself like an old man into bed.

As the silver Spider entered the town, Pip saw Jack gazing wistfully at the twinkling lights of the university on the hill. All three of them knew that the strange summer of 1963 was drawing to a close.

It had been a long journey. They had spent three more days just drifting and enjoying each other's company, passing the nights in comfortable hotels. And no matter how much Jack protested, Pip had insisted on footing the bill.

By the time they swung off the road at the familiar poplar trees and bounced along the rutted track, it was almost dark and all conversation had ceased. A feeling of nervousness settled on the returning travellers.

Outside the white bungalow Jack switched off the ignition and a deep silence fell. Pip realized that both Jack and Hannah were doing the same as him – staring across the track to Dead River Farm, scanning the yard for Erwin's Jeep. Mercifully it was not there.

Hannah was the first to move. In her flowery dress and leather boots, with guitar case in hand, she walked round the car to where Jack was sitting at the wheel. She kissed his curly head with simple affection, and by the time he and Pip had climbed out the girl had spirited herself away.

It seemed a lifetime since their first cautious meeting, but now age, education and race seemed meaningless as Jack and Pip hugged each other like an uncle with his favourite nephew.

When Pip walked wearily into the yard, with his satchel hanging from one shoulder, he heard a commotion, and there was Amigo bounding across to greet him. With tail thumping, the old dog almost knocked him off his feet.

Under a bare lightbulb on the farmhouse porch, Zachery was drinking coffee, with a cigarette to keep the bugs at bay.

'Decaided t' come back, did 'ee? Ah figured ye an' the gull run off fer good. Lemme look at ye, boy . . . Y' seem kinda diff'rent somehow . . .'

'That'll be the hat, Mr Zachery, sir.'

'Ain't the hat.'

'Wal, it's good to see you, Mr Zach. Guess I'll get some rest so I'm ready for work tomorrow . . .'

'Reck'n Lilybelle laike t' see ye now. She got awl kindsa crazy notions in her heed since you bin gawn.'

So Pip pushed open the creaking screen door and stepped into the farmhouse. There was the clock stopped at twenty to nine. There were the glass-eyed animals – although now they did not seem so threatening. He walked along the gloomy corridor and was amazed to see two live chickens pecking on the tabletop – in his absence the kitchen had become almost as chaotic as the yard.

Lilybelle must have heard him because he was greeted by the same tinkling bell and soft call as he had heard on his first visit to that peculiar house.

'Come an' show yerself. Don' be shaiy now. Is that mah precious boy outsaide?'

Pip smiled to himself, and turned the rose-petal handle. To his surprise Lilybelle was sitting with her barrel legs hanging over the side of the bed and a lively expression on her doll-like face. She had a paintbrush in one hand and a large painting on the bed beside her. In the short time he had been away she seemed to have lost weight. Her pink nightdress hung loosely around her now so that she resembled a circus tent pitched in a field.

'Oh, Pip! Ah'm so glad t' see yer. Bless yo' heart, I do believe mah li'l Pip has grown into a man.'

'And you look wonderful, Lilybelle! You're breathin's all clear, an' your face – well, it's sorta glowing! Have you been on some kinda diet?'

'Oh, look at me blush, Pip! You know how t' sweet-tawk a gull an' that's the truth. Wal, if ah've lost a li'l weight it's 'cos Zach don't know how t' cook nothin' but aigs 'n beans. Aigs 'n beans is awl ah ate since you been gawn. Makes me windy as a typhoon, but ah don' maind, Pip. Ah been real busy, see . . .'

And she *had* been busy. The room was filled with colourful artwork, pinned to the walls and propped on every surface. Pip saw wonderful imaginary worlds of forests, tumbling waterfalls, beaches and oceans, rainbows and sunsets, flying fish, wild animals of every kind, cities swarming with cars and bicycles, all populated by extraordinary people.

The half-finished painting on the bed was the strangest of them all. It showed a bearded man and a large woman in transparent nightclothes flying together through a starry sky.

'Lilybelle, is . . . is that you an' Mr Zach?'

'Sho' is!' she crooned. 'Ah painted it for a real special occasion. It was our weddin' an'versary, see. An', Pip, it makes me blush t' say it, but Zach say he's mainded t' move back into the bedroom with me!'

'That's wonderful! I'm real pleased for the both of you, because I've got something to tell you too . . . See, I love being with you, Lilybelle, but Hannah and I been thinking . . .'

She placed a stubby finger on her lips. 'Pip, whatever it is y' gotta say, ah don' wanna hear it raight now if it's awl th' same t' you. Ah've missed you like mah own son . . . Besaides, you ain't finished readin' *Great Ex'tations*, Pip, an' ah'm dyin' to know what occurs.'

'Course I'll read to you, Lilybelle. It's always my pleasure.' Pip opened his satchel and pulled out the book.

'You're a good boy, Pip . . . But ah don' even know where y' bin or what ye seen . . .'

'I don't know how to say it, Lilybelle. I went to the

past . . . I seen the future too an' it sure looked bright to me.'

When he climbed the ladder in the stable block and crawled beneath the itchy blankets, Pip was restless. He wondered how many more nights he would spend on that makeshift bed. The trip to his village had been a kind of miracle; but he knew that his life journey had barely begun. Now he reflected on the story he had been reading to Lilybelle and the equally miraculous events that had happened to his namesake, Pip. Pip had come upon an unexpected fortune too, but it had turned his head. The hero of Dickens's story had become arrogant and spoiled. He had shown contempt for the decent ordinary folk who had been his friends, and his new wealth had brought nothing but unhappiness.

But my life is not a story laid out by an author, Pip thought to himself. He resolved that he would not make the sort of mistakes people made in books; he would care for his friends, especially Hannah, and treat them with the kindness they deserved. More than anything, he would become the man who would have made his parents proud.

And all night long, Pip's dreams clinked and clanked and rustled with the sound of dollars and dimes in a cookie jar.

36

A Warm Welcome from the Klan

How is it possible for a fellow to feel so much pain?

If it hurts this much, how bad must it be to lose a lover, or a child?

He was a cat, for God's sake! And not even mine. That's what I loved about the little fellow. He belonged to himself. He belonged to no one. He came and left as he pleased, and I felt privileged that he chose to spend one summer with me.

I never owned him, or tried to own him. But now that he is gone there is something missing like the hole under the bridge when Pip removed the stone. Gaping, cold and empty.

When Hannah and Pip left, I gathered my bags and maps from the overheated car. I pulled out the suitcase with the cookie jar inside, intensely aware of what it contained.

While we were away, I had quietly resolved to leave my job at the university. A big move, I know, but I simply couldn't tolerate working for a man like Cerberus. Having said that, I'm not the sort of fellow who does things in a hurry – I'd make sure these kids had proper plans in order. Besides, this was the week in which I had agreed to stand in for the man while he was away in North Carolina, and I always fulfil my obligations.

There was just enough daylight to find my way up the steps onto the deck, my arms piled with bags and clothes and the red fedora on my head. I was exhausted, actually – I must have driven thousands of miles in the last few days and I was aching for a shower and a long sleep.

Immediately I realized something was wrong. My door wasn't quite closed! The lock had been forced!

I dropped everything on the swing seat, heart thumping like a jackhammer. Supposing the bastards were in there? Supposing that giant was waiting at my table with a rifle in his hands? Anything was possible here. People were lynched and murdered, and the judge who handled the trial would be the assassin's brother or father; the fellow who wrote up the story for the papers would be his cousin. And they'd all laugh and wink and shake hands with each other. And no one would think anything of it, until my ma received a coffin off the plane.

I crept inside the bungalow as if my belly and all my vital organs were made of concrete. And straight away I could see that the room – my lovely tidy living room – had been turned upside down. There were filthy boot marks across the white carpet. My precious books spewed from their shelves. All my files and notes were spread like apple blossom in a storm. The chairs lay on their sides, the table too. My special couch – the padded one – had been carved up with a knife . . . and – oh, God in heaven and all the saints! They had sliced three letters into the leather:

K K K

Now the concrete in my guts had turned to liquid, which swirled and slurred like a washing machine. I felt sick. Devastated. Terrified.

It was the same thing in the kitchen – every plate and mug smashed. The fridge door hanging on broken hinges, with food trickling out like bile. And I saw that these brutal villains had left me a present hanging from the ceiling fan – a dead rabbit, was it? Didn't they know I was a vegetarian?

Only this rabbit was ginger with tiger stripes.

And this poor rabbit was Finnegan!

37

The Dreamsnatcher

he has been here
he has prowled bent low beneath hannahs ceiling
and violated the sanctuary of my room
he has been here
he has touched my things with abominable fingers
and broken the web of my dreams
he has been here
i smell the stench of skin and sweat and foul fluids
where
he
has
slept
curled
like
a
vast

foetus
on

my
bed
he has been here
the dreamsnatcher

38

How the Silence Fell

The air was hot and thick as soup.

Dead leaves danced in crazy whirlwinds in the dry river at the secret valley; the long summer was drawing to an end with a last defiant heatstorm.

Two days after their return from Washington, Pip and Hannah went to the white bungalow to collect the cookie jar. They were beginning to understand that Jack wouldn't be there much longer and now it was time to find a safe place for Pip's money. Jack had told Pip about a new Black-owned bank in town, but Pip didn't imagine that a fourteen-year-old boy could stroll up to the counter to invest that kind of money without a lot of questions to answer. That was when his father's little joke had come to him again – 'The only safe bank is a riverbank'. Well, the closest thing to a riverbank at Dead River was amongst the twisting willow roots where Hannah kept her radio.

It seemed a safe enough hiding place to Pip.

When they tapped at the door, with Amigo at their heels, Jack had come nervously out onto the porch and greeted them with his back to the door. After the friendliness of the trip to Washington, he seemed withdrawn and unwilling to invite them inside. His excuse was that he was unpacking and the place was a mess. Unusually, he was unshaven and wearing sunglasses, and he muttered something about the heat and a headache. He left them waiting while he went to collect the cookie jar, looking about anxiously before handing it to Pip and disappearing inside. The encounter left Pip unsettled and confused.

Crouching side by side in the valley, Pip and Hannah lifted the flour bag from the jar one more time and marvelled at the weighty bundle of notes. They touched it again and again, hardly believing it could be real. At last they secured the lid and pushed the jar deep inside the hollow. The only living souls who saw that hiding place were Amigo and the wild birds of the valley, who seemed agitated by the oppressive weather.

Everything felt strange. Everything felt new. These days Hannah did not listen to the radio; instead she strummed endlessly on the guitar, carefully following the diagrams in the book that Pip had bought her called *Learn and Sing Along*.

C, C, C, C, play the chord named C . . .

She had mastered only a few simple tunes, but already her fingers felt easy on the strings, as if there were a natural triangular relationship between guitar and hand and ear, which had little to do with Hannah herself.

Sometimes, as she played, Hannah hummed and harmonized, and it was as if learning the guitar and learning to use her voice were one and the same. On those sultry days, Hannah talked to Pip in a small, unsteady voice, which dipped and dived in the most unexpected ways. But she never said a word in the farmhouse. Her voice was for him alone. 'Let 'em think I'm dumb, Pip. That's fine by me.'

From time to time Pip asked what had caused her long silence, but Hannah just shook her head and lowered her almond eyes, pretending to be absorbed in the placing of her fingers around the frets.

And then, at last, with her head resting on Pip's chest, the girl in the wildflower dress laid aside her guitar and began to unburden herself . . . slowly, secretly, softly . . .

'I was real young when ol' Zachery brought me to Dead River. I was so scared and unsettled I barely spoke a word. Old Zach fixed me a bed above the tool store with picks an' shovels for company. I was terrible lonesome without my daddy, but Lil'belle an' Zachery was kind enough.'

Pip stroked and twisted her hair – as smooth and black as liquorice.

'Then one day this strange giant boy come along the track and everythin' changed. Erwin scared me, Pip. He scared everyone. Shoutin' and yellin' and cussin'. Some of the kids who worked on the farm upped and ran away. Lil'belle took to her bed. Erwin – he walked about all night, rantin' an' cryin' to hisself. So I learned to disappear. Became invisible. Crept away and never spoke when he was near. Used to walk out on my own, Pip. One time I walked as far as the mauve mountains – kept thinkin' I could hear my mama callin', though I knew that she was dead. It was midnight before I returned an' Zachery was awful mad. Then I found this place – my secret valley. I used to sit an' listen to the songs on my radio an' they sounded sweet to me.'

Pip felt her body on his chest – strong and slender as a guitar.

'Then . . . something bad happened . . . I don't like to say . . .'

'Hannah, you know you can trust me . . .'

'Early one mornin' Lil'belle say she wanna treat from town – cheeseburger or somethin' . . . I set off with Amigo – he was just a puppy then. I walk down the track an' they was just buildin' them new houses where Jack live. Anyhow, down near the road I see somethin' high in the treetops. Can't figure what it is. When I get close I see it's them twin boys work for Zachery, only they was way up in the branches. They had their faces to one side, like they was tired an' restin' their heads on their shoulders. I couldn't figure why them boys should be standin' up there, restin' in the treetops . . .'

Pip stroked Hannah's forehead, and once she had started talking, it was like she couldn't stop.

'I call up to them – I say, "You boys oughta be on the yard, not restin' in the trees." Then I see . . . I see there is death in their eyes, Pip. An' their mouths is open, tongues hangin' out, an' their bodies is long an' dead an' swayin' from ropes . . . Twin boys, Pip. Beautiful twin boys, alike as two pins, swingin' side by side in the poplar tree.

'An' I jes' run to town an' buy Lil'belle's burger. When I come back there's a crowd of White folks standin' there . . . an' they lookin' up an' laughin' an' crackin' jokes. An' Erwin is there too, an' for the first time he looks easy an' at peace with hisself. I know . . . I know it's him, Pip. He done it. An' he's proud o' what he done.

'I jes' walk past, carryin' the bag with Lil'belle's food, tryin' to be invisible, an' Erwin give me this look – a terrible, terrible look, Pip – an' I hear him jes' like he's talkin' in my ear. He say, "One night ah'm comin' fer yer, gal. One night ah'm comin' up them steps in th' tool store, an' there ain't nothin' y' cin do t' stop me . . ." That's the words I hear, Pip. That's what I see. An' I go back to Dead River Farm, an' no matter how they wailed an' yelled an' cussed . . . I never spoke again.'

39
The EZ File

'Ma, I keep telling you, I don't know what I'll do back in Dublin. I'll find something. You need to understand I'm finished over here. Yes . . . Yes, I hear what you say, and I agree with you . . . It's a shame. The whole thing is a crying shame. But if I told you all the details, you'd have me on the next flight home. This place isn't safe – it's as simple as that.'

It was peculiar to be phoning home from the oak desk in the big office, with the modern art on the walls and the windows overlooking the campus. Cerberus was absent, but so was any feeling of pride or happiness I might have expected. I felt hollowed out and defeated.

I had my resignation letter all written and signed, and now I placed it by the telephone so he'd see it when he returned from North Carolina. That was when I noticed an envelope addressed to me from the man himself. I

sliced it open with his silver letter knife and this is what I found:

Dear Jack,

　　Sorry I didn't get to see you before I left, but I trust you had a good trip. Thanks for agreeing to sit in while I'm away. Go ahead and make yourself right at home – the girls will fill you in on the admin details, and if necessary I can be reached by telephone at any time.

　　Listen, Jack, I heard on the grapevine that you had some visitors while you were on vacation, and I'd like to make it very clear that I had no part in this tomfoolery. There will always be a few pranksters who enjoy that kind of horseplay, and you can be sure I will deal with it on my return. I guess it was a light-hearted way of making the point that you would do better to choose friends within your own community!

　　Hopefully there was no serious damage, and the fact that you are sitting in Mission Control and reading this suggests that you are warming to my invitation to join the Brotherhood! That's great news, Jack, and it goes without saying that membership includes an insurance policy against any future high jinks! So go right ahead and digest the literature I've left for you. Hopefully you'll realize that the Klan has a real 'point' (pun intended!).

　　When you are satisfied, kindly complete the attached form (black ink please).

　　Welcome aboard, buddy . . . or as we say in the

Invisible Empire, KIGY (Klansman, I greet you)!

Walter

P.S. Be sure to find time to practice that golf!

It was clear that the professor and I were on a different page . . . a whole different library as a matter of fact. Attached with a paperclip to this appalling note was the following questionnaire, which I understood to be a KKK application form:

QUESTIONS FOR KLANDIDATES
The Kleagle presents the initiate with the following list of questions:
NB: the questions marked with stars are used to bar Jews, Catholics, Negroes and other aliens.

1] What is your age?
2] What is your occupation?
3] * Were your parents born in the United States of America?
4] * Are you a Gentile or Jew?
5] * Are you White or of a Colored Race?
6] What educational advantages have you?
7] Color of eyes? Hair? Height? Weight?
8] * Do you believe in the principles of Pure Americanism?
9] * Do you believe in White Supremacy?
10] What are your politics?

11] * What is your religious faith?
12] What secret fraternal orders are you a member of (if any)?

I most solemnly assert and affirm that each question above is truthfully answered by me and in my own handwriting and that below is my real signature.

Signed ....

NB: If the Klandidate answers the questions satisfactorily, he must pay his initiation fees, called 'donation', and provide money to pay for his mask, robe, etc. With his money affairs settled, he is ready for the initiation, together with whatever other Klandidates there are in the vicinity. The initiation services are held at midnight, with a flaming cross, an American flag, a sword or dagger, and a Bible as the chief outward signs of the order. There is also a bottle of water on the altar.

My overwhelming instinct was to tear the thing into tiny shreds, but then the phrase 'know your enemy' entered my mind. For better or worse, I found myself sitting in the professor's well-appointed office, so why not take advantage of the situation?

I'm sorry if this sounds childish, but over the next couple of days I took a little revenge. For example, amongst his morning mail I found an official letter from the Department of Education about the possibility of de-segregation in Southern schools and universities. It seemed that the March on Washington and the numerous civil rights protests had made a real difference to government thinking, and now the Kennedy administration was looking for ways to ease race relations. The letter talked about the idea of 'colour-blind' education across America. Of course, I wrote back immediately, expressing our university's wholehearted support for an end to segregation. I enthused about our desire to open our doors to students of every creed and colour, based purely on their academic ability.

Cerberus had invited me to make use of his library, so I began reading everything I could find about the Klan. Every phrase and argument felt like digesting poison, but as it turned out, I learned a great deal more about the Brotherhood than the professor intended. It was clear that the Klan were deeply concerned about the rise of powerful Black leaders like Martin Luther King and Malcolm X, and they felt especially threatened by civil liberty rallies such as the March on Washington. With growing alarm I realized that the KKK were planning retaliation; some desperate terrorist plot was being hatched and it would be happening soon. The Ku Klux Klan was planning its revenge.

As I searched through the professor's shelves for more clues, I stumbled upon a dark green file hidden beneath some history books on a bottom shelf. The file was marked with only two letters: *EZ*.

As soon as I opened the file, I realized what it was! Stapled to the inside cover was a black-and-white photograph of a young and confused-looking soldier being escorted into a court martial or tribunal by a pair of military policemen. The prisoner's hands were cuffed together and raised to hide his face. What gave his identity away was that the burly policemen beside him looked like dwarfs – *EZ* was Private Erwin Zachery! This was something I had to read, so I slipped the file into my briefcase and carried it home.

I had fitted a new lock at the bungalow, and spent hours repairing the damage and putting the place back in order. I decided not to tell Pip and Hannah about the break-in – what good would it do? The sooner we all moved on from that terrible place, the better.

I gave notice to my landlord and booked a one-way flight to Dublin. I suppose I'm a sentimental old fool, but the hardest job of all was burying poor Finnegan in the wasteland behind the back yard. What harm had he done to anyone? Tomfoolery? Horseplay? High jinks? What those people had done was outright intimidation of which the Mafia would be proud. The fact that I was still alive was down to an accident of birth – the fair pigmentation of my skin.

To add to my troubles, the weather was unbearably close and I began to suffer from headaches and migraines behind my eyes which have been a symptom of my ocular condition throughout my life. As I mentioned, my poor old da had the same problem and it put an early end to his career.

Without even poor Finnegan to comfort me, I lay awake late into the night with the constant fear that those thugs might return to finish what they'd started. To distract myself I spread out the contents of the *EZ* file on my bed. Unless I was very much mistaken, this report on Erwin had been authorized by Walter Cerberus himself. Much of the material was marked as CLASSIFIED, so the professor must have had contacts and informers in senior positions in the military.

I was not able to copy the information, but I made some notes. The following is a summary of what I learned . . .

40

Erwin's Tale

The average American knew little of the Vietnam War until 1965, when the first television images of ground offensives and aerial bombardments spewed into their living rooms. Before long, those scenes of what looked like a rock festival from hell would become familiar around the world.

In fact, the US had been involved in an undeclared war in the region for many years. In 1961, President Kennedy surreptitiously dispatched four hundred Green Beret 'Special Advisors' to train South Vietnamese soldiers against the Communist enemy. And this was no conventional enemy – the fearless Viet Cong guerrillas moved like panthers through the jungle, setting tripwires and booby-traps, and digging concealed pits filled with sharpened bamboo spikes.

For years, American helicopter units had been

transporting troops around the country, and the controversial procedure of spraying defoliants from aircraft was
well established. These massively toxic chemicals, which
included the notorious 'Agent Orange', were used to clear
areas of jungle where the Viet Cong might be concealed.
Unfortunately, the stuff also contaminated soil and water,
thereby creating birth abnormalities for generations to
come. Vietnam was always a controversial war.

In April 1961, Private Erwin Zachery – who had
barely visited another state, let alone a foreign country,
found himself dangling from a parachute, looking down at
his huge boots high above the emerald jungle. Unlike the
elite Green Berets, Erwin and his raggle-taggle comrades
were part of a clandestine unit who had been selected for
brute muscle-power and reckless calm under fire, rather
than military experience or intelligence.

The freshly buzz-cut paratroopers, who settled like
dandelion seeds on the forest floor, had spent the last ten
weeks at a grueling military training camp in the Southern
States of America. The method used to prepare them for
battle was humiliation: these inexperienced and often
under-educated boys were constantly yelled at, referred to
as 'beasts' and exposed to terrible mental and physical
pressures. They were harassed, bullied and beaten into
shape by senior officers, many of whom were traumatized
war veterans themselves. The only way to survive was to
shed all sense of individuality. The young recruits learned
unquestioning obedience to orders, and during bayonet
training they were taught to shout, '*HATE, HATE, HATE!*'
and '*KILL, KILL, KILL!*' They were told that soon they

would be able to take out their frustration on the enemy, who were referred to as stinking foreigners or 'gooks'. The psychology was simple – the cadets were taught to de-humanize the enemy, just as they had been de-humanized by their seniors. The young soldiers would imitate their officers' aggression on the battlefield, in the same way as a violent father raises violent sons.

Of course, Erwin had not had a violent upbringing; he had grown up in a peaceable farming family, but he had always been a remote and strangely unemotional boy – something of a bully at school and not too gentle with animals on the yard. In the harsh conditions of the training camp, this unfortunate manner hardened into cold-hearted brutality. After several brawls with fellow recruits, for which he refused to acknowledge responsibility, Erwin was quickly marked out as someone with a total absence of conscience. According to the report, he was the kind of soldier who should either be '*sent to jail, or sent to kill*'.

Without further ado, Erwin was drafted into a mav-erick regiment, which had earned the alarming nickname, The Psyche Squad. Every last one of them was a petty criminal, a street fighter or an anti-social loner. Their mis-sion in Vietnam was straightforward: they were a covert advance party whose job was to 'break new ground' – give the enemy a good scare. And if they were killed in the process, well, no one would make too much fuss . . . It wasn't like losing college boys or sons of wealthy families.

Barely had he unbuckled his parachute, when Erwin and his buddies found themselves trudging through ele-phant grass and mosquito-ridden forest, laden with heavy packs and machine guns; or crawling on their bellies in saturated paddy fields. The skies above their steel helmets were thick with helicopters – known as 'birds' – which spewed machine-gun fire, and, later, the devilish substance called napalm, which sticks to skin and burns like acid.

The environment would have been horrifying for most normal boys, but Erwin was not a normal boy . . . he enjoyed it! It made him feel alive.

Within days of his arrival Erwin witnessed scenes of inhumanity from both sides. A report in the *EZ* file said:

Many in the company had given in to an easy pattern of violence. Soldiers regularly beat unarmed civilians. Civilians were murdered. Whole villages were burned. Wells were poisoned. Rapes were common.

In addition, naïve boys like Erwin discovered a strong culture of drug-taking in the army. By the later stages of the war, the majority of soldiers smoked marijuana, and hard narcotics like heroin were everywhere. Erwin had his first experience of LSD right there on the battlefield. Full details were not available, but it seems that Erwin was involved in some kind of brutal initiation ceremony, in which he was given massive doses of LSD before being thrown into a nightmarish conflict zone. Professor Cerberus's file contained witness statements saying that Erwin suffered from 'the screaming heebie-jeebies'. And in one forthright comment: 'Ain't no pretty way of saying it – this soldier fried his brains. Simple as that.'

The tribunal then moved to the question of race.

Erwin had grown up in a segregated state, but his parents had not been racists – in fact, there had been many non-White employees on the family farm. In Vietnam, however, Erwin witnessed racism in its most savage forms. Hostility towards the Viet Cong turned into hatred for the whole Vietnamese population – the 'Gooks'. The ancient rule of conflict is that it is easier to kill if the enemy can be reduced to a crude group; a lower level of humanity.

On top of racism towards the Vietnamese, the civil unrest from back home had been exported to the theatre of war. Tension between Black and White American soldiers began to emerge. Grisly practices, such as cross-burning were transferred from Mississippi and Alabama, and in some cases Ku Klux Klan 'Klaverns' were being set up at military bases.

Slowly but surely, Erwin became indoctrinated into the culture of racial hatred. He needed a scapegoat for the crazy paranoid feelings in his head and found it in the Vietnamese people, as well as the African Americans at his side. Ironically, it was in the dripping rainforests of South-East Asia that Erwin joined the Ku Klux Klan: being a Klansman gave him a sense of identity and belonging.

It seemed that Erwin gained a dangerous reputation, even amongst the Psyche Squad. The average Vietnamese is short in stature and Erwin was very tall indeed – the report paints an appalling picture of this uncontrolled giant storming into battle, out of his mind on drugs, killing without mercy. According to testimonies from the court martial, Erwin shot any 'gooks' he saw, be they soldiers or civilians, young or old. One fellow soldier reported an incident in which

> our platoon was checking out a remote village where the Viet Cong were said to be holed up. We had been taught stealth, but Erwin just runs ahead firing in the air and yelling 'Hate, hate, hate!' and 'Kill, kill, kill!' like some wacko. We hear dogs barking and babies screaming and Erwin is just firing at anything that moves. By the time the rest of us roll up Erwin has torched five or ten straw huts, and within twenty minutes the whole village is ablaze. I ain't never gonna forget the sight of Erwin coming out of the smoke real slow, with a big smile on his face like it was all some crazy game. I looked at his eyes and I knew that boy was insane.

The events that led to Erwin's dismissal from the army are more horrific still. In the heat of a firefight Erwin captured a peasant girl of about fifteen years of age. Right in the middle of battle he attempted to assault her against a tree. A Black senior officer saw what was going on and began to shout at Erwin to leave the girl alone. Erwin ignored him. The officer approached Erwin and told him that if he did not release the girl, he would be put on a charge. Erwin yelled obscene racist abuse at the officer and began firing in every direction. It took around ten men to bring him under control.

He was flown back to the United States under guard and brought before a tribunal. He refused to speak in his defence, but occasionally he could be heard muttering to himself. A member of his military guard thought the prisoner was mumbling, *'Hate, hate, hate . . . !'* In spite of overwhelming evidence against him, Erwin did not serve a jail term; he was simply let off with a BCD or Bad Conduct Discharge. A senior army psychologist described Erwin Zachery as 'suffering from acute battle trauma resulting in permanent psychological damage and severe personality disorder'.

So Erwin's military career came to an end, but the bloody Vietnam War would rage until 1975, leading to the loss of between one and three million lives.

It seemed extraordinary to me that this murderer and rapist had escaped custody – but then I came across some personal correspondence in which, strictly off the record, the same military psychologist told Professor Walter Cerberus that Erwin possessed

> many useful military skills which could be of benefit to the Invisible Empire. There is no question that this slightly alarming young man has serious problems, but in my view, if he is handled properly, he would be extremely useful to the movement.

Cerberus replies:

> If you can secure his release, I would be happy to take him under my wing. It seems to me that Erwin is exactly the kind of boy who is brave or reckless enough to take our campaign to a higher level and, let's be

frank, to take the flak if things go wrong! I believe he should remain at Dead River Farm, from where he can travel and train our recruits throughout the state. He is a simple country boy, but he has a strong drive to climb upwards through the ranks, and this can be used to encourage him. He is easily pleased by small rewards and I have already ensured that he is supplied with a vehicle and sufficient ex-military equipment to meet his needs.

Professor Cerberus signs off his communication with these chilling words:

As you know, we have plans to escalate our campaign in dramatic ways. It is my considered opinion that Erwin Zachery will be a useful puppet for the Klan – albeit a puppet of super-sized proportions! Your contribution to the Cause is duly noted.

KIGY, brother
Walt

41

Hannah in the Kitchen

hannah in the kitchen
the taste of bitter fear
erwin grab a hold of me
and whisper in my ear

ye growed up gal you know that
grown awl purty ah see
thems breasts on yer bawdy aint they
thas what they look laike t me

wal erwins taired o waitin
bin patient wi you this far
ahm comin t pay you a visit gal
so
leave
yer
door
a
jar

42

The Beginning of the End

In the yard, every chicken, turkey, duck, mouse and flea had slunk into the shade.

Even the doghouse was too hot for Amigo, who had managed to crawl below the deck of the farmhouse and collapsed there like a panting pile of fur.

With rivulets of sweat trickling through her make-up, Lilybelle lay on her back gazing out of the window at the sky, which seemed as heavy as the earth itself.

'Storm comin'. Ah feel it in mah knees.'

Pip sat motionless, his book on his lap. Even the act of thinking was too much effort.

'Wal,' said Lilybelle at last. 'Ye gonna read, Pip, or 'm ah gonna have to guess how th' story ends?'

Pip surfaced from his stupor. He opened the book and realized that only a few pages of *Great Expectations* remained unread. Then he recalled something that Jack had taught him earlier that summer. 'Wanna know somethin', Lilybelle? Old Dickens couldn't make up his mind about how to finish the story. First he writes a sad ending; then he writes a happy ending. But he just can't decide. So he thinks about it, an' he thinks about it, an' then he says there should be two endings! That way the reader can choose how they want the story to end.'

'Wal, if thar's a choice, li'l Pip, y' know what ah'm gonna say? A happy endin' every taime fer me.'

Pip smiled. What an inspirational person she was! This heat must be unbearable for a woman of her size, but she never complained. In spite of all her problems, Lilybelle remained optimistic. And lately something amazing was happening: as she continued to lose weight, her creativity expanded accordingly. Now her paintings were bolder and brighter than ever. From floor to ceiling, the pink bedroom swirled with extraordinary art.

'Ah know ah'm different, Pip. Guess ah finally decaided t'embrace th' diff'rence, stead o' hatin' mahself fer it.'

She put these changes down to Pip's encouragement and her new diet, but the fact that Zachery rejoined her each night played a part too. The thing about that weird old couple was they truly loved one another.

'I like a happy ending too,' said Pip. 'But I guess life ain't always like that. Maybe you can't separate happiness and sadness, Lilybelle. Maybe you need one to appreciate the other. Light and shade, ain't it!'

He found his place and began to read. And now his reading was fluent and easy. On that suffocating afternoon he read to Lilybelle for the last time, describing how Pip's long journey and quest for his great expectations came to an end. How the boy atoned for his arrogance and discovered the most precious treasures of all: compassion, tolerance and love.

'*I took her hand in mine,*' Pip read, '*and we went out of that ruined place . . .*' And so their storytelling sessions came to an end.

When he had closed the book, Lilybelle breathed a long tremulous sigh and enveloped Pip in her huge hot arms. The large woman and the lean young man clung together in the oppressive heat.

He said, 'Lilybelle, I've been wantin' to tell you somethin', but you just won't listen . . . I don't wanna leave you, but I need an education – you told me that yourself. Besides, things have changed, see . . . Hannah and I . . .'

'Ah know, Pip. Ah ain't blind. It wus love at first sight.'

There was that phrase which Pip had resisted. And yet he did love Hannah, and the thought of being apart from her was something he could not bear.

'Ah misjudged Hannah, didn't ah, Pip?' said Lilybelle. 'Ah'm truly sorry. Bein' silent don' make y' dumb, do it, Pip?'

'No, Lilybelle. Hannah's 'bout the smartest person I ever met.'

She lay back on the huge cloud of pillows. 'Y'awl come back an' visit me some day, tha's awl ah ask. Cin you promise tha' thang t' me?'

He swore that they would. Then he took his book and left the illuminated bedroom.

It was Saturday 14 September, the last day before Jack's return to Ireland. When Pip crossed the sultry yard to the bungalow, he found Jack looking pale and thin, but he opened the door and welcomed Pip inside. The living room was almost bare now – even the photographs of the many Morrows had been packed away. Pointing at a pile of cardboard boxes, Jack invited Pip to help himself to any of the books and records inside. Pip flipped absentmindedly through names he had heard Jack mention – William Burroughs, Jack Kerouac, Aretha Franklin, Thelonious Monk, but there was nothing he wanted. He had no precise idea of where he would be heading, but he planned to travel light.

Pip mentioned that he hadn't seen Finnegan for a while, but all Jack would say was, 'That's the thing about animals, Pip. They come and go, don't they? Perhaps we should never try to own them. But he was— he is a lovely creature, old Finnegan . . .'

That afternoon two of Jack's students came to take the beloved silver Spider. They seemed overjoyed at their purchase, and as Jack and Pip watched from the deck, the couple drove away, hooting loudly.

Jack hadn't fully explained why he intended to leave, except to say that it was a matter of principles. Now even his health seemed to be suffering; but Jack was not a man who liked to be pitied.

'Well now, Pip, I don't know what I'm doing mourning the loss of a sports car – it hardly counts as deprivation!'

It was cooler inside, so they sat together in the white room while Pip related the terrible story of Hannah and the twin boys in the poplar tree, and how Erwin had threatened her so often. Jack listened mournfully, shaking his head in disbelief and clutching his forehead between finger and thumb. Then he told Pip some of the shocking details about Erwin's military career.

'He's not a fellow who can be helped,' said Jack. 'He's not about to change his ways. The sooner you are both away from him, the happier I will be. I've met some unpleasant people in my time, Pip, but Erwin is a man without a shred of conscience and I'm terrified of what he might do.'

He talked about the guilt he felt in returning to Ireland. He felt that some act of terror was imminent but he was powerless to prevent it.

'I wish I could be around to look after you, old fellow. God knows, you're both still young. But you've got to manage on your own now. I think you can. You've a great intelligence and you're older than your years.'

He talked to Pip for a long time about developing his self-belief and using the money to build a future. As they spoke, Jack removed his sunglasses, and there were moments on that airless afternoon when Pip found himself drifting away as he stared into those extraordinary eyes. It was if Jack's voice was settling in the deepest recesses of his mind. His words of belief and encouragement seemed to take root, so that, hours later, when Pip rose and thanked Jack for everything he had done, he was surprised to find himself energized and self-confident and ready for whatever the future might bring.

Pip promised that he would be over early in the morning to see Jack leave. And when the two of them parted on the steps of the white bungalow, Pip stood a head taller than his teacher.

43

Dynamite Night

There's only one thing sadder than a stack of suitcases by the door, and that's a one-way ticket on the table.

I hate flying – I must be the only fellow on the planet who suffers from jetlag before he leaves the ground.

After Pip had gone I fixed myself a meal, but I barely managed a bite. In that relentless heat it was hard to believe that I'd soon be walking the foggy streets of Dublin wrapped in a scarf and raincoat, or sipping Guinness in a smoky pub.

I had another of those damned migraines right behind my eyes and my spirits were low. After all my fine words to Pip about positive thinking and self-belief, I felt I had failed in every way. And now I was going home to Mammy with my tail between my legs. What had begun as the greatest opportunity of my life had ended in defeat.

Now, before you get too weepy-eyed, I haven't finished

yet. If that was the conclusion of my tale, it would indeed be a sorry ending. But of course the story is not over. Before I board my flight I'll fill you in on the explosive events of my final night at Dead River Farm. You see, Pip was right – that great master, Dickens, did create an alternative ending to his tale, and although I did not realize it then, there would be an alternative ending to mine . . .

For hours I paced the white bungalow, deep in thought. So many unanswered questions kept me from my bed, but in any case I never sleep well under a bright moon, and the moon that night was a huge unblinking eye, staring down on the bungalow and the rickety buildings of Dead River Farm, which loomed like the ghostly set of a silent film.

Then I heard it! No . . . first I felt it: the floor of the bungalow began to rumble and the windows were doing their rattly thing. I peered out through the curtains, and there they were! The nightriders heading along the track towards me. The moon was so bright that they drove without headlamps.

My first thought was that someone had reported the fact that I still had friends who were not 'from my own community'. Ah, it would be a sorry thing to get lynched like Finnegan on my final night in this beautiful, terrible country.

As they drew closer, I counted them and they were fewer than before – in fact, only three vehicles in all. And maybe it was a special occasion – someone's birthday perhaps – because the man himself was leading the parade! I could see Erwin's white-starred ex-army Jeep at the front of the slow-moving procession, and he and his passengers were dressed in their full regalia like mad monks on an outing. Perhaps you're forgetting that I'd never witnessed what Pip called the 'ghost-men', so the sight made me shudder. There was Erwin at the wheel of his Jeep in crimson robes, with the pointy hood and the gaping black eye sockets and the cruel cross on his heart. And next to him was a ghost-man in white; and behind him, two more of the devils. I saw nine men in total, sitting bolt upright in the three vehicles.

I don't mean to be racist, but do all Ku Klux Klansmen look the same?

Of course, they did not stop at my bungalow; they floated by like white sails on a silver river. What I would learn later was that these fellows had far more important fish to fry that night than a nervous Irishman in his cotton pyjamas.

I went to the kitchen and swallowed a couple more aspirin, feeling worse than I ever had in my life. If only this damned weather would break – it felt like a storm brewing in my very skull.

See, Pip thinks I'm some kind of hero, because I had done the old sleepy thing on Erwin. But I'm not a hero at all. I felt like a bloody coward, if you want to know the truth. That's why I was running home, wasn't it? I was sick and scared and fed up with the whole thing – and I wasn't even a man of Colour.

Then I thought about Pip and Hannah, and how I would feel if I heard that they had met 'Judge Lynch' while I was sipping cocktails on a plane.

And I suppose that's when I started getting angry with myself. All my life I'd been the quiet one. The one the bullies picked on. But things could change, couldn't they? If an orphan boy could grow into a confident young man, if a mute girl could find a voice, then surely I could find my strength too. I remembered a powerful line my da used to quote from a fellow Irishman named Edmund Burke: *The only thing necessary for the triumph of evil is for good men to do nothing.*

And I was a good man, wasn't I? At least, I had always thought myself so. Well, the judgemental moon stared down and I knew my moment had come.

So I pulled on a few clothes and picked up my brief-case and stepped quietly into that strange silvery world from which all the colour had been bleached, and I walked quickly and quietly past the farmyard and up beside the apple trees, in the direction the ghost-men had driven.

I'll admit I half hoped that Pip or Hannah or Amigo would come out and join me. But I'd only send them home. Like it or not, this was my job, and that meant me on my own.

As I neared the red barn, I became aware of two loud noises: the first was the sound of raised voices on the hilltop, and the second was the *WHOOM-WHOOM-WHOOM* of my heart, which sounded like a bass drum at some military parade.

As I was passing the tallest of the twisty apple trees, I tripped and almost fell. Whatever it was that I had stumbled over was caught around my feet. I sat down on the hillside to get my breath back and to untangle whatever it was – and that's when I found that some anti-social litterbug had left a noose lying about on the path.

The fear rose like vomit in my gullet, but I fought it down. I knew what I had to do. I ducked behind a bush and tipped the contents of my briefcase out on the ground. It took less than a minute to get myself kitted out for the job.

To be honest, I hadn't realized how weird it would feel to be inside the professor's robe, with the baldric rope tied around my waist and the white hood over my head. Fortunately I had an almost identical build to Walter Cerberus – but in any case, the thing about the Ku Klux Klan outfit is, one size fits all: fat or thin, old or young, anyone can wear it without attracting a second glance. At least, that's what I was counting on.

I stretched up and checked the pointy pyramid on top; that seemed fine, but the thing that took a bit of getting used to was the eyeholes. I found that unless I kept my head dead centre, my vision was blinkered. But after a few moments I became accustomed to looking out through twin portholes at the moonlit world.

Then I dug about in the briefcase and pulled out the last items I had brought with me: the professor's long white gauntlets. They fitted well enough – like a glove, you might say – but of course there was one extra finger, which flapped about a bit. So I stuffed a rolled-up hanky in the empty digit . . . It's the details that count.

I'd like to tell you that I felt like James Bond or one of the fellows in the action films as I dumped the empty brief-case behind a tree and set off up the hillside; but in truth I was almost sobbing with fear and pouring with sweat under that sheet – it was literally running down my neck beneath the hood.

I took a moment to calm myself. I knew that if this was going to work, it would require absolute confidence; the slightest falter would give me away. So I employed some of the old skills I had taught so many others to empty my mind.

As I walked, I had to get used to the fabric billowing around my knees like a wedding dress. When I looked down, I gave myself a bit of a fright; you see, the moonlight was reflecting off the fabric so I seemed to be sort of glowing – exactly like a proper ghost should do!

By then I was just five hundred yards from the red barn and I began to wonder about this courage thing. I mean, we all admire courageous people, but I'll tell you a little secret – a lot of heroes are none too bright! After all, they're the first to go charging in to any situation, while the clever person is nowhere to be seen.

But now it was too late for doubts because I'd reached the top of the hill, where a strong shaft of light spilled from the open barn. I could clearly see six or seven Ku Klux clones, phosphorescent in white robes just like mine, stacking boxes neatly into the two pickup trucks, which were parked on either side of Erwin's Jeep.

Keeping to the shadows, I crept round the outside of the vehicles – and here I had to heave my skirt up around my waist so I could crawl on hands and knees, closer and closer to the barn. By now I could actually hear the grunts and the exchange of banter as they heaved the wooden crates onto the cargo area in the back of one of the pickups.

I watched carefully, and as one of the Klansmen put down his box, I seized my moment. I stood up, as calmly as I could, and simply joined the queue of men at the open doors of the barn.

At any moment I expected to be noticed, but to my amazement it worked! It actually worked! No one even gave me a second glance!

When it was my turn at the front of the line, I stepped towards the pile of boxes in the centre of the barn and a Klansman handed me a wooden box with rope handles – it was small but quite heavy. I carried it across the forecourt towards the pickup. Of course, I had no idea what was inside – bottles or tools perhaps?

When I reached the vehicle, I passed my box up to another Klansman, who was standing in the back of the truck arranging everything into a tidy pile.

Then, suddenly, the thing I had been dreading happened: the man glanced at my right hand on the rope handle and started making conversation. He said, 'KIGY, Prof. Thought you was outta town . . .'

I felt the panic surging inside me, but with as much swagger and confidence as I could muster, I dived straight in with my best imitation of Professor Walter Cerberus's relaxed but educated Southern drawl. 'KIGY, buddy. Came home a li'l early. Guess I missed y'all too much.'

To my amazement, the Klansman just chuckled, and I trotted off as quickly as I could to fetch another box from the barn. My heart was performing acrobatics in my chest, but a part of me was whooping with delight – I'd pulled it off! *I am Cerberus!* I thought as I strode about, exactly as if I had every right to be there in the red barn with my fellow Kluxies.

Within ten minutes the pile of boxes had been shifted and the Klansmen returned to the barn. I was the last person standing by the two loaded pickups, and I could see the others relaxing inside. It was still stiflingly hot, and when one of them produced a full crate of beer, the men lifted their hoods and began to bite the lids off bottles.

I listened to the light-hearted chatter in the barn and realized that no one was paying me the slightest attention. That's when I became overwhelmed with curiosity – I simply *had* to know what the Klansmen had been loading into those two trucks.

Looking at the boxes in the two pickups, I noticed something odd: one box in each truck was different. On the lids of those boxes someone had scrawled three letters in white chalk: *DET.*

DET . . . What did it mean? Every other box was unmarked, but one box on each of the two trucks was marked with those white letters. I checked again to make sure that no one was watching, then pulled over one of the DET boxes. DETERGENT? No, surely not. DETROIT? Maybe the boxes were headed there.

I found myself a hiding place between the Jeep and one of the pickups, and studied the box in my hands. It had a sliding top rather than a hinged lid, nicely made with a small thumb dip. With no difficulty at all, I slid open the lid and now, illuminated by a shaft of moonlight, I could plainly see what was inside . . . I couldn't believe my eyes! Bottles or tools? The boxes were packed with dynamite!

To be honest, I'd never seen dynamite outside a cinema, but here were the classic red tubes complete with telltale fuses. There were about ten sticks in all, in a neat bundle with strips of black tape wrapped around them.

And attached to the bundle of dynamite sticks was a round-faced alarm clock with twin bells on top. It should have been a cheerful little clock that a child might use to get to school on time – but this alarm clock was not cheerful at all. In fact it was the most alarming alarm clock I had ever seen . . . See, there were electrical wires – black and red – coming out of the back, and they were connected to the top of the dynamite bundle. To my absolute horror, I realized that the clock was gently ticking!

In an instant I realized what DET meant! DET was short for DETONATOR. One wooden box on each truck contained a timed detonator, designed to blow the entire stack to kingdom come. And unless I was very much mistaken, the alarm was set to go off at precisely 10.22 the following morning.

I forced myself to stay in control. Once you begin to panic, everything is lost. I could hear the men laughing and joking in the barn and I took a few seconds to consider my options: I could set the detonator to go off there and then, but of course everyone would die, including me, which would be a disappointment to my ma if no one else. The second option was to set the alarm to go off in, say, fifteen minutes, which would have given me time to run down the hillside. But wait a minute – that's a hell of a lot of dynamite . . . Suppose it exploded just as the Klansmen were driving past the farm where Pip and Hannah lay sleeping in their beds?

Thinking as fast as I could, I settled on a compromise – I had to pull off one of the gloves in order to adjust the dial on the back of the clock, and my shaking fingers didn't help the operation. Tipping the clock delicately towards the moonlight, I carefully set the timer to go off in exactly thirty minutes – that would be a little after midnight. When that was done, I returned the clock snugly to its resting place on top of the dynamite sticks and slid the lid back in place.

Pulling the six-fingered glove on again, I carried the box back to the pickup, as carefully as a newborn baby. Again I glanced around, and nestled the box gently into the cargo area of the vehicle.

Then I moved to the other loaded vehicle. I was about to lift down the second detonator box in order to do the same thing, when suddenly I noticed a change in sound from the barn: the Klansmen were getting up and leaving.

Groups of them sauntered towards the vehicles. I saw two men lift their robes and take a slash against the side of the barn. Quickly I remembered who I was supposed to be: I was not some petrified Irishman dressed in a sheet, I was Professor Walter Cerberus and I had every right to be there. I strode towards the others, staggering slightly for effect. I even had the presence of mind to grab a half-empty bottle of beer from a pile near the barn door.

Then Erwin was there, dressed in blood-red robes, two heads higher than the tallest man.

'Listen up,' he called. 'C'm on – gather round. I wanna say a few words afore you go. Herman, zat you? Git over here. Y' too, Casey.'

The Klansmen wandered across to the loaded pickups and gathered around their leader. I hoped I appeared to be just one amongst the faceless crowd, but I was the only one panicking about that detonator ticking away amongst the dynamite. I wondered if I had miscalculated. I thought we would all be long gone within half an hour, but I hadn't realized there would be speeches.

A man with a goatee beard settled on the tailgate beside Erwin, his hood rolled up to his forehead and an unlit cigar in his mouth. He pulled a match from a box. Suddenly Erwin turned and, without warning, lashed out with his huge gloved fist, knocking the matchbox from the Klansman's hand. With the other crimson fist, he smacked the man across the jaw, so he tumbled to the ground like a sack of garbage. It was this casual violence that came so easily to the fellow.

'Goddamn turnip-head! This boy 'bout to blow y'awl t' kingdom come. You wanna smoke, you git yo' ass a maile away 'fore you laight that thang.'

Everyone laughed as the fellow with the goatee shuffled away to smoke, rubbing his bleeding mouth and brushing the dirt from his robe.

'Git them tarps on,' ordered Erwin.

A couple of Klansmen covered the boxes with tarpaulins and lashed the sides with cord.

'Listen up,' he said. 'The Klan has had a good month. We blown up so many Negro houses in Birmingham, folks are callin' it Bombingham!'

There was a mutter of approving laughter, and although I felt sick to my stomach, I heard myself pretending to chuckle. And all the while I thought anxiously of the minutes ticking away.

'Y'all know the plan – this week we goin' in fer the keel . . .'

'*Keel, keel, keel!*' yelled the men. 'Kill, kill, kill!' I heard myself say.

'I wan' you t' strike at the very heart o' the Negro community. Teach 'em a lesson they won't f'get. Remember what ah tawt yer: *Hate, hate, hate!*'

'*Hate, hate, hate!*' yelled the men. 'Hate, hate, hate!' I called in unison.

'Bobby, Thomas, Herman, Robert, you boys raide in this truck. Rest of you in th' other one. May Gawd guide you. KIGY. Be on yer way, brothers.'

The Klansman straightened their left arms in salute – as I did too – and then the men climbed into the two pickups, slamming the doors and gunning their engines as they rolled slowly down the hillside.

And now only one vehicle remained, and that was Erwin's Jeep. And only two people remained, and they were Erwin and me. A feeling of utter powerless overwhelmed me as I realized how foolish I had been: I had prepared no exit strategy at all.

Erwin and I stared at each other – he, massive in his blood-red robes, and me, small and white in mine. The sweltering silver world fell very silent indeed. With the migraine pounding in my brain, I simply began to wander away from the barn.

'Where's your automobile, Prof?' called Erwin. He had removed the red hood and it dangled from one hand.

'Blowout,' I mumbled.

'Kinda weird y' bein' here, Prof.'

'Well, I—'

'More 'n weird, seein' as ah jes got offa th' telephone to y' in North Carolina!'

I froze. My overwhelming desire was to break into a run and tear down the hillside, but Erwin was blocking my route. Instead, I went the other way – up the hill towards the fields. As I walked, I felt Erwin's gaze burn into my back like radiation. He tossed his bottle on the ground and followed me . . . slowly . . . slowly up the hill.

Now we were above the barn in the newly-cut wheat fields, where sharp stubble scraped my ankles. My pace increased, but in that vast illuminated landscape I felt horribly vulnerable and exposed. Downhill lay my bed and my plane ticket home. Uphill lay emptiness and death. This was not the direction I would choose.

Erwin barked like a bloodhound, 'Klansman, hold it thar! Tha's an order, y' hear?'

I looked around for refuge. Far away, along the horizon, I saw a black line of pine trees, but I knew I would never make it. Half walking, half running, I set off towards the only shelter in that barren place – the first in the line of high-voltage towers, gleaming like monumental skeletons against the sky.

In great slow-motion strides, I heard Erwin coming after me, grunting like a beast as his robes swished through the stubble.

I pushed myself onwards, gasping for breath, until at last I reached the base of the colossal structure where the four vast feet were rooted like steel trees.

Now where? There was nowhere to go.

Erwin's voice came booming across the landscape: 'KLANSMAN! STOP RAIGHT THAR! Y' HEAR ME? Y' STOP NOW OR AH'LL KEEL YOU!'

In my foolish dress I stood waist-deep in the weeds at the base of the tower. Beside that soaring moon-scraper I felt as small as a grain of rice.

That man-beast was a slow-mover, but he got there in the end. I heard him breathing and cursing. I felt the cool girder against my back, and suddenly Erwin dived through the air like a crimson vulture and seized my throat in his great fingers, forcing me back against the metal column. And then, with his huge tombstone face just inches from my mask, he hissed, 'Klansman, remove yer hood!'

I felt his mighty hands tighten around my neck and the steel leg of the tower crush into my spine. The pressure behind my eyeballs was unbearable. How could I compete with this killing machine?

For a moment in the stark moonlight everything seemed hyper-real – I noticed the wide gaps between his yellow teeth and long hairs protruding from his small ears.

'Ah seed, remove yer hood!'

Obediently I took the tip of my mask in my silly

six-fingered glove and peeled it slowly upwards to reveal my strictly non-Klan face.

Blinking like a fish, he glared at me in disbelief.

I said, 'It's me, Erwin. You remember me? I live across the track from Dead River Farm. My name is Jack – Dr Jack Morrow, to use my—'

'Oh, ah 'member you well 'nuff. Yer th' freak with th' ahs.'

'Look, the thing is, I work with Professor Cerberus at the university, and as a matter of fact he invited me to join the Klan. I thought I would sort of drop in and see how I liked it—'

'Y' know wha' kaind a violation it is t' put on Klan robes? Tha's a *craime*! Tha's a *capital o-ffence*!'

'I didn't know that – but, look, it's late now and we're both ready for bed . . . You're looking awfully tired, did you know that?'

My attempt at hypnosis was laughably ineffective. He prodded the underside of my chin with one finger. 'Y' hear me, an' y' hear me good – ah ain't taired. Ah ain't taired at awl. But *you* . . . you're deed!'

In an almost workmanlike way, his hands wrapped around my throat and he began methodically squeezing out my life, exactly like a fellow wringing water from a rag. And the final thing I saw before I passed out was two tiny pinpricks of hate in those evil eyes.

Perhaps you've heard about near-death experiences. Perhaps you've heard about patients who look down at themselves on the operating table. I swear to you, as Erwin squeezed out my lifeforce, my consciousness rose

285

from my body. I looked down as if from a great height at that primeval creature with his fingers around the neck of a foolish Irishman in a white frock. And I pitied the little fellow. Apart from a thin cord of life connecting my spirit to my body, I felt totally detached from what was happening.

And then an extraordinary thing happened. From far, far away across the countryside I heard the distant *Boo-OO-OO-OOM!* of a powerful explosion. It came from many miles away, and yet it was so loud that it could only be one thing – the sound of many boxes of dynamite exploding in the night.

Erwin heard it too. I saw his small ears twitch. I saw his crazed glare turn slowly from my strangulated face towards the sound. Miles away, above the trees on the road to Birmingham, a huge purple fireball and a cloud of smoke rose into the night like an air balloon. All across the valley, as far as the mauve mountains, we heard its mighty echo:

Boo-OO-OO-OO-OOO-MMmm!

'What 'n tarnation . . . ?'

I saw the confusion on his face and felt his fingers slacken on my throat. Instantly my consciousness was sucked back into my body.

I did not hesitate for a second. I touched the side of his face gently with two fingertips and turned his head towards me. Then, fixing my eyes firmly on his, I channelled all the energy that was in me – the energy of The Voice of the Wind, and Morrow the Mesmerist, and all the Gifted Ones. And I whispered, 'Erwin . . . It's me . . .

It's Jack . . . You remember me now, don't you . . . ?'

'Huh!'

It was working! I could feel the difference. I felt The Gift awakening.

With a sideways movement, I slipped free of his grip and nudged him softly downwards with my fingertips. Then I placed myself slightly above him, so that I could look down into his eyes. And all the while I tried to ignore the fierce pain in my throat and a horrible burning sensation in my eyes.

'You've been busy, Erwin . . . so you haven't noticed how tired you are . . . and you are very, very tired now . . . It's been a long day . . . It's been a long life . . .'

'Wha' th' . . . ?'

I felt conviction growing in my voice. The surprise of finding my face beneath the hood . . . the explosion in the night – it had all disorientated him. Maintaining that soft pressure with my fingertips, I willed him to kneel before me. And kneel he did, like a conquered gladiator in the sand.

'That's right, Erwin . . . Now you can rest . . . You see the way your hand floats up . . . Maybe you would like to curl up now and rest beneath the tower – that's fine – you look into my eyes and you keep on relaxing . . . You think you can't relax any more, but you can, Erwin . . . truly you can . . .'

Now I had him. I would not let him go.

Slowly his expression changed. He gripped his head in his hands like a wounded child, twitching and blinking erratically.

'You see, I've been waiting to talk with you, Erwin . . . I've been waiting to tell you that my voice is the voice you have always known . . . It's the voice of the night and the voice of the wind and the sound of the waves on the shore . . .'

'Th' wind, goddamn it – thar ain't . . . thar ain't no wind . . .'

He was trying to resist, and yet I could tell that the aggression had deserted him. Now he began to rock and shake in a bizarre animalistic manner, forwards and backwards, making weird moaning sounds like a creature in pain.

My confidence escalated. I felt intoxicated by my power. You see, hypnosis is not about physical strength; it's about mental strength, and the more I took control of his mind, the more powerful I became.

Erwin was staring up at me with wild pleading eyes, stammering. 'Ha-ha-ha-ha . . . !'

'Now you're really beginning to relax, Erwin, and that's good . . . Let's count backwards together . . . Ten . . . nine . . .'

'Ha-ha-ha-hate! Hate! HATE!'

He half rose and I thought the spell was broken. But all I did was calmly touch the huge dome of his forehead with one fingertip, and he was back in my spell. The Minotaur was defeated!

His huge body rocked in time with the counting. His gaze never left my eyes, but he pressed his hands to his ears.

'Four . . . three . . . two . . . one . . .'

And then, to my amazement, Erwin collapsed onto his side like a falling tree in a forest. He lay curled in a foetal position, whimpering and staring up at me pathetically. The fellow was in meltdown.

'Erwin, I'm going take you right back to your happy place . . . You remember, don't you?'

He sniffed and jerked and trembled and stared. 'Yeah, ah wanna be happy . . . but . . . but ah wanna keel! Hate, hate, hate!'

'Not hate, Erwin . . . love.'

'Hate . . .'

'Love . . .'

He was on his back now, like a helpless beetle. And his eyes were gazing upwards at the endless ladders of the tower, which rose, rung by mighty rung, to where the moon hung in the wires.

Now I repositioned myself so that I stood with my legs astride him, like Jack the Giant Killer in the picture books.

As I took him deeper and deeper into trance, I searched desperately for a plan. I thought about Pip and Hannah. I thought of all the terrible things that Erwin was capable of doing.

'Relax . . . relax . . . deeper . . . deeper . . . deeper . . .'

Then it came to me! A moment of pure inspiration! How obvious could it be! Right above our heads was the steel tower. Did I possess the power to make this man climb?

I glanced quickly upwards . . . No, it wouldn't work! There was a barbed-wire canopy about twenty feet above the ground. Its whole purpose was to stop anyone foolish enough to climb.

Be calm, Jack. Be still. Stop and think . . .

I knew that the hypnotized mind could be strangely logical and precise. It enjoyed specific tasks. So how would a fellow get past that barbed-wire fence? Wire-cutters of some kind? Surely there would be some kind of tool at the farm.

But that was ridiculous! I couldn't send the fellow home to fetch the equipment to kill himself! In any case, it dawned on me for the first time, I didn't have it in me to actually kill a man – not even Erwin. I was a vegetarian, for God's sake! I didn't have the heart to eat a sausage!

And then I realized that I *had* killed a man . . . I had sent four men to their deaths that very night. It was I who had destroyed the pickup truck with the Klansmen inside.

But they were murderers for sure. The only regret I should feel is that I hadn't destroyed both vehicles with all those bastards inside. Even now, the four remaining Klansmen were speeding towards some deadly mission in Birmingham.

No. I had to be as steely as the tower above me. I looked down at Erwin's glazed eyes with their peculiar dilated pupils.

And then I thought of Hannah – that strong young woman who had lived in terror for so long. And suddenly my plan was clear: I would plant hypnotic commands deep within Erwin's mind, so that if he ever touched her, Hannah could trigger his downfall.

'Erwin, I want you to look upwards . . . Look up at the tower . . . Can you imagine how good it would feel to climb? You have always wanted more power, and up there is where the power lies . . . All you need to do is climb . . . up and up . . . Imagine how wonderful you would feel . . . Taller and more powerful than any man alive . . . When you climb hand over hand . . . up the ladder and into the starry sky . . . you would be like a god, Erwin . . .'

'Laike . . . laike a gawd . . .'

'Yes . . . Like a god . . . You would be higher and more powerful than anyone in the army . . . higher than anyone in the Klan . . .'

Erwin began to push himself to his feet. 'Ah'm gonna claimb . . . Watch me, Momma! Watch me claimb!'

'Not yet, Erwin . . . not yet . . . Look at me again . . . Look deep into my eyes . . .'

'Your ahs, goddammit!'

'I am Jack . . . I am your friend . . .'

'Yo' mah freend . . .'

'Soon I will leave you . . . You will sleep a long time and then you will wake . . . You will remember nothing about this conversation, but later you may hear some words – and they will be special words, just for you, Erwin . . . What will they be?'

'Speshul woids.'

'That's right, they will be Erwin's special words . . . and when you hear those special words, you will know exactly what to do . . . You will rise up, Erwin, wherever you are . . . You will seek out whatever equipment you

291

need to cut through the barbed wire . . . What tools will you need, Erwin?'

'Lemme see . . . Ah reck'n bolt-cutters do th' job – long-handl'd is best . . .'

'Long-handled bolt-cutters . . . yes, that will do the job . . . Then you will return, Erwin, to this very place . . . You will walk across the fields, past the red barn, and you will come back to this holy place . . .'

Maybe I was overdoing it. I'm like my ma – we've always enjoyed the theatrical!

'Then you will climb, Erwin . . . like a god. You will climb the tower, higher and higher . . . What will you do, Erwin?'

'Ah'm gonna claimb. Ah'm gonna claimb higher than evah before . . .'

'Yes, you will climb, Erwin . . . You won't let anyone stop you . . .'

'Ah'm gonna claimb laike a gawd . . . Ain't no one gonna stop me . . .'

'But not now, Erwin . . . You need to wait until you hear the special words . . . I'm speaking to your unconscious mind right now . . . These words are settling deep, deep in your mind . . . Now I'm going to tell you the special words, Erwin . . . and the special words are these . . .'

When I had told him the words and made him repeat them, I walked away across the fields. I turned once, but he was still there, curled beneath the tower. As I came to the red barn, I paused for a moment to pull off the hateful white robe. I rolled it into a ball and tossed it into the back of Erwin's Jeep.

Then I went back to the bungalow and waited by my suitcases until dawn, holding ice to the bruises on my throat.

Something had happened to my eyesight.

I did not sleep.

44

Rise Up Silent People

rise up silent people
the scared the poor the weak
rise up silent people
now its time to speak

cherokee apache navajo sioux
all of them was silenced hannah was too

rise up silent women
like birds who find their wing
rise up silent women
now its time to sing

nooksack chickasaw cheyenne crow
all of them was silenced a long time ago

rise up silent children
let your anger out
rise up silent children
now its time to shout

seminole seneca blackfeet creek
all of us was silenced

now its time to speak

45

Flight of the Hypnotist

High above Dead River, angry clouds assembled like a mob for a lynching. The air was dense with electricity.

Pip kept his promise. Early that Sunday morning, he and Hannah walked across the track to wait with Jack for the taxi.

They got a shock when they saw him. Jack was sitting on the deck of the bungalow, one hand stretched out to hold the tabletop, gazing into space like a sightless old man.

'Ah now, it's my favourite people,' he said when he heard them coming.

Pip rushed to his side. 'Jack, what's wrong? Why ain't you looking at us?'

'Well, it's true, Pip, the old peepers are playing up a bit. It's not something I talk about, but I've had a few problems with my eyesight over the years and now they've gone a bit wonky. It'll sort itself out, I'm sure, so there's no need to worry.'

'I *am* worried, Jack. I think we need to call a doctor—'

'Pip, any minute now the taxi will be arriving. I'm going home, old fellow. But if it hasn't settled by the time I get to Dublin, I'll see someone about it – although perhaps that's not the best expression!'

Pip waved his hand from side to side in front of Jack's face, but there was no reaction. He noticed another odd thing: in spite of the oppressive heat, Jack had a scarf wrapped around his throat.

'Hannah,' Jack was saying. 'Where are you, darling girl? We haven't got long and there's something very important I need to say to you. Will you sit beside me for a while? And perhaps Pip would be kind enough to carry my bags down the steps.'

Pip began the task of hauling the heavy luggage to the side of the track. As he laboured, he watched Hannah and Jack side by side on the swing seat, Jack talking earnestly to Hannah in a quiet voice, and Hannah holding his hand and nodding from time to time.

After a while the cab approached in a cloud of dust, and when the driver got out, Pip heaved the bags into the trunk. The driver ignored Pip as if he were an invisible houseboy, but he called up to Jack in a friendly way, 'Headin' fer th' airport, sir? There's one helluva storm headin' our way!'

With Hannah's help, Jack rose slowly to his feet. And just as the man had said, there was a rumble of distant thunder over the mauve mountains and jagged lightning slashed at the sky.

Carefully Jack locked the bungalow and tucked the keys

under the mat. He climbed slowly down from the deck, toes searching for each step, leaning on Hannah's arm all the while. He reached out for Pip and an expression of contempt spread across the driver's face as the Black boy and the White man embraced each other. Then the man's expression changed to utter astonishment as Jack kissed Pip tenderly on each cheek and wiped a tear which tumbled from the boy's eye.

'I'll be away now, Pip. But you'll come and see me with Hannah, won't you, old fellow? Ireland is a beautiful place – perhaps I'll move out to Kerry . . . the mountains and the sea . . . Ah, you should see it, Pip! So very blue, so very green, it is . . .'

What Pip wanted to say was that he felt the same love for this man as he had for his own father, but the words would not come. Instead he guided Jack silently towards the taxi and helped him into his seat.

'Promise you'll never forget; your names are linked – Pip and Hannah . . . palindromes, see.'

'Same forward an' backward, Jack!'

'That's right, Hannah. The same forward and backward. You look after each other, you two. Do you hear me, now?'

In the back seat of the cab, Jack wound down the window and raised his arm in a wave. One last time Pip had the sensation of falling into the wise eyes of Dr Morrow, where, just for a second, the mists of the Kerry moors seemed to swirl.

Hannah took Pip's hand as the taxi bumped away along the dirt track, and the whole world trembled with the approaching storm. They watched until the cab turned onto the main street by the poplar trees. And as the dust settled, it was lost from view.

Pip wandered sadly into the farmhouse, but just as he was about to fetch water for Lilybelle's wash, he heard a sound he had never heard before: instead of the familiar teasing tinkle, Lilybelle was clanging her handbell frantically. Pip snapped out of his reverie and raced along the corridor. He burst into the bedroom where he found Lilybelle sitting upright at the end of her bed. She seemed deeply distressed, with one hand over her mouth and the other pointing at a news item on the TV.

'Pip! Pip! Come an' watch. Thar's been a terrible incident in Birmingham . . . Jes' terrible, Pip . . .'

Pip rushed to her side. He saw an agitated reporter holding a microphone beside a pile of rubble at the back of a large modern church. The man was trying to make himself heard above the din of sirens and yelling reporters and wailing women dressed in their Sunday best.

As Pip watched the appalling sight of bodies being removed on stretchers, the reporter was saying, '*I'm standing by the sixteenth Street Baptist Church here in Birmingham, Alabama. As you can see, there is absolute chaos here . . . It's a truly dreadful sight. Details are emerging as I speak, but it seems that in the early hours of this morning, 15th September 1963, persons unknown have planted dynamite and, I guess, a time-delay system, beneath the steps of this famous African-American church. As you may know, this church is used as a meeting place for civil rights leaders, including Martin Luther King himself, although we believe that Dr King was not present today. I repeat, Dr King was not present at the time of the explosion . . .*'

The man spoke urgently into his microphone as fire-fighters hosed the smouldering debris behind him. '*Now, the information we are receiving is that at 10.22 this morning, twenty-six children were preparing for a sermon when the dynamite exploded . . . A lady has just told me that the title of this morning's sermon was "The Love That Forgives" . . .*'

Tears were streaming down Lilybelle's face as the report continued, '*Tragically I can now confirm that four little Black girls aged between eleven and fourteen have lost their lives . . .*' Visibly moved, the reporter consulted a piece of paper in his hand. '*The names of those children are Addie Mae Collins, Denise McNair, Carole Robertson and Cynthia Wesley. Police have confirmed that a further twenty-two people have been seriously injured in the blast. As you can seen behind me, every window in this church has been blown out by the explosion . . . except one – a stained glass showing Christ leading a group of little children . . .*

'*You will understand that investigations are at an early stage, but I think we have a pretty good idea of who is behind this brutal attack – as regular viewers to this station will know, we have witnessed more than fifty terrorist bombings against Coloured people in this city, which have all been linked to the Invisible Army of the Ku Klux Klan. We must conclude that the Klan are the main suspects, but this crime against innocent children attending Sunday school has hit a new low. As I speak, rioting is spreading through the city, and two more Black children . . . I repeat, two more Black children have been killed, one at the hands of a police officer . . .*'

All day Pip went sorrowfully about his tasks in the ever-building heat. There was plenty to do – Zachery had told him to board up windows and secure anything that might be damaged by the storm. As he worked, Pip tried to divert his mind from the tragic events in Birmingham and the sad memory of Jack's departure by focusing on the plans that he and Hannah had made. Before the week was out they would pack their few belongings, collect Pip's money from its hiding place in the secret valley and walk away for ever.

By the time Pip had kissed Hannah goodnight and climbed the ladder to his bed, a howling wind was raging. In the yard, ghostly doors were banging, and in spite of Pip's efforts, objects raced about as if they had a life of their own. Throughout the rackety night the storm rumbled closer, so Pip did not hear Erwin's Jeep coming down the hillside in the first weak light of morning.

As Pip tossed in a troubled sleep, Erwin leaped from the Jeep into the yard, swigging whiskey from a bottle, his clothes whipping in the wind. In the wild dawn he fought his way across the cobbles towards the tool store, where Hannah sat upstairs, wide awake in bed, staring through her swaying dreamcatcher at the flashing sky.

So how could Pip have heard the dog yelping in its kennel, or the slow *thud, thud, thud* as Erwin climbed the staircase to where Hannah had piled furniture against the door?

Amongst the clattering and crashing of the night it would have been impossible for him to hear her faintly whispering – '*Pip! Pip! I need you now!*'

Or even the loud crash as Erwin heaved aside the flimsy pile of furniture that barricaded her door. And certainly he would not have heard those menacing words: '*Ah'm cummin' for ya, gal. Ah always tol' ya ah would.*'

46

The Call of Kerry

It was a full six years before we met again. Six years before I heard the details of that awful night.

By that time I'd bought a tiny cottage in Kerry, not too far from Dingle Bay.

I'd always fancied the seaside, and now that I'm blind it's the sounds I love – the way the waves wash the pebbles, the birdsong in the hedges, the whisper of the wind dancing with the trees. Beautiful mysterious sounds, like paintings in my head.

For the first time in my life, when people see my white stick, they do not stare at my funny old eyes – or if they do, I do not know it. Soon after I left America my eyesight failed completely, but I was surprised at how little it troubled me – I have always been more interested in the internal world, the life of the mind, than what I could see in this imperfect world. Do you know what the Buddhists say? *The mind is everything – what you think you become.* Think loving thoughts and your world will be filled with love.

And my world is filled with love. I never had children of my own, but Pip, and Hannah, who sits beside me now, stroking my hand, were always like my own children.

It is 1969, and the two of them are full of excitement, having returned from a music festival called Woodstock. Now that Hannah is gaining a reputation as a singer, they spend a lot of time at concerts and festivals. Of course she has always had the flower-child look, and these days bare feet and braided hair are all the rage. Hannah tells me that Pip has grown his hair. What adventures he's had, that boy of mine. But that's another story for another day.

Ah, those festivals would be too noisy for me, but I love a little music in the evenings, and I especially enjoy Hannah's first album, *dreamcatcher*, which I listen to on one of these new-fangled devices called a cassette recorder. I think my favourite track is 'i am spirit i am sky'.

She always had a strong spirit, that woman, and last night she asked me to help her recall those final events at Dead River Farm. I'm a little nervous of the old regression these days, but she assured me that it would help her let go of all that had happened.

We went into my quiet office, and this time it was her turn to lie on the couch, and Pip's to sit at her feet and whisper words of reassurance. The old thing with the eyes would have been helpful, but it's the voice that does it . . . the Voice of the Wind, if you catch my meaning.

I said, 'I'm counting back now, Hannah . . . eight, seven, six . . . Your breathing slows . . . Your eyes fall deep into their sockets . . . five, four, three, two . . . You are deeply, deeply relaxed . . .'

'It's so hot tonight.'

'Where are you, Hannah? Tell me what you see.'

'I'm in my bed above the tool store. There's a strange light keeps flashing . . . No, no, it's the storm brewin' outside and lightning crackling in the sky.'

'Go deeper now . . . You can remember everything. Tell me, how old are you, Hannah?'

'I'm thirteen or fourteen years old – and I'm so afraid!'

'You know how to wake if you need to . . .'

'I'm kneeling on my bed. Here's my dreamcatcher blowin' at the window an' I stare through its web at the yard below. There's a whole lot of noise out there, and suddenly I see a Jeep drivin' fast through the gates. I hear doors slammin'. The dog is barking in the doghouse . . . and now it's yelping – maybe he's kicked it.'

'Who is it? Who has returned so late?'

'Erwin. It's Erwin. Oh God! He's comin' into the tool store below. I hear him crashin' about downstairs. He's drunk – I can tell because he's stumblin' and cussin'. Now . . . Oh my Lord! He's treading up my stairs . . .'

'You remember everything, but you are quite, quite safe . . .'

'I always knew he would come – that's why I never go to my bed without heavin' the chest of drawers against the door.'

'Take it steady, Hannah . . .'

'I'm out of my bed, shivering in my nightgown, and outside the thunder is crashin'. Now I'm piling chairs and the laundry basket against the door – I need to stop him getting in. I'm trying to drag the bed, but he's so strong, the door is already opening . . . Oh Lord! I see one huge hand reachin' at me, and he's saying, "*Ah'm cummin' for ya, gal. Ah always tol' ya ah would.*"

'I'm whimperin' like the dog in the yard an' I'm callin', "*Pip, Pip, I need you now!*"

'Then I'm climbin' back into bed 'cos there's nowhere else to go. I'm pullin' the blankets way up to my eyes. Suddenly there's an almighty *CRASH!* – and Erwin is here! Right here in my room! Nearly seven feet tall. No matter how many times I see that man, I am shocked and terrified. I'm tryin' to disappear into the bed and he's lookin' down at me, bent beneath the ceiling, like . . . like a shrunken head on a stick.'

'Keep breathing, Hannah. Remember, you can wake if you want to . . .'

'And now he's bendin' down, and my heart is beatin' so fast it may bust my rib cage. The smell of whiskey makes me wanna puke. His long fingers are tuggin' at my blankets, he's pushin' that tombstone face right up to mine, and he whispers, "*Ah 'magine yer 'bout the purtiest li'l woman ah ever seen.*"

'Now he's untyin' his laces and pullin' down his dungaree straps – then he trips and hits the bed so hard it knocks the breath out of me. My mouth is dry – I can't find a sound, but my eyes – my eyes are . . . *screaming*!'

'But you remembered the words, Hannah? The words I taught you?'

'I'm trying to find the words, because I know they can save me. But I been silent for so long . . . I been mute for years now, and my jaw is frozen and my tongue don't work.

'Erwin's naked and slimy with sweat. There's a big ugly tattoo on his back: a blood-drop on a white cross.

'He's kneelin' on my bed, which almost gives way, and he's pressin' his mouth against mine and pushin' his tongue inside – I can taste the chicken and onions he had for his supper.

'I feel his stubble scrapin' my skin. I'm tryin' to twist my head away. Then he says, "*Ah ain't gonna hurcha, gal. Wal, not too much anyways.*"

'And I know I'm gonna die . . . Right here. Right now.'

'But now you remember the words?'

'Yes, yes, now I remember those words. I am shaping my lips and forcing out the first words Erwin has ever heard me speak. I'm saying, "*Erwin . . . Erwin . . .*"

'He's pushing himself upright and he's staring at me in disbelief. "*Ah thought y' cain't tawk, Hannah. Yer know y' cain't tawk!*"

'Now I'm saying it loud an' clear: "*Erwin, it's time to climb.*"'

'You did it, Hannah. Those were the trigger words I taught you.'

'It's happening exactly as you promised. Erwin's strength is just *evaporating*. His long, long body and his private parts grow slack. He stands up. I'm looking down at his feet, long as canoes on the boards.

'I'm saying it again: "*It's time to climb.*" It feels so strange 'cos I still ain't used to talkin'. Something is happening to Erwin: it comes over him like a drug – reminds me of when my daddy put the needle in. There's a weird pumpkin smile spreading across his jaw. Now Erwin's turning and lopin' towards the door like a slow-motion movie. He's bending down to go under, and just then there's another flash of lightnin' and it sparks up that big tattoo across his back.

'Now he's goin' down the stairs, real slow. I see the pile of clothes he left on my floor. I hear him crashing an' tossin' stuff around like he's searching for something in the tool store. I kneel on the bed and peek out through the dreamcatcher, and I see him headin' across the yard, long and naked. He's holding a big pair of bolt-cutters in one hand.

'Now someone comes rushin' in my door and I turn round and it's Pip! Dear, dear Pip! He says, "Hannah – oh my Lord, Hannah! What has he done to you?"

'I say, "I'm feeling kinda shaky, Pip. Won't you come an' kiss me?"'

'That's grand, Hannah. You've done well. I'm going to wake you now. I'm going to bring you slowly back . . . and when you awake, you will remember everything, but you will feel calm and strong. I'm counting from one to ten . . .

'One . . . two . . . three . . .'

47

Time to Climb

One . . . two . . . three . . .

Three raindrops.

That's what woke Pip in the dawn of the storm. Not the sound of Erwin's Jeep, or Hannah's cries – it was three fat raindrops which fell on his face. There must have been a faulty tile right above his bed, because now the rain was cascading on the rooftops and finding its way through every crack and cranny.

While Pip was sleeping, the storm had rolled down from the mauve mountains. It had hurtled across the fields, whipping up scraps of dry grass. It had roared over Hannah's secret valley, wrestling with the willow trees and spitting rain onto the dusty river bed. And finally, in the deathly glow of morning, the storm began to lash the leaky roofs of Dead River Farm.

In an instant Pip awoke. He ran to the window just as a

mighty thunderclap exploded overhead. He peered into the wild yard and, to his utter horror, he saw Erwin's Jeep discarded at a crazy angle. Then he noticed that the toolshed was open wide and various implements were flying outside – a rake, a scythe, a shovel. Someone was searching for something in there. And right up above lay Hannah's room!

The storm and the crashing must have woken Zachery too, because Pip could hear the old man wailing from a window in the farmhouse. 'Ye best show yerself. Ah gotta gun, y' hear?'

In the blink of an eye, Pip had tugged on his clothes, leaped down the ladder and sprinted across the slippery yard, where the first rain in years gave off a sweet sickly smell like rotting fruit.

To his stunned amazement, a man stepped out of the tool store – it was Erwin, stark butt-naked with a pair of long-handled bolt-cutters in one hand.

Zachery came out on his porch in long johns, a gun in hand, and he was yelling, '*Erwin! Erwin! Zat you, boy? Where 'n tarnation are yer clothes?*'

But Erwin did not hear. He had a strange glazed grin on his face. He stared right through Pip as if he were made of fog, and simply headed out of the yard, long and slow, pushing against the wind and rain as if he were on a mission. He went out through the back gate and up the path to the fields. As the sky split, Pip saw the bolt-cutters dangling at his side and a terrible tattoo across his back.

Pip ran into the tool store and vaulted the stairs. All he could think of was Hannah. All he could see in his mind was

Hannah lying— No! He could not bring himself to think of it.

Her door was open wide. Pip saw a pile of furniture to one side. And there was Hannah in her nightgown, staring through the dancing web of her dreamcatcher. And she was alive!

Hannah turned and smiled at him, and her face was bright as a lantern in a storm.

He said, 'Hannah – oh my Lord, Hannah! What's he done to you?'

She said, 'I'm feeling kinda shaky, Pip. Won't you come an' kiss me?'

And kiss her he did, with arms clutched tight around her body.

In two minutes Hannah had pulled on her new dress and boots, and they rushed out into the hot rain. Now Amigo was bounding at their side, licking Pip's hand with his sandpaper tongue.

Up ahead, old man Zachery, soaked to his skinny limbs, was bent double, squealing and wheezing like a squeezebox, 'Erwin! Erwin! Goddamn him! Th' boy's gawn raight out of his maind – or lickered up – or – or sleepwalkin'. Ye come back now, Erwin!'

Way up ahead they could see the distant figure of Erwin, slickery as a silverfish in the crazy morning light.

Zachery had run out of steam like an ancient loco-motive. Half a century of smoking had halted him in his tracks. Spitting, coughing, wild-eyed and fighting for breath, he seized Pip's arm and gasped, 'Git after him, boy, ah beg ye. He's gawn crazy. Lawst his maind . . .'

Pip shouted against the wind, 'We'll do what we can, Mr Zachery, sir. Now you head back to Lilybelle – ain't nothing you can do out here.'

Hannah and Pip ran onwards, battling against the roaring wind, past the dripping apple trees, up to the red barn where all that bad stuff happened and out into the fields. The cut corn was sharp as knives and Pip felt glad for Hannah's boots.

As for Erwin, his feet must have been lacerated, but nothing slowed that mad machine as he moved across the boundless fields in that strange determined manner.

Far out on the horizon, the rising sun was battered by violent clouds, and across the landscape the army of pylons glistened beneath the splintered sky.

Erwin had seen his goal. His speed increased. The old man was far behind, but Hannah sprinted onwards, and for the first time Pip found he could equal her pace.

Now they were near the base of the first tower, and above the howling wind they heard Erwin talking to himself, over and over. '*Time t' claimb. It's time t' claimb. Higher than evah befaw. It's time t' claimb, Erwin.*'

For a moment he paused and stared up towards the soaring tip of the spire, where the sinister black cables converged. Pip was close enough to see the eerie smile on his face, and then, in one slow movement, Erwin bent his powerful legs and leaped into the air, grabbing the first steel rung with outspread fingers. With almost superhuman strength, the giant swung himself upwards, grabbing each bar like a great wet crab.

Pip was overwhelmed with horror at what they were

about to see. He cupped his hands and yelled, 'Erwin, it's Pip here . . . You remember me – I'm your friend. That's enough now. Please, climb down . . .'

But Erwin did not pause. He only shouted, 'Ah ain't gonna stop for no man. Ah'm claimbin' higher than evah before. Erwin gonna be a gawd!'

When he was twenty feet above their heads, he reached the barbed-wire barrier. It looked strong, and Pip offered up a prayer that it would prevent Erwin from climbing higher. Perhaps he would tire now and climb down so they could walk him safely home. Maybe he could get help. Maybe, with the right medication, he could live safely in an asylum.

But nothing would stop the mesmerized man. Erwin stretched up with the bolt-cutters and began to snip the barbed wire as if he were cutting straw with scissors . . . *Clonk! Clip! Clunk!*

Hannah and Pip were directly below him now, and amongst the continuous rain Pip felt something hot and sticky splash onto his face; he touched it with his hand . . . It was blood! It was blood tumbling from Erwin's lacerated feet.

By now Erwin had removed a section of the barbed wire and Hannah guided Pip backwards – she had seen that Erwin was about to toss down the bolt-cutters – and Pip heard them land with a thump at his side. With his bare hands, Erwin tore away the last strands of wire. Then he hauled his long naked body through the gap, muttering to himself all the while, '*Time t' claimb, Erwin. Time t' claimb. Higher th'n evah b'fore.*'

The morning sky was a sickly yellow glow and the storm had become a deluge.

Behind him, Pip heard gasping and spitting: somehow Zachery had made it up the hill. His white beard and hair streaming like some biblical prophet of doom, he cried, 'Pip, ye git yerself up there now, y'hear. Ye bring back my boy . . . Go on now, git after him.'

Pip placed his arm gently around the fragile old man and said, 'No, sir. I can't do that. Can't no one catch him now.'

Erwin was higher than a house. Higher than a tree. He was so high that the three of them had to step further from the base of the tower to watch. Pip longed to lead Hannah and Zachery away – he knew for sure that something terrible was about to happen – but the sight of that crazy climbing creature held him like a magnet.

At the top of the tower the girders tapered together, and now Erwin stood between them like a tiny trapeze artist, surrounded by nothing but wet steel and whirling cloud. Pip felt a sharp pain in his hand and found that Hannah was squeezing it so tight that he was forced to prise her fingers away.

Perhaps it was peaceful up there. Perhaps there was nothing but sweet tumbling rain and the whisper of thousands of volts in the wires. Perhaps Erwin felt powerful. Perhaps he felt no fear as the clouds engulfed his head.

Then came a strange noise from the sky. It was the sound of Erwin laughing like a demented being. It was as if the higher he climbed, the happier he became. And maybe in that moment he truly felt like a god – free of pain and suffering.

Beside them Zachery had fallen to his knees in the sodden earth. The white-bearded man spread his thin arms as if in prayer and stared upwards at the wild thing that was his son. Pip felt a crashing wave of sympathy for the man. What had he done except try to raise his family and look after his farm?

In one final attempt to change fate, Pip put his hands to his mouth and yelled again with all his might, 'That's high enough now, Erwin! You come back down! We all care about you, Erwin! We want you down now!'

But his words were stolen by the wind and hurled across the fields.

At the very top section of the tower, the black cables were as thick as legs. Erwin tried to reach them, but there were objects in his way – ceramic insulators, which kept him from his prize. Now he changed his behaviour to something so primal and reckless that Pip thought of an ape in a forest rather than a human being. Erwin reached up, grabbed the girder above his head and rocked his body outwards, again and again. Backwards and forwards he swung. Soles to the churning sky.

With each swing, his feet came closer to that deadly cable. A man of ordinary height could not have swung far enough, but Erwin was so very tall and agile . . .

. . . and at last he swayed outwards one final time, and the tips of his long feet must have made contact with the cables, because in that instant the sky was torn by a colossal eruption of white light. Pip heard an evil sound which he would never forget – the ripping and surging and crackling of a vast sheet of electrical power:

ZZZZZ-Z-Z-Zzzzzz-RR-R-RR-ZZZZ-TTTT-T-T!!!!

See! See! He's *dancing*! Erwin is dancing! His body is crackling and phosphorescent, and he's twisting and shimmying and jiving and dancing. It is the terrible, terrible Dance of Death. And . . . Oh! His body is alight and burning. Who would know that a human body could burn like matchwood?

As Pip stared in revulsion and horror, Erwin's blackened body dived, beautifully, gracefully, into the morning sky, where the storm was easing and a gentle rain fell. It was a beautiful sight to see a man fly, like Icarus against the delicate lemon sky. And then that great acrobat tumbled and turned over and over in perfect somersaults. He hit the barbed-wire fence, and for a moment Pip thought he would be caught there; he wondered how they would fetch him down. But no! Erwin snagged for just one moment, and then his smoking body tipped over the edge, landing with a gentle thud beside them.

Pip's nostrils filled with the smell of summer barbecues. Erwin lay right by his feet. Only this was not Erwin. It was not a man at all. The thing beside him was like a large roasted insect – a praying mantis or a huge ant burned in a forest fire – because its legs and arms were at strange, rigid angles, and there were rounded stumps where fingers and feet should be, and his face . . . his face was nothing but a charcoal skull.

In every part of his body and mind Pip felt numb. He wished with all his might that he could unsee what he had seen, and that Hannah and Zachery could unsee it too. Because once it is seen, it is always seen, and in odd unguarded moments throughout his life, Pip would see the flying man as clearly as if he were still that fourteen-year-old boy at the end of the long strange summer of 1963.

It was Hannah who guided him gently away, and her voice was so tender that it penetrated the ugliness and brutality of what they had witnessed. She said, 'It's finished. We can walk right away. The tale has ended. The tale has ended now.'

And it was Hannah who found the strength to lead old man Zachery, drenched by rain and tears, like an infant in his drooping long johns. The three mourners walked slowly down the hillside, past the apple trees and across the yard to the farmhouse, where Hannah sat Zachery in the kitchen and fixed him hot sweet tea, while Pip rolled him cigarettes and answered Lilybelle's tinkling bell.

The police officers arrived later that morning, and an ambulance with black windows drove right up the path to the barn, although the wheels spun in the mud and had to be freed with shovels. With their boots sticking in the oozing clay, the men carried a stretcher across the fields to the tower, where they collected the strange charcoal sculpture that lay there. And Pip could have sworn that two of the officers and one of the ambulance drivers were Klansmen.

The authorities were baffled about why Erwin should choose to end his life in that violent way; but everyone who knew him testified that he was always an unstable man.

From that day, Zachery seemed a little older, but somehow a little softer too. 'Th' boy's gawn,' was all he would say. 'He died in the jungles o' 'Nam. Ah don' never wanna talk 'bout him again.'

And they never did speak of it again, although something very peculiar occurred on the day Erwin died: when Pip came out of the pink bedroom where he had spent hours comforting Lilybelle, he walked into the living room and noticed that something was different. It was not the animal heads on the walls, which still stared at him; it was a gentle ticking. And when Pip looked at the mantelpiece above the wood stove, he saw to his astonishment that the clock, which had stopped at twenty to nine on the day Erwin returned from the war, had started again. At the precise moment Erwin fell from the tower the old clock had begun to tick, slowly and steadily, as if time had restarted at Dead River Farm.

Pip and Hannah stayed three more days to help Zachery and Lilybelle in that difficult time. Pip helped the old man to build a bonfire of the flags and nooses and Klan material from Erwin's room. The one thing he took, with Zachery's permission, was a small rucksack in which he began to pack his few belongings for the journey ahead.

On a golden afternoon in late September, Pip and Hannah prepared to take their leave. One last time they went up to the valley, to retrieve the cookie jar; pausing for a moment by the apple trees to gaze down at the farmyard, small and quaint as one of Lilybelle's paintings.

Behind the red barn, Hannah found that her hidden

track was almost overgrown with a late spurt of shoots and flowers caused by the storm.

As they approached the valley, Pip caught an unfamiliar sound through the trees. The place had always been so silent, but now he heard a gurgling and rushing from far below. Sprinting down the slope to the valley floor, they were amazed to find water, rushing and tumbling head over heels through the valley – the Dead River had begun to flow.

Hannah laughed in wonder – 'Take a look, Pip! Can you believe your eyes? I reckon they call it Livin' River now!'

Pip was not listening. A terrible thought had crossed his mind – suppose the river had swept away the cookie jar with his great expectations inside!

In a moment he had tugged off his sneakers and waded to his waist in cold water. After some effort, he located Hannah's hiding place beneath the twisted willow. He reached deep into the roots and pulled out, first, the radio, still wrapped in polythene, and then the cookie jar with the flour bag and roll of banknotes rolled safe and dry inside.

As Pip's father had taught him, the safest bank is a riverbank.

When he returned to his room above the stable block, Pip wrapped the cookie jar carefully inside his few items of clothing and stuffed it deep into the rucksack alongside his book.

What he found heart-wrenchingly sad was saying goodbye to that scruffy faithful old dog, Amigo. What he found harder still was the walk across to the farmhouse to take his leave of Lilybelle. But to his astonishment, as he climbed the steps to the porch, the screen door creaked, and there she stood, on her own two legs, with a walking stick in each hand. Lilybelle filled the doorframe from side to side, but her doll-face shone bright.

'Ah had ter see you off,' she crooned. 'Ah jes' couldn't lay in bed when mah fav'rite people wuz departin'.'

'Lil'belle! You're walking!' shouted Hannah rushing to her side.

'Ah'm walkin', you're tawkin' – ain't no end o' miracles!' And she gathered the children to her mountainous bosom and squeezed them until Pip thought he would suffocate in the cologne-soaked warmth of her flesh.

Then Pip went over to Zachery, in his usual place on the porch, with a cigarette in hand and Amigo at his feet.

'Mr Zachery, I'd like a word with you, sir.'

'Say what ye have t', boy.'

'I wanna thank you for the kindness you have shown me, sir. Also . . . I don't wanna cause no inconvenience, but I would be obliged if you would release me and Hannah from our employment.'

'One o' ye don' tawk, an' one o' ye use twenny words when faive will do. Listen, boy, if ye wanna go, then go. Me an' Lilybelle's perf'ly capable of takin' care o' ourselves. Always has bin, always will be. So go on, skedaddle . . . vamoose!'

But as Pip turned to leave, Zachery grabbed his arm and hissed in his ear, 'Gonna miss ye when ye gawn, boy. Gonna miss th' both o' yous.'

'We'll miss you too, sir. Truly we will. It seems long ago now, and maybe you don't recall, but when you collected me from St Joseph's, you wanted to shake my hand. I . . . I guess I was kinda wary. Wal, I hope it ain't too late, Mr Zach . . .'

The boy spat on his palm and firmly shook the old man's hand.

'Snee, hee, hee!' said Zachery.

Then they walked away – the boy with the pack on his back, the girl with the guitar. Hand in hand towards the mauve mountains.

48

This Is How the Tale Begins ...

Well now, do you hear that whispering? Perhaps it's the seagulls calling, or the waves on the shore at Dingle Bay, or perhaps it's the voice of the wind. See, my voice is the voice you have always known . . .

And now it's time to awake . . .

I'm going to count from one to ten, and you might want to gently stretch your arms . . . One . . . two . . . three . . .

It's almost time to close the book . . . four . . . five . . . You will awake feeling strong and happy . . . six . . . seven . . . eight . . . resolved to overcome all adversity and use whatever Gift you possess to live your life . . . and to love . . .

Nine . . . ten . . .

Wide awake now . . . The Hypnotist's tale is over. But yours has just begun . . .

AUTHOR'S NOTE

I didn't mean to write *The Hypnotist*. I wanted to tell a different story all together. The story I had in mind traced my own family history, beginning way back in Persia in the 1700s when our first known ancestor, Jacob Sjoesjan, led his bedraggled family across the deserts and mountains to Europe . . . just like so many poor refugees today.

Jacob and his family were Jews in a society that had turned against them. It has always been my worst nightmare to find myself in a world in which the very authorities that are meant to protect you – the police, the government, the army, the law, the educators – are on the side of the mob that is baying for your blood. You are powerless. There is nowhere to turn.

That dystopian scenario often begins with bizarre rules designed to intimidate and humiliate: *you must go here, but you cannot go there!* So Persian Jews were banned from all but the most menial jobs; theatres and public baths were closed to them; they were not allowed out in the rain or snow in case impurities leached from their skins and infected others. And here's a familiar one – Jews were forced to sew yellow stars onto their clothing, so that people could be sure they were discriminating against the right minority.

Next comes the violence – the smashing of glass in the night, the splintering of doors as uniformed bullies demand documents, which you never seem to have. Unsurprisingly my ancestors decided to flee and I bet it was a terrible journey. I wouldn't be surprised if some of them died on the roadside – the young ones, the old ones; that's what usually happens. After many months, the Sjoesjan tribe rolled up at the Dutch-German border. They were dirty and hairy and kind of foreign-looking, as many refugees are. In my imagination it was a snowy night and the official who demanded their names couldn't understand a single word they were saying. What old Jacob was trying to convey was that Jews didn't have surnames where they came from; they were named after their town of origin – Sjoesjan was just a funny way of spelling Shushan, their hometown in Persia. All the guard could think about was his warm bed and his warm wife. He stamped their papers and, to save further confusion, replaced their funny name with the sensible name of the border town where they were standing. That town was called Anholt, which suggests to me something like '*Stop and hand over your papers!*'

Jacob's family took their shiny new surname and settled into the horizontal and tolerant Netherlands. They were a creative lot and over the generations, they became art dealers and artisans, including a wonderful painter named Jozef Israels, who was much admired by van Gogh. I wanted to write about Jacob and Jozef, and the many powerful women of the family. I wanted to mention my great-grandfather,

Martin van Straaten, who went down with the *Lusitania* in 1915, so that when his remains drifted onto a beach in Ireland, only the jet-black ring on his bloated finger identified him. My sister wears it to this day – the ring, I mean, not the finger.

But the person I wanted to write about most of all was an olive-skinned, black-haired boy named Simon 'Gerry' Anholt, who became my father, although I never felt I knew him well. When Gerry was 16, that thing happened again – the nightmare I've been trying to describe . . . the one in which you are a powerless scapegoat, and the authorities that should be there to protect you are siding with the thugs. (There must be a name for that kind of dystopia, but I don't know what it is.)

Hitler's armies had invaded Holland and the cancer of prejudice, which never really goes away, oozed through the beautiful canals of Amsterdam like a foul oil slick. Up went the cry in the Jewish neighborhoods – 'Here we go again!' Along came the bizarre rules: *you are allowed here on Tuesdays, but not there on Fridays*. You had to sew on the old yellow star for easy identification. And when they heard the snarling of Alsatians and the smashing of shop windows, many of my father's family went into hiding in cellars and attics, exactly like Anne Frank's family. Those who stayed were herded into cattle wagons and freighted to concentration camps. Among the 6 million Jews, homosexuals, disabled people and Roma who were murdered by the Nazis, more than sixty members of the Anholt family also perished.

My dad was lucky . . . at least, he thought he was lucky. His parents had contacts in London and they got out before things turned nasty. My father thought he would be safe, but . . . you know how these stories go; the nightmare had just begun.

Gerry was drafted into the British Intelligence Corp and took part in dangerous missions in occupied France, Holland and later, Germany; for which he was 'Mentioned in Dispatches'. Like many Dutchmen he spoke several languages, so part of his job was to translate the often-brutal interrogations of captured SS officers. My father didn't often talk about these events, and it wasn't until the last years of his life that I learned about the worst horror of all – in 1945, that olive-skinned, black-haired boy was amongst the Allied troops who liberated the death camp of Bergen-Belsen. He said that although the stench hung over the nearby town like smog, the residents denied any knowledge. I think my father lost a lot of things in there – his youth, his optimism and even a sense of joy. What I know for sure is that the skeleton-people wandering naked amidst the heaps of bodies haunted his dreams for ever. These were his own people.

When it was all over, Staff Sergeant Anholt tried to forget what he had seen. He married an English girl. He became a Christian. They started a family. But of course my father was not ready to raise children of his own. What he actually needed was someone to look after *him*. We spent some years back in Holland and then at nine years old, I was packed off to an English boarding school, which I detested with a passion.

That was the story I planned to write. I wanted to mention that although he was not a great dad, my father was a deeply tolerant humanitarian who despised prejudice of every kind. Touchingly, he held a special fondness for Germany, which he visited many times.

But, in 2011 my father died. Suddenly the whole thing seemed too painful, and too complicated, and generally too close to home. Maybe I'll return to that story one day, but for the time being, I decided to write something completely different . . .

The problem was that some of those themes just would not go away; the stuff about powerlessness and prejudice – what it feels like to be defined by a yellow star, your gender, your sexual orientation, or the colour of your skin . . . what it's like to live in that hellish world for which I have no name; the place where there is nowhere to turn. I began searching the history books for other less personal examples. And it didn't take too long.

It starts with the bizarre and humiliating rules, like the Jim Crow laws, for instance: *You must step off the sidewalk when a White person walks by. You may not share a drinking fountain in case you pollute the water. You must sit at the back of the bus. No Coloured barber shall touch the hair of White women or girls . . .*

Then comes the fear. The rumbling vehicles in the night, the lynch mob waiting at the corner. There's nowhere to go for help because the very people who are meant to protect you are pulling on their jackboots or their scary pointy hoods.

Like my father, I despise prejudice of all kinds, but surely there has never been a more ignorant form of prejudice than colour prejudice. The idea that the pigmentation of half a millimetre of skin might somehow define the person within seems as laughable as old man Zachery choosing a goat or a horse by the colour of its coat. Colour prejudice would indeed be comical if it were not subjugating, dividing and murdering to this very day. (And let's not forget that colour prejudice can work both ways.)

The point I am making is that although *The Hypnotist* is set in the Southern States of America in 1963, it could be anywhere; anytime. For the record, I love the United States and have many friends and relatives in that great country; indeed my own daughter worked for several years at the United Nations in New York City. There is not one country on this planet that does not carry the bloody stain of prejudice and oppression. It's what we tribal humans do, and always will do until we wake up and look in the mirror.

It is not just the victims themselves who suffer – the ripples spread through the generations. The horror that my father witnessed was passed on through his inability to nurture. When I write about Pip in the orphanage, I only need to close my eyes and remember the iron bed in the cold dormitory of my boarding school. I was not an orphan, but sometimes I felt like one. And perhaps the culture of bullying and the regular canings were my personal glimmer of that nightmare in which the men with the power are your enemies.

That's all a bit miserable, isn't it! But I'm one of the lucky ones – I have a wonderful life, free of war and prejudice. Those small hardships were nothing more than the grit in the oyster shell, which every creative person needs. My father did pass on many positive things. Chief amongst them is a dream of tolerance, equality and mutual respect.

When they stayed at the Kozy Kabins Motel, Jack lay awake watching a historic moment on TV. If you know nothing about the March on Washington of 28th August 1963, I urge you to check it out! Don't let another day go by without hearing the 'I have a dream' speech, which brought Jack Morrow to tears.

Martin Luther King's dream was that one day, Black and White; Jew, Muslim and Christian; Gay and Straight; Woman and Man, will join hands and sing together, *'Free at last! Free at last! Thank God Almighty, we are free at last!'* I hope it's your dream too.

Laurence Anholt, Devon, England 2016

ACKNOWLEDGEMENTS

This is where authors traditionally thank their agent, their pets and their crumbly relatives.

Despite my best efforts I have never found an agent; instead I would like to thank the magnificent UK Society of Authors for their untiring support, and the generous allocation of an Authors' Foundation Award.

Pets? Sadly my cat, Harrods, passed away, but I gladly acknowledge his teaching and wisdom.

I owe a humungous hunk of gratitude to the whole team at Penguin Random House in London; in particular, legendary publisher Annie Eaton and editorial director Ruth Knowles, who spotted a pip of potential, watered it with encouragement and helped it to grow. I cannot overstate their contribution to this book.

I could fill another book with devotion for my children – Claire, at the United Nations; Tom, artist of genius; and Maddy, actor extraordinaire. You are my moon and stars.

And a library could not express my love for my talented wife and companion, Cathy, who had the strange experience of sleeping and waking with Zachery, Lilybelle and the Dead

River clan. You laughed at my silly voices and supported me in every way. You are my sun and sky.

In memory of my mother, Joan Anholt; one of many wise women who have inspired my life.

A rousing yell of thanks to the unsung warriors of words – librarians, teachers and booksellers!

And lastly for YOU, dear reader – sisters and brothers everywhere who share The Dream of tolerance, diversity, equality and freedom. *One Love!*

@LaurenceAnholt
www.anholt.co.uk

1963 Timeline of Historical Events

3 January – Battle Ap Bac in Vietnam is the first major defeat for South Vietnamese and American forces against the Communist Viet Cong, leading to 200 Vietnamese army casualties and the shooting down of five US helicopters.

7 January – US first-class postage raised from four to five cents.

11 January – The Beatles release *Please Please Me*.

14 January – Governor of Alabama George Wallace is sworn in and pledges '*segregation now, segregation tomorrow and segregation for ever.*'

20 March – First exhibition of Pop Art in New York City featuring Andy Warhol

20 March – General Harkins predicts that the war in Vietnam will be over by the end of the year. He is wrong by twelve years.

21 March – The infamous Alcatraz penitentiary is closed and the island reclaimed by Native Americans.

2 April – USSR launches *Luna 4*, missing the Moon by 8,500 km.

9 April – British wartime Prime Minister Winston Churchill becomes honorary US citizen.

10 April – US tests nuclear bomb at Nevada.

16 April – 'Bad Friday' Coral Gardens Massacre in Jamaica in which hundreds of innocent Rastafarians lose their lives.

12 April – Birmingham, Alabama, police use dogs and cattle prods on peaceful civil rights demonstrators.

16 April – Martin Luther King Jr is arrested and jailed during anti-segregation protests in Birmingham. He writes his seminal 'Letter from Birmingham Jail', arguing that we have a duty to disobey unjust laws.

11 May – Racial bomb attacks in Birmingham. The Klan call it *Bombingham*.

12 May – Commissioner of Public Safety 'Bull' Connor uses fire hoses, police dogs and violence on Black demonstrators during televized civil rights protests in Birmingham, Alabama.

16 May – US Army instructs its soldiers to 'emphasize the positive aspects of your activities' to the media and to 'avoid gratuitous criticism'.

10 June – John F. Kennedy signs law for equal pay for equal work for men and women.

11 June – JFK says it is 'time to act' against segregation.

12 June – Assassination of Medgar Evers by ex-KKK member. Evers was an African-American civil rights activist and member of the Association for Advancement of Colored People.

18 June – 3,000 Black people boycott Boston public schools.

19 June – Twenty-six-year-old Valentina Tereshkova becomes first woman in space.

24 June – First demonstration of video recorder at BBC Studios in London.

26 June – President Kennedy visits West Berlin and gives famous 'Ich bin ein Berliner' (I am a Berliner) speech.

1 July – The 'fab four' Beatles record *She Loves You, Yeah, Yeah, Yeah*.

1 July – First ZIP codes used in America.

28 August – The March on Washington. 250,000 demonstrate for equal rights, an end to racial segregation and the Jim Crow laws in the South. The time limit for speeches is four minutes, but Martin Luther King Jr clocks up 16 minutes with his seminal '*I have a dream*' speech at Lincoln Memorial. Many pass out from heat exhaustion and 35 Red Cross stations treat 1,335 people. Just one person, New Yorker Charles Schreiber, dies from a heart attack. The number of toilets at the march is a big concern.

The following year, on 14 October, King is awarded the Nobel Peace Prize for his role in combating racial inequality. He has many enemies amongst White supremacists and is murdered in 1968.

10 September – First twenty Black students enter public schools in Alabama.

15 September – Four young girls attending Sunday school are murdered by the Ku Klux Klan when dynamite explodes at the 16th Street Baptist Church, a popular location for civil rights meetings in Birmingham, Alabama. Riots erupt in Birmingham, leading to the deaths of two more Black youths. Four Klansmen – Bobby Cherry, Herman Cash, Thomas Blanton and Robert Chambliss

– were implicated. Chambliss, known as 'Dynamite Bob' was actually seen planting the bomb and arrested later that day. An all-White jury found him guilty of a minor charge of possessing dynamite without a permit, for which he received a six-month jail term and a hundred-dollar fine. It was not until 1977 that Chambliss was re-arrested and convicted of murder. He died in prison in 1985.

27 September – US population reaches 190,000,000.

1 October – 16,752 US military personnel now stationed in Vietnam.

5 October – In Saigon, Vietnam, a meditating Buddhist monk sets himself alight in protest against oppression by the government of President Diem. The shocking photograph appears on the front page of nearly every newspaper in the world, increasing pressure on the Kennedy administration to do something about Diem.

19 October – Beatles record *I Want to Hold Your Hand* and the term 'Beatlemania' is coined. A few years later the KKK would burn their records in disgust.

1 November – In Vietnam, rebel forces assassinate President Diem and his brother. The Kennedy government admits that they hold some responsibility. An unstable situation now arises in which the Viet Cong increase control. The US is inexorably drawn into one of the most contentious wars in its history.

18 November – Bell Telephone introduces push button telephone.

22 November – American President John F. Kennedy assassinated by Lee Harvey Oswald in Dallas, Texas. His death is never fully explained but JFK was a strong civil rights supporter, friend to Martin Luther King and to the Native American community.

22 November – Lyndon B Johnson sworn in as the 36th US President following assassination of JFK.

23 November – Launch of *Doctor Who* in England is overshadowed by assassination of JFK.

23 November – JFK's body lies in repose in White House.

24 November – First live murder on TV – Jack Ruby shoots Lee Harvey Oswald

24 November – Incoming President Johnson tells his advisers, 'I am not going to lose Vietnam.'

25 November – JFK laid to rest at Arlington National Cemetery.

26 November – *Explorer 18* launched.

20 December – Berlin Wall opens for first time to West Berliners.

22 December – Official thirty-day mourning period for President John F Kennedy ends.

31 December – 122 American and 5665 South Vietnamese soldiers have been killed in Vietnam in 1963.

Fun facts from 1963

- First C60 cassettes produced by Philips in 1963.
- Computer mouse invented by Doug Engelbart as a pointer for a graphic display screen. A wooden box rolling on wheels, connected to a computer with a cable which resembles a mouse.

- First lava lamp. Even John Lennon has one.
- Harvey Ball designs the smiley face to cheer up bored office workers at State Mutual Life Assurance Company.
- Maharishi Mahesh Yogi introduces Transcendental Meditation, inspiring The Beatles, the Beach Boys, Mia Farrow and Stevie Wonder to take up meditation.
- Weight Watchers created by Jean Nidetch. At 214 pounds Jean invites overweight friends to hear the story of her 'promiscuous eating habit' and support each other in losing weight. For the first meeting in May 1963, Jean sets up fifty chairs but over 400 people attend and membership eventually exceeds one million. Unfortunately Lilybelle is unable to attend.

Read on to discover more stories of countries
in turmoil, and the people caught up in the chaos.
You'll be gripped, heartbroken, inspired . . .

Anna
and the
Swallow Man
GAVRIEL SAVIT

Kraków, 1939, is no place to grow up. Anna Lania is just seven years old when the Germans take her father and suddenly, she's alone.

Then she meets the Swallow Man. Over the course of their travels together, they will dodge bombs, tame soldiers, and even make a friend. But in a world gone mad, everything can prove dangerous ...

'A small wonder ... worthy of the hype' *The Times*

'A bold first novel that promises more from the undoubtedly talented Savit' *Guardian*

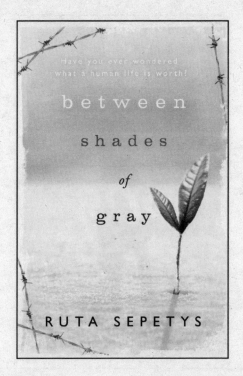

Have you ever wondered
what a human life is worth?

between

shades

of

gray

RUTA SEPETYS

This is the harrowing war-time story of fifteen-year-old
Lina and her family, as one night they are hauled from
their home by Soviet guards – and deported to Siberia.

During the terrible journey, Lina has only hope
to keep her alive. And the love of a boy she barely knows,
but doesn't want to lose.

'Heart-wrenching . . . an eye-opening reimagination
of a very real tragedy' *The Los Angeles Times*

'A hefty emotional punch' *The New York Times*

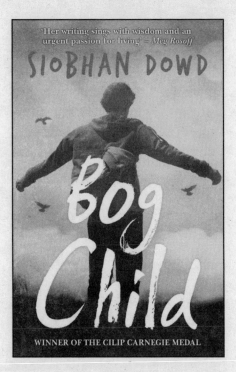

'Her writing sings with wisdom and an urgent passion for living' – *Meg Rosoff*

SIOBHAN DOWD

Bog Child

WINNER OF THE CILIP CARNEGIE MEDAL

High on the mountain above his home town,
Fergus makes a chilling discovery: the body of a girl,
hidden deep in the bog. As Fergus tries to make
sense of the mad world around him – this is Ireland
in the 1980s – a voice comes to him in his dreams,
and the mystery of the Bog Child unfurls.

'A harrowing story of choice and obligation,
peace and politics'
Independent

'Her sentences sing, each note resonates with an urgent
humanity of the sort that cannot be faked' *Guardian*